GINGER SNAPPED

BERNADETTE FRANKLIN

Happy Reading! ♡
Bernadette
Franklin
♡

GINGER SNAPPED
BY BERNADETTE FRANKLIN

Copyright © 2019 by Bernadette Franklin

Cover design by Daqri Bernardo (Covers by Combs)

All rights reserved.

No part of this book may be reproduced in any form or by any electronic or mechanical means, including information storage and retrieval systems, without written permission from the author, except for the use of brief quotations in a book review.

Chapter One

WHY HAD I believed taking on two extra part-time jobs in retail would somehow solve all of my life's problems? It solved some of my life's problems, which involved having the money to feed my twin nieces and my nephew, but it left me contemplating mass murder in the mall. As a single woman, aged thirty-four *without* children, I should've been spending the three weeks leading up to Christmas spoiling my sister's three kids rather than pretending I was qualified parent material.

I could barely take care of myself. I was not ready or able to care for a pair of twins, aged twelve, and their brother, aged sixteen and going on fifty. All in all, I only had one thing going for me: the brats made decent house guests and could amuse themselves while I worked.

If I hadn't been so worried about Michelle's disappearance, along with her husband and general partner in crime, also known as my brother-in-law, I'd be sorely tempted to kill them both for putting me in such an uncomfortable position, which involved facing off against mall moms who were convinced they knew everything and I knew nothing.

They weren't necessarily wrong, which made a mess of things.

At five minutes until closing, the store should have been empty, but a handful of men and women still wandered the aisles in search of confectionary perfection, ignoring my supervisor's notices on the intercom that everyone needed to check out. If I clocked out over my allotted time, the head honcho, Mr. Grande, would flip his lid, call a staff meeting after hours on a Sunday out of spite, and chew us all out, showcasing everyone's misdeeds.

The customer was always right, and it didn't matter if they were the reason I couldn't clock out on time.

To make matters worse, my name tag cheerfully confessed my name was Ginger, and my current part-time job involved the blasted cookies that I both loved and hated above all others.

One of these days, this Ginger would really snap, and I'd use a snickerdoodle as my weapon of choice, as gingersnaps had a tendency to break into pieces without the choking hazards of my preferred cookie. If I was going to go postal for the holidays, I'd do it right.

The headlines would be spectacular.

Fortunately for everyone in the store, it wasn't my day to snap, not with my nieces and nephew needing me to come home with groceries and somehow pay my rent before I got an eviction notice for the holidays.

When it rained, it really poured, and I still had no idea how I'd gone from comfortably living from paycheck to paycheck to being on a collision course with the nearest homeless shelter. My sister took some of the blame; she kept begging me to attend work parties with her, and I was too damned proud to ask for help buying venue-appropriate attire and accessories.

Just like I had from the day I'd turned eighteen, I'd made my own way in life without asking anyone for any help. My impressive streak would soon end, however. No matter what I did, no matter how many extra hours I worked, I couldn't find my sister and brother-in-law, I couldn't afford to pay my rent and feed her kids, and I sure as hell couldn't afford to pay all their expenses.

Add in the lawyer fees to make sure I had custody of the kids while my sister and brother-in-law were gone, and I'd learned what dire straits truly meant.

The first of the customers, an elderly woman with her cart loaded with a fortune in candy and cookies, rolled up and began the meticulous process of placing her finds on the counter. She organized by color, and while she did that, I prepared the bags so that when I rang up her purchases, I could store them in her way of choosing.

The last granny I'd crossed had verbally crucified me, and I'd learned my lesson: give the little old ladies what they wanted, because they could be meaner than a honey badger if provoked.

I began ringing up the purple candies, placing them in their designated bag. When she wasn't placing things on the counter, she watched me like a hawk, making certain I weighed everything just right. She didn't strike me as a skinflint, much to my relief; the first bag I rang up came in at slightly over a pound, and the skinflints wanted *exactly* a pound.

I might make it through the rest of my shift alive. I hoped.

My sister's kids might miss me if I perished at the hands of an angry granny.

After the purple candies, I rang up the rest of her order, cycling through the colors of the rainbow, as I figured that would appeal to her. It must have, because by the time I finished and informed her she had purchased almost four hundred dollars in candies, she grinned.

"Dear, could you get me six of those cookies?" She pointed at the snickerdoodles, and I donned a fresh pair of gloves and packaged them for her, adding them to her bill.

"Which bag would you like them in, ma'am?"

She pointed at the one with the purple candies, and I did as asked. Once done, she held up her phone. "Do you take mobile payments?"

I wanted to hug the little old granny who'd embraced technology, as our store rarely had issues with our mobile payment terminal. I pressed the button to initiate the payment and gestured to the payment interface in front of her. Two clicks and a tap later, and the register made a happy pinging noise, informing me the transaction was approved. I printed and handed over the receipt. "Thank you, ma'am. Do you need help with your bags?"

"That would be sweet of you, dear."

It only cost me a few seconds to help her put the bags into her arms, and she waddled off in the direction of my supervisor, who waited by the entry to lock up after I finished checking everyone out.

In what classified as a true miracle, none of the customers gave me any problems, and they even waited patiently for me to work through the line. Every transaction processed without event, and only one woman forgot how English worked, something I assumed was from the anxiety of trying to shop anywhere near Christmas.

My supervisor dimmed the lights to deter new customers from showing up while I helped the final customer bag his insane collection of cookies and cupcakes. Once he left, armed with enough sugar to take out an entire mall loaded with children, I heaved a relieved sigh.

Somehow, I'd survived another day of mayhem.

"Ginger, mind helping with the security gate?"

Once we had the security gate in place, no new customers would come, and we'd slip under it before securing it from the outside when we left. I abandoned my post at the register and helped her drag down the heavy steel barricade that would keep the store and its fortune of confections safe overnight. "Think we'll have enough time to clock out before the boss gets pissy?"

"We'll be cutting it close. The little old lady wants you to have the snickerdoodles, and she asked if I'd let you exchange them for whatever cookies you actually wanted. But I know you and those damned snickerdoodles, so they're all yours. She was grateful you took the time to bag her candies properly. Her granddaughter has severe OCD, and the candies are for her."

That explained the meticulous packaging of the little old lady's order. "Really? I thought we weren't supposed to accept anything from the customers?"

"She gave it to me outside of the store, so I'll let it slide this once. Stay quiet about it."

"Sure. Thanks, Tammy."

"Anytime. You did great today. It's the first time I've seen a shift with minimal insanity this time of year."

Being exhausted to the point of numbness likely helped me ignore most of the insanity and deal with irate customers who required their candies to be perfect. "Thanks. Has the roster changed for tomorrow?"

"You're still on your regular shift. If I have any extra hours, I'll let you know as soon as I know." Tammy gave me the cookies, which I'd share with my sister's children.

I couldn't give them much, but maybe they'd appreciate a few of my snickerdoodles.

While exhausted and ready to sleep in the first convenient spot, I went through the full list of tasks needed to properly close the shop, choosing to do my job right and run the risk of clocking out late versus doing a half-assed job. While a half-assed job would've gotten me clocked out on time, I'd pay for it later.

I couldn't afford to lose any one of my jobs, not until I found my sister and brother-in-law.

How I'd find the time remained a mystery.

I ARRIVED home to find my sister's business partner and best friend, Kace Dannicks, seated at my kitchen table playing a heated game of UNO with the kids. The foursome didn't notice me come in, and I debated if I really wanted to share my cookies with the off-limits man who should've been modeling rather than using his brains to develop my sister's various schemes to make a fortune and potentially take over the world.

Unfortunately for me, the pair was good at their job. A better woman wouldn't have resented her sister or her sister's business partner, but I did. They drove fancy cars, lived in big houses, and could splurge on steaks every night if they wanted. My nieces and nephew had accepted my apartment with shocking grace, treating their stay as a comfortable camping trip rather than an utter downgrade from their usual standards.

Me? I appreciated the generosity of a little old lady with an OCD candy order, and I fully meant to keep the extra cookie for myself.

I considered leaving the man and kids to continue their game and take a shower, but if I did, I had a feeling Kace would get offended and stick around longer out of pure spite. He rationed his spite into barely tolerable amounts, as I suspected he liked annoying my sister as much as he enjoyed testing my patience.

Claiming two cookies for myself, I set the bag down on the table for the four to devour. "I get two because I say so, but you all may have one each. They're snickerdoodles. And if anyone doesn't like snickerdoodles, I'm eating them."

All four dove for the bag, and after a brief but fierce battle, Amelia emerged victorious, and she handed out the cookies to everyone, saving Kace for last. She eyed the man, likely judging him and finding him lacking.

"You should give your cookie to Aunt Ginger because she's

prettier than you are, nicer than you are, and understands how not to bathe in obnoxious fumes."

A better woman would've corrected the tween, but as I agreed with her and didn't believe in lying unless absolutely necessary, I watched the exchange with interest. To side with her, I did take a few sniffs, and I recognized the scent from the mall.

"I call that one More Money Than Sense. They sell it in the mall, and I'm pretty sure it costs more than I make in a month. You really don't have to bathe in it, Kace. You might give someone an asthma attack. Take a shower when you get home, wash your clothes, and next time you apply it, put a drop on your wrist, rub your wrists together, and then touch your wrists to your throat. That's all you need for that cologne. Otherwise, you're just dumping a lot of money down the drain."

Kace took the cookie from Amelia, heaved a sigh, and offered it to me. "Please forgive me for stinking up your apartment."

I accepted the cookie, as three cookies was far better than two cookies. "I will forgive you this once." As I wasn't a complete monster, I broke the cookie in half and offered him the smaller piece. "This is a reward for understanding you made a tragic error. In very small quantities, that cologne smells nice. But the key word here is small."

He accepted my offering with a grim smile. "Your mercy is appreciated. How are you holding up? Have you heard anything from Michelle?"

Sighing, I shook my head. As I only had four chairs, I went into the kitchen, set my cookies on the counter, and went to work pouring a glass of milk for everyone. "You want any milk, Kace?"

"Please."

Huh. Someone had taught Kace some manners. I delivered the glasses of milk, got one for myself, and settled at the counter, watching them as they resumed their game, although they'd lost their gusto. I understood—the mention of my sister always deflated her children.

For all of my sister's flaws, her kids loved her. I figured Michelle had to be doing something right, although I was utterly at a loss over why she'd just up and disappear along with her husband. That her children had come to me without much sign or care their parents had taken off bothered me. I understood Michelle worked a lot, but for them to be so calm over the situation drove me to the brink of insanity.

By all appearances, everything was well in their household, but her disappearance and their general behavior still worried me.

While they finished their game, I thought about the weeks leading up to the couple vanishing without a trace. After the first few days, I'd done more than just worry. After a week, I'd developed the kind of anxiety that gnawed at my stomach. At the end of the second week, once it was apparent that there was something seriously wrong, Kace had opened up the sealed letters Michelle and her husband kept in case of death or disappearance.

They had a set for each, as they traveled around the world for work.

That had been when Kace and an attorney had showed up with the kids in tow, and I'd found myself the single mother of three.

An entire month had gone by since then, and I'd picked up every job I could to pay for three growing kids because their trust funds were locked while their parents' disappearances were investigated. The attorney promised money would come eventually, but nobody knew when.

The courts moved at a snail's pace when it came to family matters, or so it seemed to me.

I blamed the time of year; with Christmas only a few weeks

away, the courts were busier than usual, and unfortunately, that meant I had to fend for myself until a judge signed off on certain sheets of paper that Kace promised would make things easier—assuming Michelle and her husband didn't turn up.

The game ended with Saul's victory, and my nephew cackled, smacking his winning card onto the table. Kace sighed and set his cards down, bowing his head as he accepted his defeat at the hands of a teenager. The twin sisters whined, and Amelia found comfort in her cookie and milk while Wendy sulked.

"Get ready for bed, kiddos. You've got school tomorrow." Fortunately, my schedule barely gave me time to drop them off at their school, which was an absurdly expensive private school I couldn't afford even if I wanted to. To my relief, my sister had paid off the entire year upfront, which was one less thing for me to worry about. Keeping them clothed to the school's standards would bankrupt me, as their uniforms required dry cleaning, and there was no such thing as clean, tidy children.

"Seriously, it's time for bed, kiddos," I said when the laughing and groaning finally came to an end. "We have to get up early." Wendy would shower first, Amelia would protest and shower in the morning because she didn't want to be exactly like her twin, and Saul would wait until the last minute to decide if he'd shower before bed or not. I'd probably help him decide by the time his sister finished, as the last thing I needed was the teen languishing in front of the bathroom mirror for an hour trying to make certain his hair was perfect for school.

Judging from his muttering, there was a girl he liked, and he lived to impress her.

I really needed to pull him aside and make sure he knew about life's important lessons, what women actually wanted, and how to avoid being an asshole women hated but wanted for his money later in life. For some reason, I expected my sister had forgotten some elements of the talk.

She still blushed if I asked if she'd had a good night with her husband.

Life was hard, and I only made it harder on myself each and every day.

The kids scattered, guzzling their milk and setting their glasses in the sink before fleeing in the general direction of the bathroom. After a brief skirmish in the hallway, the twins won, and to my surprise, they opted for a shared bath. A shared bath meant one thing: the bubbles were coming, and because Saul was inherently a gentleman-in-training, he'd be determined to help me clean up the mess before it could ruin the floor.

Then Saul would need to take a shower, as would I, but I'd have to wait until morning. In the morning, chaos would surely reign, and I'd be forced to wear a braid to work again to contain the disaster my hair would become.

I missed my quiet life.

Saul skittered into the living room long enough to grab his bag, which warned me he hadn't done his homework yet.

Argh.

"You look harried," Kace murmured, leaning back in his chair and looking me over. "At least come sit. It seems there's now space."

Armed with my milk and cookies, I obeyed, as I'd learned some fights weren't worth having. Kace would fight me to death on the little things, as he enjoyed nothing more than verbal sparring. "Why aren't you an attorney?"

"I like money too much, and I only want to argue with people I like. As an attorney, I'd have to argue with people I didn't like on a daily basis and get paid a lot less to do it."

Huh. The sensible response hadn't been what I expected from him. At all. "So you went into business with my sister?"

"She has good ideas, I have better sense. Mitch has decent sense, but he's happiest working on investments, so we let him handle that part of things. It works out. Or it had until they up and disappeared. Any luck with the attorney?"

"Outside of the letter including their requirements for the kids and their care, plus the trust release terms, no. The six-month window started last week."

If no one heard from them within six months, they would be presumed dead, their wills would be read, and it would be assumed I would become the permanent mother of my nieces and nephew. I wasn't sure what I thought about everything, especially the idea of becoming their mother. The kids had taken their parents' disappearance too calmly.

"That's quite the expression on your face. What are you thinking?"

"I'm thinking everyone is taking this far too well, which leads me to believe this is the shittiest prank anyone has ever pulled on me in my life."

Kace shook his head. "I don't think it is a prank. I think Michelle and Mitch ran into bad luck, went somewhere they shouldn't have, and are now up shit creek without a paddle. It could be their idea of a joke, but if they are pranking us, they'll show up on Christmas Eve to drive us both crazy. They'll succeed this time, too. You know how they are."

I did. Their idea of a vacation was to skip off for a week, leaving Saul to watch his sisters while they did humanitarian work in some out of the way country.

The last I'd heard, they'd been planning a venture to Nigeria. At a loss of what to say, I shrugged. I couldn't complain about their humanitarian efforts, but I would've appreciated some warning that they were planning an expedition.

Had I known they were heading out on such a venture, I would've been better prepared for disaster. Then again, even with warning, I doubted I could ever be truly ready for my sister to vanish out of my life. Sighing, I began the process of packing the cards up and returning them to their box.

"I can't tell if you're unsurprised by my opinion, annoyed I have an opinion, or annoyed with Michelle and Mitch for putting you in this position."

"You have equal reason to be annoyed. As for your speculations, a little of each applies. If it weren't for the kids, I'd be just a little annoyed and a lot worried."

"But the kids have you pretty miffed."

"Yep. It isn't just about them and their globetrotting anymore, and they should know this by now." I grimaced at the anger in my voice, glancing in the direction of my guest bedroom, which had been converted into an indoor campground for three kids. "I wasn't ready for this."

"And it was unfair of them to presume you would be, and equally unfair for them to have locked the kids' trust funds like they had."

"I should make it until the first payment processes." I hoped.

The nastygram I'd received two days ago promised an eviction if I didn't pay in full within ten days, but as soon as my next check hit on Friday, I'd be better off. I hoped. I just couldn't afford to miss a single shift and needed to earn as many bonuses as I could over the holidays.

"How bad is it, really? And none of your normal prideful bullshit, Ginger. What's your actual situation?"

Damn, Kace was on a roll. I drummed my fingers on the table, glanced again in the direction of my bathroom and guest bedroom, and heaved a sigh. Getting to my feet, I went into the living room, dug through my desk for the folder of bills and other important things I needed to deal with, along with the receipts for everything I'd purchased for the kids to show I wasn't being completely irresponsible with my money when I came knocking at my sister's door later to be paid back—assuming she came back at all.

That left me feeling more than a little guilty.

At a loss of what to say, I tossed the folder in front of him so he could figure my situation out for himself, sat back down, and made friends with my cookies.

Snickerdoodles couldn't fix anything important, but it made things a little better for the short period of time it took me to enjoy them. Milk couldn't wash away the bitter pills of life, but nothing short of my sister showing back up would make things right.

Kace sorted through the bills, eviction notice, and receipts, and his brows furrowed. "At the risk of facing your wrath, why didn't you speak up about this earlier?"

"I don't like whining."

"Ginger, going from getting by to responsible for three children on limited funds is not what I'd consider whining, especially if you need the money. First, it's unfair to you; you weren't even asked if you'd take custody when it was popped on you."

"It was a choice of accepting custody or the state gaining custody. I live close enough that they can still go to school, and their school bills have been paid for the year, including the extra fees."

"You're spending a hundred a week in dry cleaning for their clothes."

"I know. And don't tell me what I can't afford. I know."

"How many jobs are you working?"

"Part-time, full-time, or both?"

"That you're asking me to specify is concerning."

"I still have my full-time job. But I have two new part-time jobs in retail for the holidays to make up for the extra expenses."

"You're working retail. For the holidays."

According to his tone, I was attending torture sessions and having my toenails ripped out every day. As a general rule, I agreed with him. If anything, having my toes ripped out daily would be a general improvement to my situation.

I had a brand-new respect for retail workers over the holidays, and I'd do my best to shop online whenever possible—and not bother any retail worker with unnecessary questions or petty problems. I lifted my chin and engaged Kace in a glaring contest. "Well, yes. I have to. Where else am I going to get a job on such short notice this time of year?"

Kace stared at me as though I'd grown a second head. "You have got to be kidding me."

"Life isn't all sparkles, sunshine, and unicorns farting rainbows, damn it."

"No, it's not, but this is not fair to you."

I shook my head. "Life isn't fair, Kace. That's the one truth in life you can rely on. I'll do what I've always done, and make do. I'll be able to pay off the rent issue on Friday, and I'll figure out everything else from there."

The look Kace shot me informed me that I was full of shit, and the arching of his perfect brow sent a clear message I wouldn't like what he was about to say. Then, he opened his mouth and called, "Saul?"

My nephew scampered out of the guest bedroom, a pencil shoved behind one ear and a marker dangling out of his mouth. "What'd I do?"

"You didn't do anything," Kace promised with a crooked grin. "But we're going to do something bad."

Nothing revved a teen's engine like permitted naughtiness, and Saul's eyes widened. "What are we doing?"

Kace pointed at me. "We're kidnapping this train wreck, taking her over to my place, and camping out there for a while. Pack stuff for your sisters, don't forget any of your homework, and yes, all three of you are going to school tomorrow. While you do that, I'll wrangle the woman."

I waited until Saul bolted for the guest bedroom before I hissed, "Like hell you will."

Kace rubbed his hands together. "Try me, Ginger. You can

run, but you can't hide, and one way or another, I'm taking you home with me tonight."

I rolled my eyes. The first thing I needed to do when my sister came home was give her a stern talking-to, as she needed to stop making friends with smug, egotistical, but hot men. "You are so full of it, Kace."

"Just wait until the kids are ready, then you'll see just how full of it I am."

Chapter Two

SAUL, Amelia, and Wendy joined forces with Kace, and the quartet cornered me in my bedroom. Along the way, Saul had discovered I kept a set of bungee cords in the closet, and he armed himself with them. "Aunt Ginger, this is for your own good. Come quietly," the teen ordered.

How was going to Kace's house for *my* good? If anything, it was for theirs, and the little jerks would gloat over their victory if I gave them their way. I thought I'd done well; I'd escaped the quartet for an entire hour before they'd gotten smart and coordinated their capture attempt. Kace blocked the doorway, also armed with various items from my closet, including some rope I'd used to lash my trunk closed after hauling furniture for my sister, who couldn't bear the thought of her SUV's paint possibly being scratched.

I needed to have a long talk with my sister about the facts of life.

"You are not tying me up and dragging me to Kace's house," I announced in my firmest tone.

Unfortunately for me, I stood against an egotistical rich

man, a teen, and a pair of tweens. I didn't stand a chance, and judging from their smiles, they knew it.

"You're coming home with me," Kace announced. "If you come quietly, you'll get six hours of sleep before you have to get up and drive these precious children to school. If you're nice to me, I'll drive the children to school so you can go straight to work. You'll have to call the school to let them know they'll be coming to my house for the foreseeable future, but there's a bus stop right down the street."

"We've taken it before, and it's on the list already, so you just need to authorize it," Saul announced.

I was surrounded by brats, four unapologetic brats. One of the brats was an adult and should've known better.

"This is ridiculous," I muttered.

My statement served to encourage the tweens, and the girls pounced, latching on to my arms and using their body weight to drag me to the floor. After seven days of all work and no play, I proved easy prey for them, and I went down with a startled squawk.

Saul joined the fray, but thanks to the hooks on the bungee cords, he aborted his effort to restrain me, and he looked to Kace for guidance. "How am I supposed to use these things?"

"You're not supposed to use those things on a woman. First, the bands are elastic, so you could cut off circulation to her hands and hurt her." Kace grinned, stepped into my bedroom, and held up his pilfered rope. "This is what you use if you want to tie someone up. That said, we're just going to escort her to my car and shove her in, as I think she's been properly subdued. Right, Ginger?"

No wonder my sister had disappeared. After making sure she'd arranged for a sucker, me, to care for her brats, she'd run away to avoid the terrors of her life. "I just have one question, Mr. Kace Dannicks."

"Ask away, but know that you're coming home with me. If

you're good, I'll swing by McDonald's on the way. You look like you could use a milkshake and some fries."

Damn. Kace meant to play dirty. "Twenty nuggets, just for me, with sweet and sour sauce. If the brats want nuggets, you have to get them their own. That means *you* have to feed them, and if they want forty nuggets each to go with their fries and drinks, you will order it for them without complaint."

"This is called negotiations, kids. It's much easier to get what you want when you have what the woman wants."

I was so cheap, but I wanted dinner so damned bad, and instead of dinner, I'd gotten an hour-long chase around my apartment. "I still get the milkshake and fries."

"If the milkshake machine isn't on, I'll get you a Coke, which I'll turn into a vanilla Coke float when I get you home."

"I am changing my order to a vanilla Coke float, a large order of fries, and a twenty-piece nuggets. Don't forget my sweet and sour sauce."

"Come along quietly, then. Amelia already grabbed clothes for you for tomorrow."

Uh oh. If I trusted her clothing selection, I'd show up at work dressed like I was ready to take on an entire town of randy men. Then again, I only had one slutty dress hidden in my closet, but Amelia would find it. Amelia liked dressing adult women up, and the less clothing involved, the better.

"I grabbed three dresses, matching heels, two pairs of slacks, dress blouses, and the necessary things," my niece announced. "Boys don't need to know about the necessary things."

According to the tween's look, Kace was the top offender.

I almost laughed at being chaperoned by my sister's daughter.

"I won't poke my business into her necessary things without invitation."

The innuendo flew right over my nieces' head, and even my nephew seemed confused by his solemn promise.

Somehow, I kept from laughing. The logical, sensible, and single woman in me didn't want Kace's business anywhere near me, but the wild child I continuously insisted on repressing wanted to test what an invitation would win me. "Thank you, Mr. Dannicks. That's appreciated."

"Anytime. Consent is important, especially when it comes to a woman's necessary things."

I doubted the message would get through to the teenage boy, who operated purely on hormones, spunk, and spite with a dash of proper manners, but I appreciated the effort Kace put in.

"That's right," Amelia chirped, and she tugged on my hand. "Kace has a *pool*."

"It's December, Amelia. It's December in Delaware. In case you missed it, it snowed two days ago."

"It's an *indoor pool*."

Well, then. "Why didn't you just say that an hour ago? I would've surrendered without a fight if you'd told me he had an indoor pool."

Only an idiot refused an invitation to a house with an indoor pool during the hell month of December. As I doubted the tween troublemakers had raided my closet completely, I shook free of my captors and dug through my closet, grabbing the shoebox I used to store my bathing suits and bikinis. I held the entire thing out to Amelia. "And this is my box of things necessary for swimming. Guard it with your life."

After working myself to the bone, I would enjoy a trip to Kace's pool or die trying. With my luck, it could go either way.

Amelia beamed and held my box to her chest. "This was more fun. I put your bag near the door, and we cleaned the bathroom when we were finished in the tub."

I refused to question the act. I would not show a single grain of doubt, and while I would grab a few things from the bathroom before we left, including my favorite shampoo, I would accept the kids would likely never clean to my standards. "Thank you, girls. I appreciate that. I just need to grab my shampoo—"

"It's in your bag, and I put it in a baggie so it wouldn't leak!" Wendy chirped.

Wow. I sensed a conspiracy, and when I turned my attention to Kace, he smirked.

Double wow with a snickerdoodle. I'd been truly played. I blamed hunger and working too much. "How long have you four been scheming this?"

Kace checked his phone. "I came over at eight, and I was regaled with tales about my own swimming pool."

Kids. "I see. And how did this turn into a sleepover party?"

"Well, I initially told them I would talk with you about it, but then you showed me that nice stack of paperwork, and I decided to skip the talking phase and go straight to the decision phase. Following the decision phase is the late-night McDonald's run phase. And yes, I will pay out with however much you gluttons want to eat."

The kids cheered while I sighed. "All right. You win. Take the kids in your vehicle—"

"Nope."

I blinked. "Nope? What do you mean by that?"

"I also talked to them about your working schedule. You're too tired to drive. As such, you're not driving anywhere. The brat can't drive this time of night, so I'm going to take us in my car, and I'll bring the brat over here after school tomorrow. I'll drive your car, and he'll drive mine. I'll take you to and from work."

"Have you lost your mind?"

"I do that from time to time. Don't worry. You'll get used to it."

I would? "But I need my car. You'll be at work when I need to head to the mall, and there's no easy bus route from the office to the mall."

"I'm sure I can force my boss into allowing me to take the proper time off to retrieve all individuals in my care at the appropriate intervals. As I happen to be my own boss, I'm sure I won't have any difficulties arranging my schedule. I'm slightly concerned, as are the kids, about your current work schedule. We'll talk about that tomorrow, as I'm well aware your work ethic will not allow you to miss a shift even if you're dying of plague or about to faint from exhaustion."

Someone had been paying attention, and I was curious who in the lot had the good observation skills. "Fine. We'll talk about it tomorrow."

My tomorrow would end at eleven, and I doubted the man would be eager to string late nights together, as my sister often complained Kace liked being in bed no later than ten, which meant she couldn't indulge in her night-owl tendencies. Generally, I liked Kace's way of thinking. If I could choose my bedtime, I'd be in my pajamas with a plate of snickerdoodles and a glass of milk, wrapped in my favorite blanket, and reading a book by six every day. At no later than nine, assuming I'd finished my book, I would go to bed and enjoy a minimum of eight hours of uninterrupted sleep.

I missed sleep. I missed milk and cookies at my leisure, and I definitely missed my favorite pajamas.

I wore plain, boring ones to keep my sister's children from ruthlessly mocking me.

Kace rested his hands on my shoulders and directed me towards the door. "Grab everything and load the trunk, kids. I will make certain the woman is imprisoned in the front seat. Prisoners get the front seat, so no arguing in the back, either."

In what had to count as a Christmas miracle, the kids did as told without comment or complaint.

There was nothing left for me to do but cooperate, so I followed their excellent example.

※ ※ ※

MY TWENTY NUGGETS, scarfed down so no one would steal them from me, clubbed me over the head and dropped me straight into a food-induced coma. I had vague memories of dragging myself out of Kace's car and into his house, but everything afterwards disappeared into an exhausted blur.

Damned nuggets. Damned hot man who could keep his hands to himself. Damned soft, cozy blanket I'd have to steal.

Two of the three items in my list were okay, but after the few weeks I'd had, I didn't want the hot man to keep his hands to himself. If my thoughts kept wandering back to my sister's business partner, I wouldn't have to snap, crackle, or pop to be fired. I'd be let go for daydreaming at work.

I had enough problems at work. I definitely didn't need a man making even more of a mess of things—or making me look like even more of an idiot than usual.

I refused to regret the nuggets, I definitely regretted wanting the damned hot man more than the nuggets, and I really wanted to keep his blanket.

Stress accounted for most of my thoughts, and my bone-tired state took the blame for the rest of it.

Emerging from my daze without a soft, warm blanket or nuggets annoyed the hell out of me. I had no recollection of making it to work in the first place. Had I gotten my way, I would've stayed lost and only semi-coherent throughout the entirety of my shift and woken up in possession of more nuggets—and snickerdoodles.

I needed an obscene number of snickerdoodles to get me through the holidays.

There was only one thing worse than working retail over the

holidays, and it was working in inventory management over the holidays. Helping companies figure out what they should stock for the holiday rush—during the holiday rush—stressed everyone at my job on a good day.

Any day between October until January counted as a bad day.

One day, I would figure out how big firms could pay out millions for logistical work while I got paid the equivalent of pennies. Without me, the merchandise and materials had no chance of making it from factories in China to the United States without incident and in a timely fashion.

My boss, who likely hadn't touched a contract negotiation, inventory, or anything relevant in at least twenty years, ran home with the big bucks. Half the time, I couldn't find another soul to help coordinate anything, as extra employees were "too expensive."

On my own, I almost made a living wage, and I crossed the threshold with weekly overtime.

I refused to think about how many extra hours I worked.

I wanted to hate my sister for screwing around with my life, but I couldn't. When she wasn't being impulsive, she did a good job raising her kids alongside her work. All things considered, I just wanted my sane life back—and sleep. Sleep would do me a lot of good.

Well, more sleep. The few hours I'd grabbed thanks to some nuggets and Kace's blanket would get me through the rest of the day. Probably. Hopefully.

Maybe, assuming I appealed to the correct deity. Which deity would work? Technically, I counted as a Santa's helper. Would Santa give me some sleep for Christmas?

Rubbing my temples, I tried to make sense of the inventory in front of me. Someone had thought it was a good idea to route a shipment meant for Des Moines through San Francisco, which would ensure chaos while attempting to get the containers to their appropriate destination within the company's budget. Upon closer inspection, I discovered the cause of my life's problems: the owner's beloved son.

One day, when I no longer cared about having a job, I would make heads roll and tell the incompetent idiots down the hall to invest in a map and stop sending shit to the wrong side of the damned continent. The CEO could afford to send his son to a good school—the type of school I only dreamed about attending. His son had gone to said school and had emerged as Fancy Pants Whatever He Was that was in Latin and meant jack shit to me as a general rule.

I wanted to tell Mr. Chaplon's precious baby boy to get some relevant job skills—and shove his precious Latin up his ass right along with his fancy, expensive degree.

Iowa was *not* located anywhere near San Francisco. Had everyone in the firm forgotten Chicago existed? I would've accepted Detroit without complaint. I would've even been happy enough if the container had sailed into Baltimore, New York, or even Charleston.

Anywhere but bloody San Francisco.

Wait. They could've shipped to Alaska instead, or even San Diego. Houston was also a frightening possibility, as was Miami.

In my field, anything could—and did—happen, and I would be the one to pay the price for someone else's mistake.

I drummed my fingers on my desk, shot the inventory a final look, and picked up the phone to begin the tedious process of transforming chaos to order—and getting one of our largest big-box clients their next batch of in-demand goods they planned on selling between next week and Christmas.

In good news, the container was flagged for arrival at their local warehouse in seven days, which meant I had a solid chance of getting it to Des Moines without having to creatively insert my foot—or the damned shipping container—into someone's ass for making a rookie mistake.

In logistics, sometimes cheaper really wasn't better, and for a few hundred dollars extra, the container could've been routed to somewhere sane rather than requiring a few extra weeks and luck to make it to its final destination. As I did every time I went to work, I longed for the day I didn't care about my professionalism and suggested that the firm get rid of the idiots who couldn't read a map.

My third call of the morning involved convincing a snobbish Chinese transport manager the container really did need to go to Des Moines instead of Denio, Nevada. I had no idea how they'd screwed up the transport when the zip code on the damned container was correct.

I needed to put in some serious thought about where I could go that paid better without nearly as much stress.

It took spelling Des Moines and asking how Denio was spelled to convince the man someone on his team had made a severe mistake. Then, when I politely asked to confirm the zip code and run it through the post office's system, I'd won the war. Any other day, I might've savored the uncomfortable silence.

After securing a soft promise to make sure the container would reach Des Moines, where it belonged, on their dime rather than mine, I hung up.

Mr. Chaplon wouldn't find out his son was a complete idiot this time, but next time, I'd be severely tempted to let his half-assed efforts blow up in his face.

"Denio?" my boss asked, his tone displeased.

Crap. My boss had been standing behind me, listening to me work—an unfortunately common occurrence. Screw it. I hated my job, I hated the holidays, and while I adored my nieces and nephew, I hated everything about how my life had turned out lately. "Mr. Chaplon, the younger, neglected to confirm the actual shipping destination with our Chinese supplier, resulting in a rather important shipping container being freighted to San Francisco. I have corrected the mistake. The shipper is paying the difference for the adjusted shipment route." As my boss would find some way to criticize me anyway, I copied down the confirmation numbers on the spare copy of the inventory printout and handed it over to the older man. "This will update by the end of the day with the new route."

As the mistake had been committed by the owner's son, nothing would happen to him. I'd probably get scolded for daring to peep a word of criticism. But if the company wanted to lose money, that was their problem and not mine.

I handed over the sheet with the confirmation numbers written on it, looked my boss in his dark eyes, and said, "I am paid insufficiently to negotiate with Chinese management to correct novice errors. It is also outside of my job scope to reroute entire shipments due to those errors."

"Mr. Chaplon will not be happy to hear this."

"Which one, sir? The one who can't read a map, or the one who paid for his son's degree to learn his son can't read a map?"

My boss frowned, and then, to my shock, he heaved a sigh. "Both, because this is the third time in a week you've had to do a major reroute of critical inventory thanks to, as you say, novice errors. A large contract was just dumped on my lap. One of our larger stores requires a shipment of trendy toys to be distributed to all of their stores for arrival six days before Christmas. They want to be stocking shelves five days before Christmas to take advantage of the rush. I will not be handing this contract off to someone who has made this many novice errors lately, so I need you to take care of it."

My mouth dropped open, and I checked the calendar. There were two weeks and five days left before Christmas.

I needed an entire batch of snickerdoodles to myself, a box of tissues, and some alone time so I could cry. Since crying wasn't permitted at work for any reason, I'd have to wear a shield of sarcasm. Sarcasm probably wouldn't get me fired. If it did, I could handle working two part-time jobs while seeking a new employment opportunity.

Everybody needed logistics managers. I could probably pitch a position to one of the big stores we worked for and save them a fortune handling shipping directly rather than through a logistics firm.

"Well, just call me Santa and ask for a miracle!" I eyed my stapler, the kind meant to tackle thirty pages at once. It would make a very impressive hole through my window, which had a lovely view of the chemical storage and refinery plant polluting Delaware's not-so-pristine shores.

"They specifically requested a split shipment to make certain all containers reach their individual destinations on time. In good news, the supplier isn't too bad to work with. The order is large enough that every container will be full, so you won't have to worry about shared containers."

"And what is the toy of the hour this time?"

"It's a talking doll that can be controlled and customized with phones. They can be taught how to speak using some AI program. It's supposed to be an educational tool to help teach younger children to improve their talking skills. I expect the toys will rise up and take over the world by Easter. It gets better."

When my boss said something got better, he actually meant that the situation was about to get a great deal worse for me. "How does it get better?"

"The accompanying contract is for the line of accessories for the toys, and those need to arrive hot on the heels of the first shipment so the stores can draw in a second wave of people hoping to get the accessories for their new dolls. A third batch, with even more accessories for these dolls, needs to arrive two days after Christmas to encourage sales after the holidays and into January."

"Why weren't they planning this in October?" I whispered.

"Upper-management changes, I'm afraid. I haven't figured out how they got the manufacturing companies in China to work with them on such short notice, but here we are. The manufacturing was finished yesterday, and their initial shipment plan fell through. We're being paid a premium to get these goods to the United States on time and ready for sale for the last leg of the holiday rush."

"It can't come by sea. It takes over twenty days to arrive by sea, excluding transit to their stores. Air freight is their only option. Do we know how many containers they have, the container sizes, and the container weights?"

"I ran the estimates, and you're going to need to arrange for at least twenty full cargo flights for the first wave of toys. They're fairly large, the packaging is obscene, and they want these toys to be noticeable when purchased."

Where the hell was I going to find *twenty* empty cargo planes during the Christmas rush? I closed my eyes and pretended counting actually helped anything. "Can I make a request, sir?"

"What do you need?"

My request would count as unprofessional, but I no longer cared. With luck, I'd be fired. "If you want this done in time, someone is going to have to handle bringing lunch to me, as I will not have time to take a lunch break. In a perfect world, someone other than me will buy my lunch until this disaster is sorted."

"I'll have my secretary take care of it. If you get this done right, I'll talk to Mr. Chaplon about a bonus and a raise. You'll have earned both."

Huh. Maybe Santa was real and miracles could happen. It wasn't the sleep I'd wished for, but it would do.

Chapter Three

MAYBE THERE WERE a lot of idiots in the office, but my boss's secretary and our floor's receptionist, Marianna, knew just what a woman needed to get through the day. Tacos couldn't fix everything, but the tacos came with a slushy, and when I took my first sip, I discovered the slushy was actually a margarita.

Armed with my consolation prize, I wandered across the office to her desk. "You are the best friend a woman could have. This lemon-lime slushy is spectacular."

"And needed, if the word on the wire is right," she replied with a smile. Then, leaning towards me, she whispered, "The lemon-lime slushy is a gift from the man upstairs, who says you obviously needed one after seeing the shipments you're handling."

My brows shot up, and I pointed in the direction of the CEO's corner office, one floor above ours. "That upstairs?"

"That upstairs. He asked me to make it extra strong, and if you needed a cab, that you're to charge it to the company's account. You won't make much progress on the shipment today, anyway."

I hated that she was right—and that I would need my little

slice of alcoholic heaven to get through the day. I took another sip of my slushy. "Thank you very much. I'm going to work, and this drink is the only reason I won't be crying in my office."

"That was a factor," she replied with a smile. "Good luck, Ginger."

If I wanted to make a Christmas miracle happen for a big department chain with poor planning skills, I couldn't afford to waste an entire afternoon drunk. I nursed the tacos and the slushy and went through my contact list of transporters to find every square foot of available cargo space on American-bound planes.

Once in the United States, I'd be able to hire transports with relative ease; the transport industry always needed full loads, and I'd need every available truck in the damned country to get the goods where they belonged. I'd already failed to secure train freighting; early and heavy snowfalls had turned the tracks into disaster areas, and one pass had been obstructed due to an avalanche; repairs were already underway and scheduled to be completed within a week, but not in time to ease the backlog of goods needing to be shipped.

Planes might be an option for the United States, too—even if I had to give a call to some of the more expensive shippers.

I kept a close eye on the clock, and with only a few minutes to spare in the day, I'd secured transportation of the goods from China to the United States.

Tomorrow, I'd arrange for the rest of the shipments and do a check-in call with the manufacturing warehouse to make certain every single container met the import specifications. There would be no delays at customs if I had anything to do with it.

The last call of my day would be a doozy, but it would make certain there were truly no issues. Hiring drug-sniffing dogs for a pre-inspection of Chinese goods toed a few lines, but I'd been in logistics long enough to know that there was an asshole born every minute, and I was not going to be one of the idiots who let their goods become a vessel for drugs and other smuggled contraband.

"Dodson speaking," an old man with a thick Chinese accent answered. The man never failed to amuse me, as he spoke better English than most without having even a drop of American blood—and he'd picked an American name for the sake of convenience, as I couldn't pronounce his real name no matter how hard I tried.

He found my attempts amusing.

"I'm sorry for bothering you at this hour. It's Ginger from LDYJ Logistics. How have your family friends been?" I never understood why he called his sniffing dogs family friends, but I rolled with it; he liked that I didn't just call his beloved animals dogs or pets.

Happy contacts remained contacts, and good contacts made the logistics world go round and round.

"Ah, Miss Harriet. It's been a while. My family friends are doing well. How can we help you?"

"I have a large shipment of toys scheduled to fly out of Shanghai in two days. Can your family friends go have a look-sniff for me? I'd rather there be nothing unscrupulous in children's toys."

"For you, it will be done. Do you need us to see the goods safely onto their planes?"

Santa existed, he loved me, and he wanted me to have a happy holiday. "That would be marvelous. We're on a tight schedule, and the owners didn't plan sufficiently. The cargo is flying out on many different planes, but I have all of the information you need. I can send you the appropriate customs forms and the details for your family friends and the government."

"Excellent. I will eagerly await your information. How long will it be?"

I clicked a few buttons, copy-pasted the entire cargo log,

and sent off an email including the signed authorization forms for his work. "Ten seconds, give or take a few," I answered.

"Which means you have just sent it, as you're always well-prepared for every eventuality."

"On days like today, I wish that were true. I'm about to leave the office, but if you email me back with a confirmation of your fees, I'll make sure my end of things are handled as soon as possible; if it's your standard fee for the goods, there'll be no problems with invoicing."

"It will be my standard fee, no worries there. You are lucky; most companies have already shipped out for the American holidays."

"I'd say I'm anything but lucky right now. This was put on my desk this morning for delivery before Christmas."

"Well, the receiver is lucky you are in charge of their file. I will make sure everything goes smoothly on my end, and I will email you back with all transit information, customs confirmations, and inspection results. I will call you if we discover anything amiss."

"You're a lifesaver, Dodson. Do you need anything else from me?" He wouldn't, but I'd found taking the extra few moments to be polite—and double-check—made a huge difference.

"I have everything I need. Rest well tonight. Looking at the manufacturing sources, I do not expect any trouble. It has been many a year since I've seen issues with this factory."

That was something. "Call me if there are any issues; if it goes to voice mail, I'll call you back as soon as I can."

"I will give you the important details in a message, and I will text you as well."

After the holidays, I would have to nudge my boss to send Dodson and his family friends a gift to thank him. "Thank you. I'll speak with you soon."

We exchanged a few more pleasantries before I hung up, double-checked I had everything I needed for my harrowing adventure to the mall for another stint at the candy store. According to the clock, I had a minute to make it out front before I was counted as late, which would earn me Kace's ire.

Kace hated being late.

I hated being late, too.

To my dismay, my sister's partner was in the reception area chatting with Marianna, and according to her expression, Christmas had come early, and she wanted Kace to take her home with him.

I needed another slushy, a swift kick in the ass for thinking the wrong things about untouchable territory, and a cookie. I even considered buying a cookie or two from work. My cookie fixation would likely lead to weight gain, but I wasn't sure I cared.

Did being so busy I barely had time to breathe help with weight loss?

Marianna spotted me, and she smiled. I blinked, wondering what I'd done to earn her favor.

"I was about to call you. Mr. Dannicks is here to see you."

Kace turned and showed off his sinful smirk. "Ready to go?"

Marianna's brows shot up, and she pointed at him. I foresaw a great deal of explaining to do, but at least I could defuse some of her assumptions. "I am. Thank you for offering to take me to the mall and pick up my car later tonight. It's appreciated."

"I have some bad news about your car." Kace grimaced, and then he scratched his head. "It won't start. I took the brat over to go get it, and it appears to have had irreconcilable differences with its engine. Then, I went to have it towed, but the tow truck skidded on ice."

My eyes widened. "The tow truck skidded?"

"In good news, it only hit your car." Kace cleared his throat, refusing to look me in the eyes. "The tow truck was dinged, but that's about it. The driver looked at your car, and then looked at what was left of your engine, and said it might be for the best.

Your policy number was in the files at my place, so I contacted the company about the incident for their records. There was a police report done because that's the tow company's policy."

"I'm going to need a lot of snickerdoodles to deal with this today, Kace." All things considered, I viewed it as another Christmas miracle, but I kept my tone even.

He reached into his wallet, pulled out a twenty, and handed it to me. "Get snickerdoodles at the mall, however many a twenty will buy, and I will provide the chicken nuggets and the Coke float to get you through tonight."

I accepted the twenty. When disaster came calling, and the source of the disaster was paying for my cookies, only a fool would reject the money. "I might need a slushy, too."

Kace frowned. "A slushy?"

"Margarita, extra large, heavy on the alcohol," Marianna replied, rising from her seat and coming around her desk to pat my shoulder. "Will you need a ride to work in the morning? I live near you."

"I've got her," Kace replied. "I've decided I'm taking her home for the foreseeable future."

So much for attempting to defuse any assumptions. "Thank you, Marianna, but I'll be all right."

I don't think she believed me, as she sighed. "Call me if you need anything."

As my pride had already left the building, I nodded. "If I do, I will," I promised.

I'd do everything in my power to make sure I didn't, but a new—or used—car wasn't in the cards, and I'd seen molasses flow faster than my insurance company when it came to making a claim. No matter how I looked at it, I was screwed.

But, I'd be screwed with cookies, nuggets, and a Coke float, which went a long way to convincing me everything wasn't all bad. I just had to get through the next few weeks. That was all.

A WISE WOMAN napped whenever possible, and I had no shame about dozing in Kace's car. If the man needed help finding the mall, he'd have to ask his fancy phone, which made mine look like I'd fetched it out of a dumpster—which wasn't too far from the truth. I'd gotten it from a batch of phones work handed out for those who might need to take work calls in the middle of the night, also known as me.

Technically, I owned a phone, but it lived in the bottom of my purse. I paid for it by the minute, used it only when necessary, and worked hard at pretending it didn't exist. Most of the time, I even got away with it, taking it out of my purse every now and then to charge it. I'd kept it charged for the past week hoping to hear from my sister.

I hadn't.

"Should I go around the block a few times to give you a few extra minutes of sleep?"

"I am fortifying myself against the holiday rush. Better just drop me off before I lose my nerve and run away."

"If I told you losing your nerve and running away was an option, would you listen?"

"I'm afraid not. If I don't show up at work, I can't get my cookies."

"This is the honest truth. What time should I pick you up?"

"I should be done shortly after eleven, give or take thirty minutes."

"I'll be here at eleven. I don't want you to wait that late at night." Kace muttered something under his breath before asking, "Which entrance?"

"Macy's is closest."

"Hell is a mall near Christmas. I'm not sure it's safe to leave you here."

"It's a lot safer than leaving your nice house in the clutches of two tweens and a teen unsupervised."

Kace shuddered. "You have a terrifying point. I think I'll just drive you up to the doors and drop you off like a proper gentleman. If you don't see me when you get off your shift, wait somewhere safe, please?"

"I can do that."

"Call me if you need help with anything. You have my number, right?"

Digging through my purse, I found my phone and checked to make sure it hadn't died on me. It still lived, much to my amazement. I checked my contact list. "Apparently not."

He told me his number, and I dutifully added it to my phone.

He pulled up at the doors, and before he could come up with some excuse to make me miss work, I thanked him and bolted out of his car, taking care not to slam the door before hauling ass into the mall. The mall mayhem had already begun, but I made it to the store in plenty of time for the start of my shift. To my horror, the pet store down the hall was open for business and was in the middle of an adoption fair, the kind destined to bring screaming children and overwhelmed parents through our doors.

To add to the chaos, the toy store had a sale sign proudly displayed, and beleaguered mothers on the hunt swarmed the place.

Children.

Animals.

Toys.

The ingredients for an utter disaster waited in close proximity to each other, and I wasn't sure if I wanted to laugh or cry. A pen of white puppies took over a chunk of the hallway, and their huge paws on their tiny bodies promised they'd become behemoths in a few months. A lone husky puppy shared their pen, and the poor thing cowered as far from the crowd as possible.

I considered asking if Kace was accepting applications for a house sitter who came armed with one or two puppies. If I could con him out of affordable rent, I could have a puppy—or two. My boss would even let us bring dogs in to work as long as they were trained and quiet.

After Christmas, I wouldn't have to work retail, either, so I'd have the time needed to take care of a dog.

Tammy snagged me as I drew close to the cookie shop, leaned close, and whispered, "The puppies are going to kill us all."

I stared at them, gulping. "I want the husky."

"You and me both. Along with every single kid in the mall. It's a trap. They have lovebirds, too. An entire flock of lovebirds."

Uh-oh. I could take care of birds. Hell, who was I kidding? If I could adopt the entire pet shop, I would. "An entire flock?"

"Go look. Quick. I'll hold down the fort; you still have ten minutes before you're on shift anyway."

When Tammy said I needed to check something out, something spectacular or horrific was going down. I headed for the pet shop, afraid of what I would find.

To my delight—and horror—the pet shop had twenty cages with pairs of lovebirds seeking new homes. They even had a toucan, and one of the pet store employees was letting children pet the massive bird, who seemed to love the attention.

Since a pack of puppies wasn't enough to draw in a crowd, another playpen featured more kittens than I could count. I fought my urge to squeal over the fluffy little balls of joy I wanted to take home and cuddle for all eternity.

They had orange balls of fluff, gray balls of fluff, tabby balls of fluff, patchwork balls of fluff, and even black balls of fluff.

The unfairness of it all made me want to wail. Keeping a

close eye on the time, I went to the puppy pen and tried to make friends with the husky. After five minutes of cooing to the little baby, it wiggled closer, allowing me to reach in and stroke its gray, white, and black fur.

I needed to take the puppy home, and I knew nothing about puppies, their care, or anything. I also couldn't afford a puppy, which killed any hope of actually having a pet.

According to the sign, the white puppies were three hundred dollars each. The husky, which came with papers proving her status as a purebred show dog, cost a thousand dollars. Her price tag shocked me, and I floundered to breathe.

If I had a thousand dollars, I wouldn't be scraping pennies to pay my rent.

If I had a thousand dollars, I wouldn't be quite so panicked about my dead car.

If I had a thousand dollars, I'd be the mommy of a frightened little husky puppy.

Reality stated there was no way I could have a puppy, and I couldn't even adopt one of the hundred-dollar kittens, either — even with a sign nearby proudly declaring all pet necessities were on sale for anyone who purchased an animal during the adoption fair. There was even a representative from a local shelter, who looked ecstatic, as her cages no longer had any pets available for adoption.

Heartbroken I wouldn't be going home with a furry friend, I returned to work. Tammy met me at the entry. "It's terrible, isn't it?"

"I love the puppy, and she costs a thousand dollars." It helped admitting the truth. I couldn't have the puppy, but Tammy would share my anguish. Tammy loved dogs, too. Tammy loved anything that wasn't human and had a pulse.

Tammy patted my shoulder. "Everyone is sharing your heartbreak. She's a looker, isn't she? Poor thing is so scared, though. She definitely needs a loving hand. I bet you'd be an amazing puppy mom. Huskies can be energetic, but puppies are the spice of life. And we could both use some spice in our lives."

Ah, the truth sucked. We did need some spice in our lives — and not the troublesome sort, including Kace, my sister's disappearance, or my destroyed car. However much I pretended to complain, I loved my nieces and nephew, and they were the right kind of spice, although I preferred them in limited doses. "She let me pet her."

Tammy nodded. "You were so patient with her. She's precious."

"I have twenty dollars to spend on cookies. I plan to eat my feelings tonight." Kace's offerings of nuggets and a Coke float would help soothe my anguish, too. If an alcoholic lemon-lime slushy came my way, I'd go to work severely hungover but well on my way to healing.

Raising a brow, Tammy looked me over. "That's a lot of cookies. I suppose a milkshake or two wouldn't hurt you at all. It looks like you've lost weight."

Raising my sister's kids on a budget had something to do with that. "I'm going to need a lot of cookies after this. Anything I should know?"

"Unfortunately, yes."

Uh-oh. That didn't sound good. "What's going on?"

"There are three drunk Santas in the mall, and the rumor is that the mall elves are about to go on strike in protest of the drunken Santas."

I couldn't tell if it was a Christmas miracle or a disaster. "It's going to be an interesting night, isn't it?"

"That's one way to put it. Buckle up, girl. It's going to be a wild ride."

Chapter Four

THE MARCH of the Slutty Elves began at the pet shop. I didn't have the heart to blame the puppies for attracting the women. I had no idea why there were over fifty scantily clad Santa's helpers, where they came from, or what they were protesting, but they had signs, made a lot of noise, and drew everyone's attention.

About ten minutes after they started their commotion, the Santas showed up, and as warned, some of them were drunk. Most of the drunk Santas tried to "talk sense" into the women, and if I didn't need the paycheck, I would've joined the crowd watching the drama unfold.

The customers fled the candy store, and I stared out the window, delighted at the reprieve from helping parents calm their hyperactive children with bribes of sugar. I doubted their efforts would work well for them, but I wished them the best.

Tammy and one of the stockers, a high schooler saving up for college, joined me at the register to stare out the window at the insanity. Rufus covered his mouth and tried his best not to laugh—or stare—at the women.

It didn't take me long to figure out he was an ass-man in training.

Oy.

"Oh no. That Santa is looking at your puppy." Tammy pointed, and sure enough, one of the Santas was looking at the husky while talking to a store employee. I classified him as a drunk Santa, but he seemed to be standing stable enough that he wasn't just shooed away from the animals.

He gestured to the lovebirds, too, which made the store employee look positively delighted.

"And the lovebirds, too." Screw it. I'd had a bad enough day to justify sulking. "At least he's not bothering any of those poor women."

"Don't poor-women them, Ginger. See the blonde with the melons that belong at a farm fair competition?"

I bet her breasts could be seen from space without requiring a zoom lens. "It's hard not to see her, Tammy."

"She's a stripper. The drunk Santa she's protesting is her husband."

I stopped and blinked. "Wait, what?"

"He probably looked at another elf's ass and pissed her off, so she organized a revolt. She loves being Santa's helper, but she only goes on shift with her husband. This happens every year. She gathers the prettiest elves, and they start their march. They're an hour later than normal, truth be told."

"The March of the Slutty Elves happens every year?" What the hell had I been missing at the mall? If this was a yearly ritual, I would have to start hanging out at the mall to enjoy the chaos when I didn't have to work. "Are you serious?"

"That is the best name ever for the Santa's helper protest. They're protesting this year because they cut an inch off the skirt size again. They either have to buy their own dress, or one is provided—most take the provided dress because they're a little too expensive to buy, or they have to make it themselves to keep them decent. But this year, they can't bend over without giving the entire mall a show. Crouching presents a hazard, too."

I considered the skirts, which had gone from mini to microscopic territory. "I would have worked extra hours to buy my own dress."

"Me, too."

Sure enough, the Santa who'd opted to ignore the protest bought the husky puppy and a pair of lovebirds, a cage, and enough pet supplies that it took four huge bags to hold it all. Then, because the toys, bed, and other accessories wasn't enough to satisfy Santa, he bought five huge bags of food.

Even Rufus stared at the Santa, spluttering at the insanity of it all. Finally, he pointed and said, "Is he supplying his new dog for an entire year?"

"It looks like it," I replied, somewhat relieved the dog was going to someone who was willing to go overboard for her sake. It didn't change the fact that I wanted to find a thousand dollars and beg Santa to let me buy her from him. The puppy, wearing a new collar, harness, and leash, tried to hide among the bags.

The protesting elves waved their signs, complained to the Santas, and offered the entire mall free entertainment. The shine wore off after about ten minutes, and I went through the motions of preparing for the next wave of customers.

"If you stop fighting," a deep voice boomed, "I will buy you all cookies."

Shit. I spun around, and to my horror, the one making the proclamation was the new owner of my puppy.

I hated Santa. He needed to assign himself to the naughty list for bringing our candy store into their protest.

Tammy paled. "Oh, Holy Mary Mother of God. We're doomed."

"Miss Tammy?" Rufus asked.

"Yes?"

"The word you're looking for is fucked. We're fucked."

That we were, and neither one of us could bring ourselves to correct him. In the face of encroaching disaster, only the f-bomb would do, and if I hadn't valued my professionalism quite so much, I would've flung a few with vehement vigor.

"Rufus, wash your hands and get a pair of gloves on. You can pack cookies and anything else from the shelves. I'll handle the register," I said, and I looked around the store, wondering how the hell Tammy would manage the floor on her own. "I'm so sorry, Tammy."

"I'd rather you go a little slower and make no mistakes than hold the line up for longer because of one, because there's no one as hungry for sweets as angry Santa's helpers. The March of the Slutty Elves has begun."

Sure enough, the women spent all of twenty seconds discussing the situation before they decided that cookies and other sweets beat protesting. The Santa even managed to recruit several of the women and two of the Santas to ferry his new pet supplies across the hall to our store.

No matter what, I would not cry.

Who the hell was I kidding? If they bought out all of the snickerdoodles, gingersnaps, or even the chocolate chip cookies, I'd take it beyond mere crying. I'd be in a corner sobbing and rocking.

Tammy patted my shoulders. "If they buy out all of the snickerdoodles, I will start a batch so you have them to take home with you. They don't take that long to make, and the ingredients we need are in the back. I'll even tell the boss we had a March of the Slutty Elves trample through the store to make up for clocking out late. But honestly? When he sees tonight's profits, he won't care at all."

It really would be the little things that got me through the holidays without snapping.

THE MARCH of the Slutty Elves and their drunken Santa cohorts stormed through the store and left ruin, a pair of lovebirds, and a puppy in their wake. Their supplies had, somehow in the chaos, been moved into the store, out of the way, where they'd gone unnoticed until the puppy's whining drew our attention.

Rufus and I exchanged looks, then we stared at the pile of supplies and the birdcage carefully placed so the birds wouldn't be disturbed. The puppy had somehow hidden behind the bags, but I could see the dark tip of her tail peeking out from near one of the many food bags.

"Uh, Tammy?" I called, not sure how to break it to our manager we had a major food safety violation in progress. Fortunately, the birds and puppy had been stashed in the packaged goods closer to the front of the store, which would make our lives easier. I checked the clock, astonished so much time had gone by.

The mall would close in ten minutes, and there was no sign of the Santa responsible for the birds and puppy being abandoned in the candy store.

Tammy walked over, and when I pointed at the corner, she sucked in a breath. "You have got to be fucking kidding me."

"I hadn't even noticed because it was so busy in here, but then the puppy started to cry." I left the register and hurried to the bags. A bright red-and-green envelope placed on top of the white bag caught my eye. "There's a card?"

Tammy joined me, snatched up the card, and flipped it over. The envelope hadn't been sealed, and with a shrug, she pulled out a Christmas card featuring a puppy wearing a Santa hat. She blinked several times before bursting into laughter. Then, shaking her head, she handed the card to me.

The card was addressed to the "Pretty little blonde who was

nice to the puppy" and wished me a Merry Christmas. The card included a gift receipt for everything in the store, including the puppy and the lovebirds, along with a phone number to call if I couldn't have any of the animals for any reason and a promise they would be cared for.

My mouth dropped open, and I stared at Tammy, stared at the card, and stared at Tammy again.

"Rufus, we're going to pull down the security gate a little early and make some snickerdoodles. If anyone asks, we have to restock. We're also going to have to do extra cleaning because of the dog and birds tonight."

Considering the damage the March of the Slutty Elves had done, we really did have a lot of restocking work to do. My eyes burned, and I waved the card, unable to think of a single thing to say.

Rufus frowned, and he took the card, reading it over. "Damn," he said, shaking his head. We all stared at the card for a long time. "I'm sixteen, and I learned today that Santa is real, and he really likes you, Ginger."

"Santa is insane." Who bought some random person a puppy and a pair of lovebirds? It didn't matter I'd wanted the puppy with every fiber of my being. It didn't matter I'd adore the lovebirds and would do the best I could for the pair.

Only a crazy person bought animals for a stranger who couldn't afford the food bill or vet bill.

I regarded the bags, which were so loaded with supplies I'd probably be able to feed my puppy and birds for at least six months before I needed to buy anything else. I checked the puppy's papers, which were in a white packet. According to the sheet, she had all of her puppy shots and would be due for another round in March.

Huh.

I could afford to have a puppy and lovebirds.

While Rufus and Tammy waged war with the security gate,

I gingerly moved aside some bags, set the birds where they'd be safe, and tried to coax the puppy out of the corner.

It didn't take her long to decide I was safer than the corner, and she wiggled onto my lap while whining and whipping her tail. While worried she'd pee on me from excitement or anxiety, I petted her and did my best to calm the poor baby down. She hid her nose under my arm.

Yep, I was doomed. Nope, I wasn't just doomed. I was fucked. I had a puppy, and she wanted to hide with me, and there was no way I could call the number on the card and give up the puppy who viewed me as a safe haven. I would find a way to make it work. I'd have to move, and since I faced eviction anyway, I could move to a place that allowed a dog.

Tammy looked in my direction and burst into laughter. "Looks like Santa got the puppy a human for Christmas."

Tammy was not wrong.

"I will help close in a few minutes," I promised.

"Rufus can handle most of it, so just coach him if he needs help," Tammy replied.

My life had turned upside down on me again. I had a puppy on my lap, my part-time job manager was telling me to slack off, and I had a pair of birds to comfort, too. The birds seemed happy enough to keep each other company in their cage.

All I had to do was call Kace, swallow what was left of my pride, and beg to keep a puppy at his house until I could figure out what to do.

It would be the strangest call I'd ever made in my life.

Unable to think of any reason to delay, I twisted around and asked, "Rufus, can you hand me my purse? I need to call a friend of mine. He doesn't know I have a puppy and birds to take home in his car. Mine broke earlier today."

"You really are having a rough day, aren't you?" The teen skipped into the back where we kept our personal items and returned a few moments later with my purse. "Here you go. Do you want me to do the cash?"

"After I call my friend, I'll have you do it while I guide you," I promised. Then, drawing a deep breath, I located Kace's contact in my phone and called him.

"Hello?" Kace answered.

"It's Ginger," I replied. "There's an issue."

"What's wrong?"

"I wouldn't exactly say something is wrong. Not exactly. It's not wrong as much as it's unexpected, possibly an inconvenience, and after the day I had, I'm really going to need some extra nuggets tonight. Okay, it's definitely an inconvenience. But it's a good inconvenience. I think."

At the rate I was babbling, Kace would think I'd lost my mind.

"Strangely, I'm all right with being inconvenienced. You're working retail before Christmas. I'm expecting to be making late-night runs to McDonald's to keep you sane. What happened?"

"A drunk Santa bought me a puppy."

Silence.

I wasn't sure if I wanted to laugh or cry.

"Could you repeat that? I couldn't have possibly heard you correctly."

"A drunk Santa bought me a puppy, and he left the puppy—and a pair of lovebirds—in the store with a Christmas card, a gift receipt, and a bunch of stuff to take care of them. None of us noticed until after the March of the Slutty Elves ended."

"Until after the *what* ended?"

"The March of the Slutty Elves."

"Where do you work in the mall? I'm already here, and I feel like I need to come in before they lock the doors."

"The candy store across from the pet shop," I replied.

"I'll be there in five minutes." Kace hung up.

Five minutes wasn't a lot of time to close the cash, but then again, I expected we'd be waiting for the cookies. Santa's helpers had cleaned us out of every single cookie, there was one sad cupcake left, and I had no idea how the morning staff would make enough for tomorrow. As I expected the puppy would flee to her supplies, I eased her off my lap and placed her near the bags.

She followed me to the register and crowded my feet.

"You have an attachment," Rufus said, peering down at the husky. "Don't tell anyone I said this, but she's possibly the cutest thing I've ever seen in my life."

I loved teenaged boys, who were so determined to be manly but fell head over heels for puppies, kittens, and many other adorable things. "It's okay to like cute things. I tell my nephew this every time I see him. Don't listen to what any of the assholes say. It's *always* okay to think a puppy is cute. And if the person you are speaking to doesn't believe the puppy is cute, back away slowly and with great suspicion. If they're cat people, you can test them with kittens. If they dislike puppies and kittens, leave and go to a safe place with people who like kittens or puppies."

"That is the best advice anyone has ever given me."

"You can tell a lot about a person from how they treat animals."

"That's also really good advice."

"I try. So, the register isn't hard, but you need to be careful. It's always better to take your time and do the job right rather than mess this up, because heads roll when the accounting doesn't add up."

Rufus listened, which put him head and shoulders above most of the other people who worked in the store. I showed him how to close the register for the night, how to properly count the money, and how to lock everything up. The entire time, my puppy sat on my foot, pressing close to my legs.

A few minutes after starting to work with Rufus, Kace arrived and sat on a bench in the walkway watching the store like a demented humanoid hawk on the hunt for some fresh meat. That I was his choice of fresh meat disturbed me more than a little.

If he hadn't been stupidly wealthy, my sister's business partner, and otherwise unavailable, I likely would've worn something brightly colored and pranced around to draw his attention. In the wild, I would've been the male, Kace would've been the watchful female, and things would've been a lot more complicated.

Fortunately for me, we weren't in the wild. Unfortunately for me, I needed to keep my hands off him.

Having a puppy around would be all the distraction I needed. Why did I need a man when I could have a puppy?

When I found out where my sister had gone and dragged her back to the United States where she belonged, I would scold her for daring to have Kace as a business partner, thus evicting him from the pool of eligible single men.

It was an exclusive club featuring only him, and I planned on scolding my sister for a full hour over that alone. She deserved it.

It took twenty minutes longer than usual to close the register, but I didn't mind that Rufus took his time. He did the job right, and when tomorrow rolled around, the employees opening the store wouldn't want to murder us for leaving them with a mess they'd have to clean up.

The real mess was the store itself, which would take a lot longer than twenty minutes to fix. "Tammy? How do you want us to handle the cleanup?"

"Blitz. I've already contacted the morning shift about the situation so they know they'll have extra work."

I considered Kace, who sat patiently on the bench in the

hallway. "We could recruit the guy on the bench to help. He's driving me home because my car broke."

"If you don't tell I won't tell," Tammy replied before disappearing back into the store's kitchen, where most of the candy magic happened. "Your cookies will be done in ten minutes."

With a little help from Rufus, I lifted the security gate enough so Kace could come in. "You can enter, but you have to help us clean if you do."

"You drive a hard bargain," he replied. To my amusement, he didn't even hesitate before entering the store.

The fool.

"It looks like a storm swept through here. What happened?"

"The March of the Slutty Elves," Rufus and I chorused.

Giggling, I pointed at the closed pet store. "They had a lot of puppies and kittens up for adoption in an event. It seems to be a yearly event, but all of the Santa's helpers protested their shortened skirts. One of the Santas is married to one of the helpers, and they're the primary instigators. Or so Tammy says."

"They have six kids. The holidays fry their brains," my manager announced from the kitchen.

My mouth dropped open at that piece of news.

"That's a lot of kids," Kace muttered. Then he stared down at my feet at my new puppy, who insisted on sticking to me like a burr. "Are you aware that your new puppy is a husky?"

I nodded. "She's not just a husky. She's a purebred husky with paperwork. She hasn't been spayed yet, but she's still a little young. I don't know when I should spay her."

"She's really a purebred?"

I nodded.

"You'll want to check her bloodline before you spay her. If she's from a rare or dying bloodline, you'll want to breed her once or twice. Purebreds can have major inbreeding issues, so it's usually advised to look into the bloodline to keep the breed diversified."

I stared at Kace with wide eyes. "You know about dogs?"

"I fucking love dogs," he announced, his gaze locked on my puppy.

Rufus stared at Kace a lot like Kace stared at my puppy.

There were worse role models Rufus could pick. "Rufus, this is Kace. He's my sister's business partner. Do you want to show him the ropes of cleanup while I handle the front and keep the puppy away from the stock?"

Tossing Kace into the care of a teenaged boy was likely pushing my luck, but the young man in training successfully made off with the gentleman to restore the store to rights while I handled the front with my new loyal companion. I would need to find a doggy therapist, as I expected I had a puppy with severe separation anxiety in the making.

I could live with my new puppy adoring me, but I wanted her to be happy when I couldn't bring her with me, and I refused to become one of those pet owners who ignored the signs and took their dog everywhere. Hopefully, a doggy therapist, if such a thing existed, could help me figure out how to ease my baby's anxiety.

Then again, I'd be anxious, too, if I'd been dumped in a cage at the mall and put on display. I'd likely attach myself to the first kind soul to come my way with every intention of never leaving the safety of their presence.

I couldn't let Kace learn that, not when my defenses were already lowered. He'd already discovered one of my dirty secrets, and he could get me to eat my prized nuggets right out of his hand with little work on his part.

Who needed grapes when I could have nuggets instead?

Add in my shameless love of snickerdoodles and their nefarious cousin, the delightful gingersnap, and I was a lost cause. I could be bribed into doing just about anything when presented with nuggets or cookies.

Cleaning might help purge me of my inappropriate thoughts—or not.

Kace was cleaning, of his own free will, and there was nothing sexier than a man who was willing to help with housework. If he knew how to wash the dishes, clean the bathroom, and do the laundry, I was doomed.

When I got my hands on my sister, I was really tempted to kill her for convincing Kace to be her business partner. It wasn't fair she got to hoard two good men, one through marriage and the other through legitimate work arrangements, thus making him off limits to me.

I wanted to scream—and march in protest of the situation. After my marching, I'd have to make friends with some cookies.

Damn. Maybe the Santa's helpers had had the right idea all along. I couldn't even blame them for marching. After seeing the length of their skirts, I would've marched in protest, too.

I was all for a woman embracing her inner slut and going out for a night on the town, but she deserved the right to pick when she showed off her ass rather than have it forced on her by a bunch of perverted Santas and their boss.

To clear my thoughts of Kace and his wicked ways, I cleaned like I meant it, careful to step around my puppy whenever I moved. She followed me around, wagging her fluffy little tail and occasionally pouncing—and mouthing at—my shoe. Were huskies oversized cats? My shoelace interested her a great deal, but as it kept her quiet and amused, I pretended I wasn't encouraging her to develop a bad, destructive habit later.

Who needed shoes when I could have a puppy?

It took us an entire hour, with help from Tammy, to restore the store to rights. My manager exchanged my twenty for a massive box of cookies, which smelled so good I wanted to find a corner and begin my rampage.

"Thank you for your help, Kace," my manager said, showing off her most charming smile.

Kace smiled, too, and I put some serious thought into heading for the corner rather than figuring out how to haul everything to his car.

Before I could retreat and indulge in a cookie-fueled sulk, both Rufus and Tammy offered to help carry everything downstairs, and we took turns guarding the supplies we couldn't ferry down in one run. It took us three trips, and Kace's car barely had room for everything when we were finished loading it up.

Once my co-workers left, I got into his car and settled my new puppy on my lap while Kace secured the seatbelt around the birdcage in the back. "I'm really sorry about this."

"Don't be sorry, Ginger. It's obvious you like dogs, and I'm not going to say no. My house has plenty of room for a puppy. The only reason I don't have a dog or two right now is because I wasn't sure how to handle my work hours while giving them enough attention. Mostly, that's just an excuse. I'm the CEO. I could bring a puppy to the office if I want. I just didn't want to get too busy for the puppy. It never occurred to me to get birds, though. These are pretty cute."

"They're lovebirds. I presume one is a male and one is a female, but I'm really not sure. I'm going to take my puppy to work with me, but I'll need a dog sitter when I'm working in the mall."

"I volunteer."

"I am prepared to offer you a share of my cookies as thanks."

"I am prepared to accept your offer of cookies to babysit your puppy. What are you going to name your new pets?" Kace got behind the wheel and started the engine.

"I have no idea. I haven't gotten beyond having a puppy or birds." I hoped I hadn't done something stupid like hit my head on something. "It's not something I could afford."

"It looks like Santa realized that. He bought out the entire store, I think. I'm impressed it all fit."

"Me, too. Do you think nuggets will fit in this car somewhere?"

"There's a small amount of space in the trunk I reserved for your nuggets. I have to get stuff for the kids, too. It seems they also want McDonald's."

"We should try to feed them something healthier tomorrow."

"Agreed. Today is for junk food that's horrible for us. Tomorrow, we'll negotiate with the teenager and his sisters."

"You can't negotiate with them. The instant you negotiate, you lose. It's a rule. You have to go the dictator route—but you have to be a benevolent dictator, so they think you're doing things for their benefit. That's when you start tricking them into doing their chores." I laughed at that, shaking my head. "I had to teach them how to clean. It's been a daunting task. They have no life skills."

"That would be because your sister lacks life skills."

My eyes widened, and I sucked in a breath. "I haven't checked on their house."

"It's still standing. I drive by it on the way to work. I have no idea what the state of the inside is, though."

I groaned. "I'll find time tomorrow to check in on the house."

"Is it even possible for you to find time in your schedule tomorrow?"

"Not really, but I'll have to. I'll swing by after work."

Kace made a show of checking the time. "Are you seriously telling me you're planning on going to your sister's place at midnight tomorrow to check in and possibly clean the house?"

"Yes."

Shaking his head, he heaved a sigh. "Okay. I'll drive you to Michelle's house, but I'm giving you exactly sixty minutes inside. I've heard about what happens when you start to clean.

If someone doesn't stop you, you'll clean until the entire house is finished. I've been warned about you."

I stroked my puppy, lifted my chin, and refused to look him in the eyes. "I don't know who warned you about me, but they're wrong. I know how to stop!"

"Everyone who knows you, Ginger. You hate a dirty home. But I've taken steps."

"You have?"

"I hired a maid service this afternoon, and the kids have been keeping an eye on their activities. There will be nothing you can clean in my house."

"Kace! You didn't have to do that."

"I didn't have to, but I had three kids desperately worried you'd clean my house. If Michelle left her house a mess, I'll hire a cleaning service to handle the problem and give her the bill when she comes back home."

If she came back home. "Have you heard from her?"

"No, but you received a letter from Botswana today, and it's in Michelle's handwriting. It was dated from a week ago."

My sister would be the one to finally make me snap. "I really might kill her this time."

"Can we wait to see what the letter says before you decide to kill her? I put it in the safe at my house. I haven't told the kids you received a letter."

"That was wise of you."

"Look on the bright side. You'll have all the nuggets and cookies you can eat when you deal with Michelle's letter. That's something, right?"

"The letter better tell me my asshole sister is fine, and it better include her bank card so I can rob her blind," I muttered. "I'll even deal with her lawyer again if it means she's fine and is just delayed getting home."

"If she didn't include her bank card, I'll handle the expenses and make her pay me back, and there's nothing I enjoy more in life than making Michelle pay me back for things. She hates it."

She'd always hated owing anyone anything. "I'll think about it if you charge interest."

"Not only will I charge interest, I will make her pay for your nugget therapy program. I expect this will be quite expensive. I underestimated how many nuggets such a tiny woman can consume in a single sitting."

"And I need every last one of them to get through the day."

"After seeing the candy store, I'm not going to argue with you. But the nuggets come with a condition."

I could make a few guesses. "I can't kill my sister."

"That's right. You can't kill Michelle. It's a good deal. Unlimited nuggets in exchange for leaving her alive—and I'll make her pay for them."

"Deal. But if the letter says something I don't like, I'm charging extra."

"You drive a hard bargain. Dare I ask what you'll have in addition to your nuggets?"

"Copious amounts of alcohol."

Chapter Five

EIGHTY NUGGETS, enough fries to feed even a teenaged boy, and milkshakes filled Kace's dining room table. I squished the momentary pang of guilt over forcing the man to feed me before descending on dinner like a starved beast.

My puppy, who still needed a name, sat on my foot and played with one of her new toys.

"There's an important lesson here, kids. Keep the women in your lives fed. When hungry, women are terrifying."

"Is that why Mom gets pissy some nights?" Amelia asked, waiting until I'd secured my box of nuggets before selecting one for herself. "Mom breathes fire sometimes."

"Possibly hunger, possibly pissed at me because I told her she shouldn't pursue one of her crazier ideas. She hates when I tell her no," Kace replied, snagging a box for himself. Then, to make it clear he didn't want anything to do with dealing with a hungry woman, he fished out several of his nuggets and transferred them to my box. "Feed the beast, kids. Feed the beast."

Thanks to his demonstration, I received a payout of six extra nuggets from my nieces and nephew.

I accepted their challenge, thanked them for their payment, and addressed the serious business of eating dinner.

Food was sleep, and sleep was a scarce, precious resource—and would be until my sister showed up.

I'd wait until the kids were fed and in bed before finding out what Michelle's letter said.

"Mom's probably just wandering again. Mom does that, and she talks Dad into it because Dad thinks Saul should be a mature adult-in-training and can take care of us without help," Wendy said, snatching a fry and pointing at Kace. "And Mom is mad you wouldn't go with her last scheme."

"Wendy, your mother wanted me to invent a self-flying kite so she could sit on a beach and watch a kite without having to do any work."

I considered that, rather liking the idea of a self-flying kite. "I don't see anything wrong with that."

"It's too lazy. If she wanted me to invent a kite designed for weather monitoring, security monitoring, or something cool like that, I'd be game. She just wants to watch kites, though. Toys can be fun, but we're not in the toy business."

"You should be. You should see how much this one company is paying for an emergency shipment of a talking toy."

Kace cringed. "I've heard about that disaster in the making. Latest trendy toy, you can teach them to talk?"

"Yep."

"I'm officially banning those things from this house."

My sister's kids pouted.

"But they sound cool," Wendy complained.

"They sound like the end of the world, as these robotic demons will rise up and take over."

I choked on a nugget. When I could breathe again, I grabbed my milkshake. "Robotic demons?"

"That's what those things are. Robotic demons."

"Have you seen one of these toys?"

"I have a prototype in my office at work. The company that makes them uses some of our software for their AI abilities. They really might rise up and destroy us all."

"And here I thought you'd be proud some of your software was used in them."

"Disgusted, really. Disgusted by how much the manufacturer spent on our software. They paid out half a million."

My brows shot up. "How the hell are they going to earn that much back from toy sales?"

"They're selling them for north of a thousand dollars each. That's how. There are five different models, and the first edition will be numbered. The second edition will sell for just as much, also be numbered, and introduce five new models. Last check, there would be five editions, all numbered, before a general release. We get paid again for a new license for the general release, too."

Who would pay a thousand dollars for a *toy*? My mouth dropped open. "Repeat that for me. I couldn't have heard you correctly."

"Each toy costs over a thousand dollars, and there will be twenty-five different variants, all numbered. The general release will have all of the models, but they won't be numbered. Their generation will be listed on the toy to help them be more valuable down the road." Kace shook his head and handed me another of his nuggets. "It looks like you're going to need another nugget to deal with that."

My head hurt. "That explains why they're so determined to get these out for the Christmas rush."

"That would be the last color batch, I bet. They released the first four color batches a month ago, and then they announced there would be a special edition releasing for Christmas." Kace chuckled. "Those ones will sell for closer to two thousand each."

"Who the hell can afford two thousand dollars for a talking toy?" I snatched a nugget and chomped on it. With two thousand, I could buy a cheap junker to get to and from work instead of relying on Kace to drive me around everywhere.

"That's a really good question, and it's one I don't have an answer to. And no, I am not buying any of you that toy. That way leads to madness. If you want the toy, you'll have to get a part-time job and earn the money yourselves."

Damn. Kace didn't pull his punches.

Wendy and Amelia, too young to legally work yet, pouted. Saul considered it. "Aunt Ginger? How long would I have to work part-time to earn enough to buy one of them?"

"Three months, give or take a few weeks. You have to pay your taxes, travel expenses to get to and from your part-time job, and so on. That's assuming you can only work four hours a day after school and on weekends. Assuming you're working seven days a week four hours a day, you'll make a little over two hundred a week after taxes and expenses."

Saul's eyes widened. "You didn't even think about that. At all. You just knew."

I saluted the teenager with my next nugget victim. "I am the undisputed queen of part-time jobs right now. They'll pay you minimum wage because you're young and desperate for work to pay for a toy that'll talk back."

"Is that really it? That's all I'd be paid?"

"That's really it, kiddo."

"Please tell me your regular job pays you more."

For all of my sister's faults, she's gotten one thing right: she's raised her kids to care about others. "They do."

Kace snorted. "She isn't paid even half of what she deserves. If her company had half a brain, they'd double her pay. I'm thinking about hiring her out from under them."

My brows shot up at that, but rather than make a comment, I focused on my dinner.

My nieces and nephews locked on to Kace, and I imagined

the *Jaws* theme playing while they circled, ready to devour his flesh from his bones—or interrogate him. Possibly both.

I needed to talk with my sister about whether she was raising young lawyers.

I wasn't sure if I could deal with three young lawyers I liked. They might take over the world if they joined forces, too.

"All right. I see I have captured your interest. Ask your questions."

"Why do you want to hire Aunt Ginger?" Saul demanded.

"She's smart, she's a hard worker, and she'd be the prettiest woman on the executive floor."

"But Mom's on the executive floor."

"My commentary stands."

My nieces and nephew turned their attention to me, and I ignored them in favor of drowning a nugget in sweet and sour sauce and devouring it. As I expected, they redirected their curiosity back to Kace.

"Okay. Aunt Ginger is pretty, but you can't hire women just because they're pretty," Amelia announced.

"Please note that I ranked her third in appearances, with her work ethic and intellect taking the top spots."

"If you think Aunt Ginger is pretty, you should marry her," Wendy declared.

I choked on my nugget. Of course my niece would come up with a gem like that and spit it out while I was eating. I grabbed my milkshake, wheezed, and somehow evicted the nugget out of my lung. "Wendy!"

"What? It's true. Then you can be the prettiest woman on the executive floor. Mom totally lets couples work together in the company. She loves it because if something happens with the couples, she can help get them therapy and stuff. And it lets her keep an eye on the other ladies. Sometimes, if there's trouble, she'll step in. Last month, she helped a nice lady get out of an abusive relationship. That dude didn't work at the company, though. She fires abusers."

Kace sighed. "Wendy, that's supposed to be confidential information."

"Not my fault the jerk tried to come to the offices and start problems. I saw it, so it's not confidential. It happened in the lobby."

Maybe my sister had run away after dealing with nightmares at work, and if that was the case, I couldn't even blame her. I'd be tempted to run away, too. "When did that happen?"

"A month ago, I guess. That guy was a real class act." Wendy wrinkled her nose. "Mom went ballistic, called the police, and even escorted the woman to her home to pack. He was arrested for assault because he hit the lady. It was filmed, and he's still in jail for it. Mom was getting as much dirt on the loser as she could before she left on vacation."

My sister was out to give me gray hairs, I was certain of it. "Please tell me she didn't get physical with this man."

"She wanted to, but security got involved first. Kace got really upset over the whole thing."

"Did you really have to bring me into this?" Kace grumbled. "Don't worry about it, Ginger. The guy will probably rot in jail for a long time. He was denied bail, and his trial will start in January. The police found a lot of evidence of wrongdoing, so he's got a charge list a mile long. Our employee has moved, and she's still with our company, but we transferred her to a different office so she would feel safer. There's also a restraining order in case he's released from prison."

"Please tell me that's the only serious case like that at work."

Kace, my nieces, and my nephew refused to look me in the eyes.

"Michelle ran away because her work life is insane, didn't she? And she took Mitch with her. Did you three brats help drive your mother crazy?"

"Yes," they replied.

I had no idea how they could take everything in stride. Shaking my head, I resumed munching on my nuggets in the hopes of having enough energy to deal with my sister's letter. I bit in to discover the nugget cold and unsettlingly squishy. I snatched a napkin and spit it out.

While I'd heard rumors of unfortunate souls receiving a raw nugget, I'd never dreamed I'd become one of them. My stomach churned, and the sight of the raw chicken meat did me in. I bolted for the bathroom, leaving my puppy to squeak and whine at the table.

Life sometimes just wasn't fair.

※※※

MY PUPPY FOLLOWED me into the bathroom and pawed at my side while I regretted having fallen prey to my favorite food. How could my precious nuggets betray me?

Why had I drawn the shit lot and gotten a raw nugget?

I hoped I hadn't swallowed any of it, and even if I had, I suspected I'd thrown up everything I'd eaten last week along with dinner. Then again, with my luck, I'd be down and out from salmonella within a week.

When it rained, it poured.

"Ginger? You okay?" Kace asked from the doorway.

"I'm never going to be okay again. I ate a raw nugget. I've been betrayed, Kace."

"At least you threw it up. Hopefully you won't get sick. In good or bad news, however you want to view it, that was the only bad nugget in the lot."

"I'm going to die from food poisoning, which will result in the lamest headstone message in existence. 'Here lies Ginger. Her love of chicken nuggets killed her.' I don't even have a will. Who is going to take care of my puppy?"

"You're going to take care of your puppy, because you aren't going to die from a raw chicken nugget. However, I will be watching you closely, and I already spoke with the manager at the McDonald's while you were occupied. I requested the relevant corporate information, and should you get sick, I'll make sure they handle the situation appropriately."

"If appropriately is a lifetime supply of chicken nuggets, I may need to be restrained."

"With how you attacked those nuggets, I don't think you'll be able to say no to them for long."

"You're right. I'll just break my nuggets in half before eating them in the future."

"That's the spirit. Can I get you anything? A drink? The kids tossed the rest of the nuggets and raided the freezer for frozen pizzas. They'll be ready soon if you want some."

Food was sleep, and sleep was a precious resource I lacked. Without my nuggets, I'd have to eat something or be worse off tomorrow. "I'll try a slice."

"Shout if you need anything." Kace retreated.

After he left, I stroked my puppy to convince her the world wasn't ending quite yet. "We're both having a rough day, aren't we?"

I underestimated the jumping abilities of husky puppies, and she washed my face with her tongue before I wrangled her and set her on my lap. Laughing, I rewarded her with another round of petting before taking the time to clean Kace's bathroom. With all evidence of my nugget mishap erased, I returned to the dining room.

"I'm not sure I'll ever be able to eat a nugget again, Aunt Ginger," Amelia whispered.

"I think I'll be taking a break from them for a while, too." I shuddered. "I don't want to know if they're made of real chicken, but I have the feeling I'll find out soon enough."

"They're made of real chicken," Kace said, returning to his

seat. "The pizza will be ready in a few minutes. I expect these three brats to scarf down their pizza and head right to bed."

My sister's children saluted Kace.

I sat, and my puppy picked up her toy, flopped over my foot, and resumed playing. "I'm sorry I inflicted that disaster on you."

As one, my nieces and nephew rolled their eyes.

Amelia looked me in the eyes and replied, "You shouldn't apologize for something you didn't do. You didn't ask for a raw nugget, did you?"

"Despite appearances, I have sufficient common sense to avoid doing something that stupid."

"Despite appearances? You are not stupid," Kace retorted. "No one who can juggle as much as you do plus wrangle three brats could ever be stupid."

"I think he likes you, Aunt Ginger," Wendy announced in a false whisper.

A beep from the kitchen spared me from having to answer, and the kids bolted for the oven. I shook my head, wondering if I should let them test their luck. On second thought, they might burn Kace's house down. "Don't forget to use the mitts and turn off the oven!"

"Yes, Aunt Ginger!" the three chorused.

"I hope two pepperoni pizzas will feed us."

If it didn't, I'd be concerned. "Are they qualified to handle two pizzas on their own?"

"We're about to find out. In good news, if they somehow destroy both, I have more in the freezer."

"Is your freezer stocked solely with frozen pizza?"

"I would be lying if I said no."

I stared at him, my mouth dropping open. Even I, who scraped pennies, managed better than a freezer loaded with frozen pizza. "How often do you eat frozen pizza?"

"Never. I cook them first."

No amount of ibuprofen would be able to conquer my growing headache. "That's something."

"It's a good, quick dinner on nights I work late."

Kace worked late? I didn't believe him. I narrowed my eyes. "Define late."

"After seven."

His late was closer to my normal. "You're an old man trapped in a young man's body, aren't you?"

"Michelle likes to say the same thing for some reason."

"Should I be concerned about how often you eat frozen pizza?"

"I already told you I cook them first."

Kace would be the one to finally drive me completely insane. Before I had a chance to reply, the kids returned with the pizzas and set them on the table. Amelia picked the slice with the most pepperonis and offered it to me on a paper plate. "We're being classy tonight, Aunt Ginger."

I raised my plate in a salute. "This is the best type of classy. Someone fetch the snickerdoodles. We may as well be properly classy."

There was no way the snickerdoodles would betray me. Tammy made the best snickerdoodles, and I'd never seen her mess up a batch of cookies since I'd started working for her.

Wendy bolted from the room to fetch the box from the kitchen. I expected the cookies would last less than ten minutes in the hands of three starving kids plus Kace. I'd take two and hope my stomach handled them and the pizza without resulting in another dash for the bathroom.

I claimed my two cookies and settled in to watch the feeding frenzy. Kace grabbed two slices before the three kids rampaged and devoured the rest of the pizzas. Once they finished, they cleaned up, said goodnight, and ran from the room.

I doubted I'd ever understand my sister's children.

"That was different," I muttered.

"I suspect they have gotten certain ideas." Kace shook his head. "I'll get the letter and be right back. If you start feeling sick again, let me know."

"I'm pretty sure it takes up to a week for salmonella to kick in, but should I start feeling like I'm plagued, I'll let you know."

Kace shot a glare my way before leaving his dining room. I checked the box of cookies to discover three had survived the feeding frenzy. I'd probably regret eating another one, but I did it anyway.

Then, as I'd already crossed the line of no return, I went after the other two like they were the last cookies on Earth.

When Kace returned, he set a plain white envelope on the table beside my cookie box. "I was tempted to open it and read it, but I decided I'd show some patience. It was hard."

I bet. Kace had almost as much to lose as I did with my sister's latest stunt. I pushed the empty cookie box aside, straightened my shoulders, and tore into the envelope.

Glitter spilled out, covering my hands and the table.

"This time, I'm really going to kill her," I announced in my coldest voice. "She's in fucking Africa, disappears on me, and her first communication is to send me fucking *glitter*?"

"Please don't kill your sister."

"Where the hell did she find glitter in fucking *Africa*?"

"Why wouldn't there be glitter in Africa?" Kace eyed the mess on his polished wood table. "That's going to be awful to clean up, but it could be worse."

"How, exactly, could it be worse?"

"She could've sent powdered glitter. These are pretty big pieces. That's easier to clean up, right? Imagine if she'd sent powdered glitter."

My sister would. I sighed and tipped the contents of the envelope out onto the table. More glitter spilled out along with a pair of earrings and a slip of paper. I unfolded the paper and read, "Will be back for Christmas. Will call the lawyer to let him know my return date. Don't kill Kace, say hi to the kids."

Not only had my sister lost her mind, she'd also lost her ability to write in complete sentences, too. Sighing, I set the sheet down and looked at the earrings, which were made of beaten gold shaped into discs. "She included a pair of earrings as a bribe to avoid killing her, I see."

Kace retrieved his cell phone from his pocket and dialed a number. "Gerry, sorry to wake you at this hour, but did Michelle call you? Yes? What did she have to say?" Kace's expression soured, and he spent a long time listening. "Why didn't you call me right away when she contacted you? Okay. Thanks."

While Kace looked like he wanted to send his phone on a short flight to the nearest wall, he set it on the table instead.

"That doesn't bode well."

"She called him yesterday, didn't tell him where she was at, where she was going, or when she'd be back, but asked to have funds released to you. The catch? You'll have to go to her house and find the debit card she had drawn up in your name. Apparently, she abused her power-of-attorney rights and opened an account for you and put money in it."

"She had a card brought up in my name?"

"Never give your sister power of attorney, Ginger. You did that. You fool."

Fuck. I had. "I have made some serious mistakes in my life, Kace."

"It's all right. This isn't a complete disaster."

"It's not?"

"She said she's coming home for Christmas, so you only have to last until then, right? And she has a bank card for your use. You won't have to work yourself half to death."

If only that was so. "I'm not going to abandon my part-time

work right before Christmas, Kace. That would be an asshole move."

Kace stared at me like I'd grown a second head and possibly informed him the world was going to end within the next ten minutes. "I underestimated your work ethic."

That didn't surprise me. "Most do."

"Obviously, I'm going to have to be on my guard. You might attempt to maintain your work ethic even when ill."

"If I'm that sick, I do stay home."

"That's something, but I question what you consider 'that sick' to be. It's likely much different from my own definition."

Kace really was out to drive me insane. "If I think I'm contagious, I stay home."

"I don't think salmonella is contagious."

"Then there's no reason to stay home, is there?"

"Yes. You'll be sick, so you should stay home. I can make an arrangement with your part-time job if needed. The older brat could use some real-life job experience. He's old enough to work. If Michelle didn't want him earning his keep, she would be here telling me no. But no, she's in Africa, doing her best to drive us crazy for the holidays."

"I think I threw up last week's lunch, so I doubt I'll get sick."

"I've met you, Ginger. A week from now, you're going to be so sick you're not going to be able to crawl to the bathroom without help. Your car got taken out by the tow truck that was supposed to take it to the mechanic for repair."

"I'm trying to forget about my car for a while."

"It's just a little extra evidence you have awful luck. You're going to be sick next week. It's better to plan for it now."

I snorted. "Want to make a bet on that? I'm not going to get that sick."

"I'll make a bet, sure. When you get sick, you get to be my

captive prize, and you have to even pretend you're being cruelly held hostage to the three brats sharing the house with us. Except you're not allowed to escape me, so you have to stay in the house unless I'm taking you to the doctor. That means you have to accept pampering from me and the kids, as I'm sure they'll side with me."

"Why the hell would you consider me a prize? I'll probably be throwing up everywhere. That's not a prize. That's a punishment."

"You're a treasure I get to claim as mine for the duration of your illness. You'll be a captive because I can't imagine an independent woman like you willingly accepting pampering from a mere man such as myself. I can see you accepting pampering from the kids because you'd appreciate the effort they'd put in."

Damn. Kace had categorized me rather accurately. Worse, I could find a certain appeal about being his captive for a while, especially if the chicken nugget rose up from its grave in a week, seeking revenge. "Since when have you counted yourself as a mere man?"

"The instant I realized I was outclassed by my partner's sister," he replied with a sly grin. "I'm debating if I should hire you to be an accountant, my executive secretary, or find an even better role for you. And before you get upset over the executive secretary line, it's one of the most important jobs in the office, and the position requires someone who can do a lot more than handle a calendar."

"I'm a logistics manager, Kace."

"You can still do that as my executive secretary."

I rolled my eyes. "My sister would kill you if you hired me as your executive secretary."

Kace only smiled. "I recommend you don't get sick in a week, because I will use that time to convince you to work for me."

"This is a dumb bet. What do I get if I don't get sick?"

"It seems only fair if you get to take me as your captive prize."

I stared at him, wondering if he'd hit his head while we'd been hauling puppy supplies to his car. "How does that benefit me?"

"I'd be forced to drive you around, feed you whatever you want, allow you to rule over my home—anything goes, really. I'd be your captive prize to do with as you please."

"All right, but only because I don't have the time or the money to get a new car until after the holidays. But you have to drive me around until I don't need a part-time job anymore."

"You have a deal."

Chapter Six

TAKING my puppy to work created all sorts of problems and interruptions, but she behaved better than my co-workers, who wanted to become friends with her. Upon discovering her, almost everyone abandoned their work to raid a pet store several blocks down the street to bribe their way into her affections.

As the demonic robotic toys of doom wouldn't ship themselves, I worked around the chaos, doing my best to ignore everyone who couldn't get over my puppy. I expected a few of them believed I was the last person on Earth who would fall prey to a puppy. More than a few likely whispered to each other, wondering how I could afford a dog in the first place.

Secrets didn't last long among the gossips, and one of the most notorious gossips in the entire company worked in HR. Salaries were supposed to be private, but news of how underpaid I was started spreading within ten minutes of showing up with my puppy in tow.

Maybe I'd take a few blind leaps of faith and ask Kace if he'd been serious about hiring me. A job upgrade, better pay, and an infuriatingly handsome boss seemed like a good way to celebrate the holidays to me.

As I did most days, I checked my email. Dodson confirmed his work order, left the results, which removed some of the stress; there was nothing amiss with the pricey order of talking dolls, although as part of the inspections, someone had pressed the button to activate it, resulting in a short sound clip and general chaos in the inspection facility.

I needed to have a long talk with Kace about the responsible leasing of his software.

With the shipments cleared to enter the United States and the appropriate inspection and customs forms prepared, I could work on the next stage of turning chaos to order: finding shippers to send the goods to the stores eagerly waiting for their ridiculously expensive toys.

In good news, the phone calls made it easy to keep my co-workers out of my office; I hung a sign on the door notifying them I was working on a critical shipment and that any interruptions might lose us a contract. The threat did the trick, giving me several uninterrupted hours to make miracles happen.

Fortunately, I had a number of contacts in the industry to get the job done, although I struck out for several hours before finding enough reliable shippers willing to take on the challenge. It would cost more than I wanted to spend, but it would get the toys to their destinations right on schedule.

As promised, a lunch of tacos and an adult slushy appeared right after noon, and I only left the office long enough to walk my puppy, who waited with admirable patience. While I provided pee pads for her to use, someone had already trained her to do her business outside.

I assumed someone had taken her out in the middle of the night to prevent any accidents.

While I worked, my puppy's new collection of toys kept her amused, for which I was grateful. I did indulge in taking off my shoes and rubbing my toes in her fur, something she didn't seem to mind.

It took an entire day with her to decide she was an embodiment of all virtues. Virtue was an odd name for a puppy, but she was mine, and nobody other than me needed to like her name.

When the end of the day rolled around, Kace showed up with the kids in tow. Between the four of them, the rumor mill at work would be interesting tomorrow, especially as the resident gossips had stayed later than normal, likely hoping to continue their campaign to charm Virtue.

I suspected I would be asked how old my kids were, how long I'd been married, and why I hadn't talked about them in the morning.

Kace smirked, and I bet he'd come to the same conclusion and enjoyed the idea of me having to explain I wasn't his wife.

Virtue stuck close while I hauled her supplies and new toys to the car. "I see you have fetched the brats."

"Aunt Ginger!" the three protested.

Well, that would save me some trouble tomorrow. I'd have to find some way to thank them. "What? I checked the dictionary. I found a family photo next to brat in the dictionary."

They pouted.

"And what do you have to say for yourself, Mr. Dannicks?" Hopefully the difference in our last names would put an end to the rest of the gossip and spare me from my version of a living hell.

"They begged for a trip to the mall, but I told them if they wanted to go, they'd have to stay there until you were done with work. Once you're done with work, they'll watch the puppy while we run your last errand of the day."

The last thing I wanted to do was go to my sister's house, but I couldn't push it off forever—especially if I wanted to survive through the holidays with my sanity intact. "Thanks. I named her Virtue."

"Cute name. How'd she earn it?"

"She demonstrated an understanding of all-important virtues while I was working today. I almost named her Patience, but she's a husky. They're work dogs, aren't they?"

"They are."

"I'm going to have to enroll her in some courses. Think she'd be good at showing?"

"I have no idea, but I do know who to ask. I'll make some calls while you're at work tonight." Kace helped load his trunk before evicting Amelia out of the front seat so I could have it. "I made arrangements for dinner for you tonight. Tell the brats what time your dinner break is, and they will kidnap you so you can eat the finest fare the food court has to offer. Afterward, they're going to cook us something for a late-night snack. I've been told they won't burn my house down, and that you have been teaching them the basics of cooking."

We were all going to suffer from food poisoning within a week. I'd managed to teach them the basics, but I hadn't done a good enough job to prevent illness. I hoped they would surprise me. "And will these children be using a proper cookbook for their efforts and follow the directions exactly? No shortcuts?"

Amelia joined her siblings in the back of the vehicle. "We're using a cookbook! Kace took us to a bookstore on our way here to pick up what we needed, and we ordered the ingredients online."

All I could do was pray for a Christmas miracle. If they screwed it up, I'd have to teach them how to do it right in the future—and choke down their efforts with a smile. When my sister came home, I would go out of my way to torture her.

I'd enjoy every minute of it.

"All right. Be careful. The last thing any of us needs is one of you getting cut because you're playing with knives."

"We'll be careful," Saul promised. "We want to cook for Mom when she comes back."

Kace got behind the wheel, and I stared at him in silent questioning.

He chuckled and started the engine. "I showed them the letter when I picked them up from school today. I think they're planning on cooking all of your favorite foods, prioritizing the dishes Michelle hates so she has to be appropriately grateful while also being tortured."

"I really like tacos."

"Mom hates tacos so much," Wendy replied, and I loved how the tone of her voice shifted to one of pure, gleeful evil. "Mom's wrong about tacos. Tacos are life."

"There's a taco joint in the mall, and it's perfect if you want to hate yourself while you eat it. It's so bad it's good."

"I'm in!"

Her sister and brother held out for a few moments before they decided a meal of awful Mexican sounded good to them, too.

I would return my sister's children fully corrupted, and I would be proud of it.

"How about you, Kace? Are you going to come have awful Mexican with us?" I smirked, well aware he'd view my question as a challenge.

"Well, now I have to. What time?"

"Nine, and I'll only have half an hour. What are you going to do with Virtue while you're eating with us?"

"I'm going to invest in a puppy crate, which I will set up in the house. As I'm the one neglecting my puppy duties, I'll pay for the crate. If I was doing my duty properly, I wouldn't need the crate. I expect she will howl upon separation from her chosen human, but she'll be all right. I have a camera, so I'll film her to see how she does."

"That'll work. Make sure you offer all the cuddles she wants, but don't force her into cuddling unless she wants to."

"It didn't take you long to become a protective puppy mother."

"I am determined to be the best puppy mother on this planet." Money would be an object later down the road, but I'd figure something out. I always did.

And unlike yesterday or the day before, I had options. The options might lead to dark places with Kace as my boss, but if I needed to climb the work ladder to care for Virtue, I would.

I'd fight with my sister over the situation later.

CHAOS REIGNED AT THE MALL. I supposed the elves liked our cookies so much they staged a second protest to get some more. Instead of dinner with Kace, my nieces, and nephew, I helped hold off the masses, sparing the few seconds I could to text Kace with a warning I'd have to skip out on them due to holiday-induced insanity.

Everyone in the mall wanted a snickerdoodle, and they were willing to wait for the batches to finish baking to get them. While they waited for the cookies, they tore through the store. The March of the Slutty Elves expanded to include retail workers on break and in dire need of sugar, children with beleaguered parents about to get an unpleasant reminder of why it wasn't wise to feed their children sweets so close to bedtime, and an entire herd of police officers.

The cops came at the request of mall security, who couldn't believe our store could be the actual target of so many shoppers. To keep to the store limits, a pair of cops kept a head count of people in the store, organized shoppers into a line, and otherwise maintained order.

My stomach gurgled a complaint, and after a shift of smelling snickerdoodles bake, I wanted nothing to do with my favorite treat. If I hadn't known it took time for salmonella to incubate, I might've thought my chicken nugget was already rising from its raw grave to kill me. I clung to the only silver lining of my day: holiday-induced indigestion could be resolved with dinner and an antacid. I kept a stash of the antacids in my purse, and chewing on one would buy me time until I found something to devour.

Despite knowing my sister would be coming back for Christmas, despite having the understanding I could take a step back, I couldn't bring myself to quit the insanity.

I'd given my word to work as much as I could until the holidays were over. That meant I needed to show up until the end of the month. No matter how badly I wanted to crawl into a corner, have a good cry, and sleep for a week, I'd do what I did best: I'd keep putting one foot in front of the other.

I might need to grab a few weapons along the way. A cookie sheet might work—and make a satisfying thunk when connecting with the thick skull of an asshole shopper. I couldn't afford bail, nor would I accept it from anyone, not even my sister. Understanding I wouldn't be leaving jail for a long time if I went postal and rampaged kept me smiling and pretending everything was okay when it wasn't.

By the time the end of my shift rolled around, I shook from exhaustion, and I would need to buy stock in antacids to survive until I found something to eat. I went over my work two extra times to make certain I hadn't made a stupid mistake before tossing in the towel.

Kace and three disapproving children waited outside of the candy store when I finally emerged. Virtue sat on Kace's foot and wagged her tail when I slipped beneath the security gate. With five choices of who to greet first, I went for my puppy, crouching so I could pet her. She made excited puppy noises and washed my face with her tongue.

"To bring the puppy into the mall, we were forced to buy her presents from the pet store. We're not sorry for this," Kace announced, holding up a small bag from the pet store next door. "We have decided this will be our usual ploy to bring Virtue inside the mall whenever you're working."

Nothing was more dangerous than a sexy and clever man who brought me my puppy after a hard shift. "Thank you. I'm sorry I skipped dinner on you."

"We peeked in at dinnertime and saw the madness. We decided that you were serious that it was insanity and opted to offer you our forgiveness for neglecting us so terribly."

"You're insufferable."

He smirked. "Michelle likes telling me that often. While I'm insufferable, I'm good at what I do, so she can't get rid of me. You can't get rid of me, either."

"I can't?"

"You'd choke before paying for a cab to get to work, and you can't walk that far. I wouldn't put it past you to try, but you don't have enough hours in the day. You're stuck with me."

He was going to drive me crazy. I looked to my nieces and nephew for help.

As one, the little traitors shrugged.

"I see how it is. Well, you three brats have late-night cooking to attend to while Kace and I run an errand. The faster you three are delivered to the kitchen where you'll serve as underaged slaves, the sooner I get to bed. March!" I took Virtue's leash, and as I'd had a hard day and needed my puppy's love, I picked her up and cuddled with her. "I didn't get any cookies today because I've been smelling the damned things bake all night, and if I look at another cookie today, I might get sick."

Literally.

Kace dared to laugh at me. "You've had a rough day, haven't you?"

"Rough doesn't even begin to describe it."

"It'll be all right," he promised. "One day at a time. This'll be over soon enough."

In some ways, that was exactly what I hated the most about my situation. All good things came to an end, and soon enough, I'd have to return to my old life.

I already loved Virtue, but I wasn't sure if she'd be enough to fill the holes when I returned to living alone. Despite myself, I'd fallen in love with having kids underfoot, being too busy to breathe, and dealing with Kace and the many troubles he brought with him whenever he showed up. Once the holidays were over, I'd have to have a long talk with a bottle of wine and get myself sorted.

I thought I'd been happy before life had blown up in my face.

Life liked proving me wrong.

KACE DISABLED my sister's alarm system using a blue fob on his keychain. The fob also unlocked the door, which both amused and bothered me. Regular keys seemed far more secure than some tech doodad some hacker could have a field day with. I kept my criticisms to myself and peeked into my sister's house, which ventured into mini mansion territory.

The stench of old dishes left unattended sucker punched me. I clapped my hands over my mouth, my eyes watering at the unfair assault to my nose.

Kace frowned, leaned closer, and took a single sniff.

"Someone left dishes in her sink or an animal somehow entered the house and died. I'm not sure which."

I was so glad I'd left Virtue with the kids. The puppy would've gone ballistic at the scents, which were pungent enough I considered finding a Walmart and spending some of my little money on a gas mask. "I'm billing my sister two hundred an hour to detox her house."

"I think you're underselling yourself. Charge three hundred. Add fifty dollars per vomit event. My nose says one of us is going to lose this battle, and I'm man enough to admit it might be me. That smells disgusting. What the hell did she do?"

"I bet she left dinner out on the counter to rot. Possibly breakfast, too. She loses her fucking mind when she's about to go on a trip. And the kids? Until they came to me, they didn't know how to clean anything properly. Training has been a slow, tedious affair, but I have made progress with them."

"You might need to give Michelle some parenting lessons. I'll add a parenting surcharge to the invoice for the care and training of her kids. I'm also going to require a confidentiality clause. If the other gentlemen figure out you're mother material, you'll be swarmed."

I snorted at that. "Have you been drinking?"

"Not yet. That's going to happen after we get home. After dealing with this, I'm going to need a stiff drink. I'm probably going to work from home and rock in a corner to get over the trauma. And my nose? My nose is telling me there is trauma ahead."

"Whoever pukes first loses."

"You make it sound like we're both going to puke."

I pointed into my sister's house. "The kitchen is on the other end of the house, and we're smelling this from *here*?"

Kace gulped. "You have a disturbing point. Maybe we should call in professionals."

"No. I refuse to be defeated by my sister's slobby, chaotic ways. I will make this house presentable."

"I would like to remind you that you only have an hour to do this."

I faced Kace, looked him in the eyes, and replied, "I am not leaving until this place has been detoxified."

"No matter what I say, I'm going to say the wrong thing, won't I?"

"I hope you're trained in how to clean."

Kace grimaced. "I'm really not."

Just like my momma had done to me as a child, I snatched Kace by his ear and dragged him into my sister's disaster of a house. "There's no time better than the present to learn. You're a damned full-grown man. You need to know how to cook, clean up after yourself, and otherwise function as an adult. I hope you're a quick study, or we'll be here all night."

"I'm not that bad, I swear."

"I don't believe you, Mr. Dannicks. As such, you can prove it."

He whimpered, and the hopeless sound made me laugh. "Mercy, please."

"Hell no. If I have to deal with my sister's messes, so do you. You encourage her, and don't you even try to tell me you don't."

"I surrender. I'm guilty as charged. I promise I'll help clean properly, just let go of my ear."

"If you run, I will find you, and when I find you, I will create even worse messes for you to clean. I will recruit the kids to help make the worst mess possible, all so you can clean it. I recommend against running."

"That threat is absolutely terrifying."

"It's not a threat, Kace. It's a promise."

✻✻✻

A TOXIC WASTELAND of rotting food, dishes that should've been cleaned weeks ago, and a mold infestation in the sink did me in. I lost my bet, detouring straight to the bathroom, which likewise suffered from neglect. My lack of dinner only made things worse. Kace held my hair out of the way, a gesture I'd appreciate if my stomach ever settled. "It's even worse than I imagined," I whispered.

"We'll figure this out, even if I have to find a service to clean it."

"I won't lose. I will not. I refuse. I will not be defeated by her damned kitchen. Find me a damned clothespin."

"Clothespin?"

"Wooden clamps for hanging laundry. She keeps them in the kitchen drawer near the back door."

Kace gulped. "I think I can hold my breath that long. Will this hurt our noses?"

"I don't care if I hurt my nose."

"But won't we taste it if we breathe out of our mouths?"

I gagged at the mere thought of tasting what I'd smelled in there. "Maybe I'll take my chances. Scented candles? Febreze? Anything?"

"I'll check her cleaning closet, but don't get your hopes up. She hires a maid service, too."

"I will kill my sister when she gets home."

"You won't kill her. You'll just teach her how to clean. It'll be a rehabilitation program. I'll help. You can teach me how to clean at the same time, too. I won't run away." Kace shuddered. "I don't think we'll have that kitchen detoxified in an hour."

"I don't think we will, either. If we do, will you reward me?"

"Ginger, if you clean that kitchen in an hour, I'll have to marry you, because it's going to take a miracle to get that place detoxified in an hour."

My brows shot up at that, and I regained enough control over my stomach to stare at him. "Have you lost your mind?"

"No, I just saw that kitchen. My father told me the instant a woman capable of performing miracles crossed my path, I should marry her because I'll never get another chance for someone like that. Seems like good advice now. Because that's exactly what it's going to take to clean that kitchen in an hour. A miracle."

"Does it still count as a miracle if you're helping?"

Shaking his head, Kace laughed. "Ginger, I'm man enough to admit all I'm going to be in that kitchen is a liability. I'll cost you more time messing up your work than helping. That's what always happens when you dump someone into a new chore for the first time."

Kace underestimated my ability to calm chaos and restore order. "I'm not going to hold you to any bet like that. Don't be an idiot. You don't just marry someone because she can clean efficiently."

"I saw that kitchen, Ginger. That's not just cleaning efficiency. That's exorcising the devil from Michelle's home. We've entered devil possession territory."

The mess must have broken Kace. Cleanliness would hopefully restore him to sanity. Taking a few moments to control my breathing and force my stomach to obey me, I thought the problem through. "You will begin timing me the instant I step into that kitchen. When I tell you to do something, you will do it, even if it sounds absurd. Questioning why I want you to do something costs me time, and I will be very upset if I have to spend even an extra second in that kitchen like it is. Are we understood?"

"Understood."

I straightened my shoulders, glared at the filthy toilet, and spent five minutes restoring it to order while Kace watched me with a brow raised. When I got tired of his silent questioning, I said, "One or both of us will be in here heaving again, Kace. It's inevitable. At least let us worship a clean porcelain throne."

"I hate how serious—and right—you are."

"Ditto."

TO WIN A WAR, a strategy was required, but in the middle of a toxic emergency in my sister's kitchen, the worst sources of evil had to be vanquished first.

Michelle might never forgive me for my method, but there was nothing quite as satisfying as ordering Kace to hold open a garbage bag while I ruthlessly threw out every contaminated dish on the counter. My sister could view replacing her dishes as another part of her bill. I doubted even her fancy dishwasher could fully decontaminate anything she'd left sitting around for weeks.

Gross, gross, gross.

I indulged in a cursing fit, spewing f-bombs without remorse, sprinkling them in multiple times for every sentence and offering Kace a running commentary of the various ways I'd make my sister and my brother-in-law pay for their various crimes.

He held garbage bags for me, and each time I filled one, he hauled it to her trash cans for disposal.

I pitied the garbage truck operators when they arrived to remove the evidence of my sister's sins.

Once the worst of the mess was outside stinking up the entire neighborhood, I tackled the next chore: the salvageable dishes. As I'd misplaced my last fuck, I hoped her fancy dishwasher was as badass as Michelle believed, neglecting to do more than scrape the dishes before dumping them into the machine. If the machine broke, she could afford a new one—and I would count it as yet another lesson learned about not leaving a disaster in her home before leaving on a long trip.

"You're ruthless," Kace observed from the safety of the doorway. To make it clear we waged a losing battle, he spritzed more air freshener into the kitchen. "You're terrifying."

"Are those compliments or insults?"

"Compliments and expressions of awe. I had no idea a human could get up at five in the morning, go to work until almost midnight, and then rampage through a disgusting kitchen without collapsing. You're doing this on a small breakfast of a bagel and whatever you had for lunch. Honestly, I'm terrified you didn't have lunch."

"I had lunch. It contained an adult slushy. The adult slushies make everything a little better. You know your life is bad when the boss is sending you adult slushies during the work day to help you get through it."

"Your boss is sending you margaritas? During the work day?"

"And tacos."

"Do you run on tacos and chicken nuggets? I know my diet has room for improvement, but I'm really starting to be concerned."

I thought about the past few weeks, grimaced, and started the dishwasher before tackling the grime encrusting the counters. "Is it bad I wouldn't say no to a chicken nugget as a reward for dealing with this shit?"

"Only if you break each and every one in half before you eat it."

"Extra sweet and sour sauce. And we don't tell the kids I ate nuggets after the incident."

"Your secret is safe with me. I'm also impressed with your willingness to court salmonella again so soon."

"It's not courting it if I break every nugget in half first."

He chuckled. "Is there anything I can do to help?"

"Do you know how to scrub a counter?"

"Can I just put soap on a sponge and rub enthusiastically?"

I pointed at the second-worst section of countertop, which had various forms of alien lifeforms growing on it in a myriad of blacks, greens, and blues. "There are gloves beneath the sink. Attack that with extreme prejudice. Rub enthusiastically, rinse your sponge often."

"I vote we don't tell the kids the house is this bad."

"Agreed. They've had a bad enough time of it lately. The last thing they need to know is that their parents are certifiable."

"As what?"

"Residents of the local looney bin. Also, residents of a filthy sty."

"Not a pig sty?"

"Pigs are cleaner than this."

"Harsh but possibly true."

I remembered something that would likely ruin my hopes of chicken nuggets on the way to Kace's place. "The kids are cooking, aren't they?"

"You can have six nuggets on the way home. And we'll pray they followed the instructions."

I foresaw yet another disaster, but unable to do anything to dodge the inevitable, I sighed and focused on cleaning so I had some hope of getting some sleep before diving back into the fray for another long day of work.

Chapter Seven

FORTY-SIX MINUTES after starting my cleaning spree, I declared the kitchen to be a somewhat habitable space. While still a sty, I doubted anyone would throw up upon entering the house. Even better, Kace and I had both avoided a sprint to the nearest bathroom despite facing moldy horrors. The remaining clutter wouldn't stink the place up, everything that needed to be cleaned was in the dishwasher, and if I wasn't careful, I'd get high on cleaning fumes and air freshener. I blamed my light-headed state on my crazy schedule and inability to quit before I was done with whatever I set out to do.

Kace checked his phone, staring at the kitchen with his mouth hanging open. "You really did all that in less than an hour."

I nodded. "It's easy when you throw everything away. We didn't clean, Kace. We shoveled."

Kace pulled out his phone, dialed a number, and held it to his ear, tapping a foot while he waited. "Hey, Dad. Sorry to wake you, but I have a question."

I rolled my eyes and debated if I wanted to punch Kace in

the right or the left kidney if he asked his father a stupid question.

"Remember when you told me if I met a woman who could perform miracles that I should marry her? How does this work, exactly? Remember Michelle? Yes, the walking disaster area Michelle. Well, her sister has been watching the kids, and we went to do a check-in on Michelle's place. It was bad. It was so bad Ginger snapped and cleaned it up in under an hour. I'm pretty sure this is a miracle. What should I do?"

I fought the urge to laugh. If I started laughing, everything would come tumbling down, and I would start to cry. I'd laugh and cry my way to a breakdown.

"Yes, Dad. I did say that. Ginger snapped. That's the only way I can describe it. Yes, Dad. Her name is really Ginger. Anyway, she made this kitchen her bitch. It's a huge kitchen, and she attacked it. It was a slaughter. I think she exorcised the devil. Actually, forget think. I know she did. It was that bad. We opened the front door, and she almost threw up last week's lunch. I was a few seconds from joining her, truth be told."

I covered my mouth so I wouldn't laugh. Laughing would be the end of me. Kace would have to scrape me off the floor, drag me to his car, and explain to the kids why he was bringing a comatose body back rather than their conscious aunt.

"You're the one who said to marry the first woman I met who could perform miracles. I have no idea how to get her to agree to it, though. She's resistant to my charms."

No, I really wasn't, but I was putting on a good show. Maybe if I kept working on my act, he wouldn't have any idea he drove me crazy and could end my single streak with some light flirting and the removal of his shirt. I bit my knuckle to cling to my dignity. I couldn't afford to let a single giggle slip.

"I know, Dad. It's inconceivable. Thoughts?" Kace raised a brow and stared at me, and he took his time looking me over. "I was actually thinking about hiring her as my executive secretary. She's underpaid as a logistics manager at her current firm, and if they're not going to treat her right, I will."

I matched his expression, and if he wanted to eye me like I was a choice piece of meat up for sale, I had no problems following his example. I got the better deal of the two of us; my unintentional weight loss plan of overworking and skipping meals wasn't doing me any favors.

"I think I've either upset her or interested her, and I can't tell which. I think this is my cue to hang up." He disconnected the call, returned his phone to his pocket, and raised his hands in surrender. "He's the only man I know who has managed to stay married longer than twenty years!"

I had to give him credit—that was a good reason to call his father for advice about women. "I think you're tired and need a nap."

"Says the woman who has turned gray and keeps swaying. Also, if you faint, I will catch you, but I will have the kids take pictures of you being carried. I haven't determined if I'll toss you over my shoulder or pretend you're a princess yet. I won't do the fireman carry, as that's not dignified enough."

"And being tossed over your shoulder is?"

"It makes me look manly."

He didn't need to do anything to look manly, but I refused to give him the satisfaction of admitting that. "If I sit on the ground, have a temper tantrum, and cry because I want a nap, will you count that as fainting?"

"If you fall asleep, you're being carried, children will be notified, and pictures will be taken."

Well, I was motivated to not fall asleep in unauthorized places. He'd probably show the pictures to my sister, and I'd never hear the end of it—and she might join Kace's campaign to marry me off. To him.

I needed to put in some serious thoughts on the advantages and disadvantages of leaving single life behind me. "I'm going to your car, and it doesn't count if I nap on the way back to your place."

"It's only a few minutes, Ginger. If you nap in my car, you're being carried, children will be notified, and pictures will be taken."

Kace did not play fair. "I can't believe you told your father you wanted to hire me as your executive secretary."

"I'm going to lose a lot of sleep trying to figure out a hiring package that'll actually convince you to take the job. And then I'll have to get into a fight with your sister as I break every company rule in the book trying to convince you to marry your boss."

"You're something else."

"You only have yourself to blame for performing miracles, working hard, and being smart. I'd say your looks factor into it, but honestly? You look like hell right now. But that's okay, I value brains over beauty, but I won't say no when the brains come with beauty."

I was tired enough that if he took off his shirt I'd jump him and embarrass myself in the process. "I'm too hungry for this conversation."

"And that's my cue to find that damned bank card, take you to my car, swing by McDonald's for some nuggets to tide you over, and see if I still have a house standing after leaving three kids and a puppy unattended for an hour. I will hope we can discuss this again at a later date. Perhaps tomorrow?"

"Tomorrow will be like today but possibly worse, as we're one day closer to Christmas. Every day until Christmas is going to be like today but possibly worse. Even if I had the money to go buy a new car, I don't have the time to deal with it." I gestured to encompass the entirety of my sister's house. "And I expect to be coming here every night for an hour until hell freezes over or she comes home and makes this place presentable. And I've volunteered her house for any holiday celebrations, as that'll make a huge mess she'll have to clean up."

"You don't just get mad, you get even, I see."

"I've only just begun."

✶✶✶

I MADE it to Kace's house to be greeted with the drool-inducing scent of roasting turkey. My stomach gurgled a complaint, deeming the light snack of six nuggets slathered in sweet and sour sauce was no longer acceptable.

Somehow, the children had figured out my weakness and meant to make me wait pathetically for hours to be fed. Then again, I could nap until the turkey was ready, wake up in a few hours, go on a feeding frenzy, and go back to sleep before heading out to work. Every problem had a solution, if I took the time to think it through.

Saul, wearing an apron declaring him the King of the Kitchen, skidded into the entry armed with greasy tongs. "We have successfully spatchcocked the cock."

My mouth dropped open, the world crashed to a halt around me, and I stared at my nephew in utter disbelief. "You what?"

With a delighted grin, he pointed the tongs in the general direction of Kace's kitchen. "We have spatchcocked the cock, and he's resting now because he's tired."

Maniacal laughter rang out from the kitchen.

"You spatchcocked a cock?" I asked, unable to comprehend what cocks had to do with the smell of turkey determined to ruin the little peace of mind I had left. I swallowed so I wouldn't be caught drooling.

"Violently. We liked it."

After several long moments, I figured out the turkey was the cock and spatchcocking was the grisly act of crunching through bones so a bird could be grilled or baked lying flat, which dramatically reduced cooking time. If spatchcocked correctly, a turkey could be finished within an hour—with the appropriate preparations.

I could make a few guesses who had helped with the preparations, and I turned a baleful glare on Kace.

As always, he smirked. "A friend of mine helped them, so they were supervised while working on this project, and we actually skipped back to the house while you were working to do the preparations. I figured you'd murder me if I let them spatchcock a cock without appropriate supervision."

"Can I eat now, or do I have to nap before I can eat? Napping on my plate is always an option, too," I confessed.

"How's dinner looking, Mr. King of the Kitchen?"

"It's done. Amelia and Wendy are just getting the stuffing out of the oven now. You can't go to sleep until you have a proper meal, Aunt Ginger. If you get much skinnier, you'll freak Mom out. Mom does not like when she can count ribs."

I lifted my shirt just enough to do a rib check, and sure enough, I'd lost enough weight for my ribs to be visible. Only a curse would do, but I tried not to curse too much around the kids. No matter what I said, I lost. "Kace said he'd be mean if I fell asleep in an inappropriate place, so please feed me so I can go to bed. I'm exhausted."

"Your mother left the kitchen a disaster area. I'm on a mission to marry your aunt now. I'll require your assistance, as she's resisting this idea."

"That's because Aunt Ginger hates skirt chasers who want in her pants. She don't got time for no man," my nephew announced, and the brat sounded rather proud of my status as a strong, independent woman. "Go sit in the dining room, Aunt Ginger! We'll bring everything so all you have to do is eat."

My sister's children must have been switched or reprogrammed. Bemused and more than a little concerned, I obeyed the teen. As though aware I toed the line between conscious and dead to the world, Kace kept close while Saul ran back to the kitchen to resume his cooking and serving duties.

"I'm so freaked out right now," I whispered.

"It's difficult realizing the children are growing into capable human beings. If you blink a few times, they might become adults on you. Then you'll have to deal with two women just like your sister and a man who might end up like her, too."

Trying to imagine three other people just like my sister stopped me dead in my tracks. "No. Don't say that. That's wrong, Kace. That's so wrong. There can't be four Michelles. The world will end if there are four Michelles."

"I'm pretty sure Michelle couldn't spatchcock a cock even if she tried," Kace muttered. "Also, there's nothing quite as scary as asking a friend to help three kids brutally break the bones of a dead bird so it cooks faster in the oven."

"I think you all just like the name of the cooking method."

"Your expression was priceless, Ginger. He came in, said that, and you looked like he'd smacked you between the eyes with a baseball bat. When it clicked what he said, you looked so disgusted. It'll be a cherished memory."

I bet the brats, with some help from Kace, had planned for that to happen from the very beginning. "And then you just had your friend sneak out the back door?"

"It's better if you don't see the supervision. It's psychological for the kids. They felt guilty you had to work so hard today."

Maybe Michelle tended to make some poor decisions, especially when it came to her adventures out of country, but she'd taught her kids what really mattered in life. "They have nothing to feel guilty about."

"No, but they know it's because their mother went and did something dumb again. They're mad at their dad, too."

Poor kids. "I really need to remind Michelle that she's a mother and can't ditch her kids until all of them are eighteen."

"I wish you the best of luck convincing her of that now that Saul's old enough to keep an eye on them."

"I'm buying my sister birth control for Christmas, and I'm also leashing her. Where's my puppy?"

"Considering how quiet it is, she's probably asleep in her crate." Kace placed his hand between my shoulders and propelled me towards his dining room. "Don't tell the kids I said this, but they were whining for turkey, and this was the only way I could prevent a three-way temper tantrum. As a bonus, you get turkey dinner."

"I will eat it even if it double downs my chances of salmonella poisoning."

"I think you'll be fine. My friend? He's a chef, and he's a pretty good one. Eat, be merry, and get some sleep. Tomorrow's another day."

That it was. I laughed at the thought of what I'd have to do over the next few weeks to survive the holidays. I expected the incident in my sister's kitchen would be the last time I had enough energy to actually snap. Time would tell, however.

There were still over two weeks until Christmas.

"I'm not going to sleep at the table," I swore. "So don't you get any ideas. I will not be defeated by a damned turkey."

Kace laughed.

※ ※ ※

UNDER THE GUIDANCE OF A CHEF, the kids had made the best damned bird I'd ever eaten in my life, served with enough gravy to sink a battleship, the majority of which went into my stomach where it belonged. Someone must have snitched about my love of sage, cranberries, nuts, and bacon; the stuffing had it all, and I gorged on it as much as I did on the juicy turkey with its crisp, herb-encrusted skin.

Saul applied for sainthood, giving me his share of the skin.

I had serious issues with turkey.

Sometime after gobbling down the skin, a fourth serving of stuffing, and gnawing a drumstick into submission, I started nodding off at the table.

"My earlier promise still stands, and I make no promises which bed you'll wake up in should you fall asleep at the table," Kace announced. To make it clear he considered himself the undisputed victor, he dished out another serving of cranberry sauce. "Go ahead and fall asleep, Ginger. I dare you."

In about thirty seconds, I expected to be defeated by a damned turkey, and there was nothing I could do about it. I thought about getting up, but I gave up after a few moments of contemplation. "I can't move. I'm too tired."

Kace inhaled his cranberry sauce in record time, pushed away his plate, and rubbed his hands together. "And that means I win, you have to submit to being carried, and the girls can take photographs of my victory."

"I'm still conscious. It only counts if I'm not conscious. You haven't won yet."

Challenging an egotistical man likely wouldn't end well, but I had to maintain my status as a stubborn, independent woman.

My sister's children snickered, and Saul asked, "What are you two talking about?"

"I told your aunt if she wasn't able to get to bed on her own steam, I would toss her over my shoulder or carry her in some other fashion to bed. As a part of this, I would have pictures taken to immortalize the moment."

My nephew looked me in the eyes and said, "Sleep now. I demand you sleep now. Go to sleep, Aunt Ginger. I want to see this."

Of course he did. Saul was my sister's son, and my sister lived to witness my humiliation. "Why do you want to see this?"

"It's funny."

I couldn't argue with that. "I'm going to go crawl to bed now to spare myself the shame of being carried."

Maybe I wouldn't be defeated by a damned turkey after all. I pushed my chair away from the table and got to my feet. While my head was all on board with giving the instructions on how to walk, my legs opted out of performing their basic duties. I sat on the hardwood floor hard enough to rattle my teeth, blinking as my body decided it weighed several thousand pounds more than usual.

Kace cursed, knocking his chair over in his hurry to get to his feet. He knelt beside me, placing one hand against my back. "You all right?"

"My legs are broken," I complained. "I told them to work, but they just went plop."

"Normal people call this severe fatigue. You're so tired you're shutting down for the night, like it or not. Can you work from here tomorrow?"

I shook my head. "I really can't. The shipment has to be monitored, and I need to use my work computer." In reality, if I owned a laptop, I could've done the work from home; when I needed to work in the evenings, I tended to go to work since I didn't have the money for the kind of computer needed to do my work efficiently. "I have to go to work, Kace."

If I didn't go to work, everything would fall apart.

"It's okay, Ginger. I'll let you sleep in as long as you can and make the kids take the bus in the morning. I'll even handle the cleanup after you're in bed. You're not going to miss work. If you can't walk, I'll carry you, and I won't let the kids take pictures."

"It's no fun if your target legitimately collapses?" I guessed, poking at my uncooperative legs. "That's never happened before."

"Stress, fatigue, and malnutrition can result in legs no longer functioning properly. And you're right. It's only fun when my target is more of a challenge and just dozes off. Hitting the floor wasn't in my plan. If it had been part of my plan, I would've caught you when you fell."

"Appreciated, I think."

Kace hauled me to my feet, and I had better success at staying upright. "I'll clean up after I get Ginger to bed. You three get ready for bed. You do have school tomorrow."

Wendy bounced to her feet and started gathering plates. "We'll do the dishes. Don't let Aunt Ginger escape. She's slippery and stubborn. You should lock her in your room for the night."

"You're an entity of pure evil," I informed my niece.

"But you love me anyway."

I did. "Why do *you* want Kace to lock me in his room, anyway?"

"I like weddings, and you'll be really pretty in a white dress."

Right. I should've guessed. "That's not a good reason to marry someone."

"I think it's a perfectly good reason for you to marry me. I agree with her. You'd be really pretty in a white dress."

I needed sleep, I needed my legs to work properly, and I needed to knock Kace down a few pegs and possibly invest in a baseball bat for protection purposes.

As long as he didn't take his shirt off, I could resist his wicked charms. Probably.

Maybe.

It took a few steps with Kace's help before I convinced my legs they needed to work. I aimed for the guest bedroom before I could be lured elsewhere. If Kace managed to lure me to his bed, it would be game over.

I liked being a strong, independent single woman. I didn't need no man.

But damn, for the first time in a long time, I really wanted one.

"I'm going to bed now," I announced. Before my legs and brain could get into another dispute that resulted on my ass hitting the floor, I retreated to the safety of the guest bedroom.

Kace hovered every step of the way, even when I flopped on the mattress. I passed out before my head hit the pillow.

Chapter Eight

I WOKE up in such a daze that Kace refused to let me shower without an attendant. Wendy and Amelia brawled for the honor, resulting in all three of us sharing space in the bathroom. Any other day, I would've been annoyed by the restriction, but after trying to use toothpaste as shampoo, I acknowledged I needed all the help I could get.

According to the mad giggling, the twins would never let me live down my semiconscious blunder.

"Can I ask you to keep that quiet until after Christmas?" I begged.

"Maybe," Wendy answered.

"For a price," her wicked twin continued.

Great. I was dead on my feet, and I was going to be hoodwinked by a pair of kids cursed with their mother's questionable ethics and creativity. With the frosted glass protecting the little modesty I had left, I went to work transforming the bathroom into a sauna. "What do you want?"

"Why don't you like Kace?"

Great. The twins were on a quest to see me married off to

my sister's business partner. "There's a rule, girls. We don't date the business partners. Kace happens to be your mother's business partner. Him dating or marrying me becomes a major conflict of interest. Me becoming his executive secretary? Also a major conflict of interest. That, plus he's probably the type who wants to take his secretary into his office for reasons other than work."

With my unhealthy interest in him, I feared I could easily be talked into such a thing.

"We could use some cousins," the twins announced.

"You have our permission," Wendy chirped, and she put the toilet seat down and sat on it. "Really. You do. Mom would be thrilled, and she'd totally not care you're shacking up with her business partner. Mom's totally keen on your shacking up with her business partner. If you shack up with him, she won't have to worry about you. And Mom says you're a big worry because you're all by yourself."

Sometime after bringing my sister's children into my life, being single had lost its shine. The shift of perspective bothered me almost as much as admitting I liked having three precocious kids underfoot all the time. The purposes that had driven me from day to day also lost their shine.

I did well at work, but Kace had a point: They could treat me better and pay me more for what I did. Always bailing out the asses of those treated better—and paid better—took its toll on me. It'd been a long time since someone had cared about me rather than what I could do for them.

I'd been getting that treatment in spades, and I wasn't sure what to do about it.

Things would be easier if I could get some alone time with my puppy. Puppies made everything better, and I bet the husky could give me some good advice—or at least a listening ear.

"I made promises," I finally replied, unsure of how to get the twins to leave me alone about Kace without slipping and letting them know I held unfortunate interest in the man. "I have obligations."

"Delaware is an at-will state. If they're not paying you right or treating you right, you can walk unless your employee handbook requires you to give notice, and the labor board will often vote in favor of the employee if they're quitting due to mistreatment because of the state's at-will laws. You don't have to keep promises that result in your employer abusing you," Amelia announced with the confidence only a child possessed. "We talked about this in history class."

In this specific case, she was right.

My sister had created miniature versions of herself, and I wasn't sure why the world hadn't come to a destructive end with more than one Michelle in it.

Wendy joined her sister in assaulting my work ethic with a derisive snort. "You're worth so much more than they're paying you."

"How would you know that?" I grabbed my bottle of shampoo and went to work on my hair, hoping the bubbles might somehow offer an escape from the twins out to trash my peace of mind.

Wendy and Amelia huddled over the toilet, discussing something in whispers before Amelia said, "We caught Kace going through the papers you gave him. Your pay stubs were in it along with your bills. We asked questions. He answered them, and he showed us his employee guidelines for salaries. He explained why they paid people what they do, and then he compared your position with his logistics managers."

Uh oh. I was about to lose a discussion with a pair of kids armed with facts, knowledge, and research.

Life had it out for me, and there was nothing I could do to make it behave for once. "All right. In Kace's opinion, how much am I worth?"

Amelia paced the tiny bathroom, and I glared at her through the frosted glass. "We talked about this, because you are stubborn and he is stubborn, and well, you're both stubborn, and you might listen if I tell you. Maybe. You're really stubborn, Aunt Ginger. He said he would pay you a starting salary of a hundred and fifty with bonuses and full benefits. He also said logistics managers are valuable. As his executive secretary, you'd make more, plus he would pay for all of your travel expenses, as you have to follow him around everywhere."

Okay. That was three times what I made, which stung enough I considered sitting and hoping the shower would drown me. "And executive secretaries are paid how much?"

"Oh, they're usually only paid fifty a year, but Mom and Kace don't agree with that because they're so important, or so they say. Mom thinks we should join the company when we get a little older and be executive secretaries, too. Then, when it's our turn to take over the company, we'll be ready. A good executive secretary will bring in one hundred and seventy-five plus all the extra stuff they seem to think are really important. A good executive secretary makes or breaks a business."

How the hell could my sister and her business partner afford to pay an executive secretary so much money? Were they waving their hands and willing diamonds into existence? While I'd known my sister's crazy ideas had turned into wealth, I hadn't really thought about just how well her company had done since its inception eighteen years ago. I also hadn't known my sister had been integrating her children into her work life. "If I go back to bed, will everything go back to normal?"

"No, Aunt Ginger. You have to go to work," Wendy replied. "You said so yourself last night."

I needed to give my work ethic a kick in the ass. "Does your mom's executive secretary get paid that much?"

"More. She's been with the company for a long time. You'd have to work your way up like everyone else."

I admired Kace for his ruthless cunning. Had he been telling me about the pay, I wouldn't have been nearly as receptive. "I'll think about it, but you two need to keep your mouths shut."

"We promise!" they chirped.

I knew my sister well enough to recognize her children might last a few hours before they tattled to Kace and turned my life upside down yet again.

※ ※ ※

VIRTUE WANTED TO PLAY, and all I could offer her were a few chew toys and my feet. While I busted ass making sure a bunch of talking robots likely programmed to take over the world made it to the shelves in time for Christmas, I sacrificed my toes to my puppy. Puppy teeth hurt, especially as I'd removed the protection of my shoes to make them last a little longer before Virtue had her way with them.

I needed to check over her papers, as I suspected I'd been given a kitten thinly disguised as a puppy. Why else would her little teeth hurt so much? As she wasn't mouthing me with any malicious intent, I let her play, kept wiggling my toes for her amusement, and tracked each shipment to make certain they arrived intact.

My precautions paid off, as the containers made their way across the United States without incident.

If the rest of my work went so smoothly, I would've been happy being paid only fifty thousand a year fixing other people's mistakes. When I wasn't monitoring the wretchedly expensive dolls, I located more of Mr. Chaplon's mistakes, mistakes that cost our company time and money.

Ultimately, I'd have to defend my work while toeing the line of outing the mistakes that led me to having to do the work in the first place. That annoyed me. Instead of extinguishing the fires the CEO's son started with his inability to plan ahead and use his brain, I read over the employee handbook and also checked into loopholes in Delaware's laws to make certain I could, in actuality, walk out at any time.

It took me less than ten minutes to confirm that the company had tried to keep at-will for themselves while strongly recommending that employees give them two weeks of notice. Two weeks would put my departure date close to Christmas. The timing would make my life a miserable mess until I found a new place to work.

Two weeks would let me finish the work on the toy shipments. I could also enjoy watching the company meltdown as they realized how many times I fixed problems that shouldn't have existed in the first place.

I had enough food and supplies to keep Virtue happy for months, and after the holidays, if I didn't have a new job, I could invade my sister's place for a while.

If I ignored my pride, I had options.

If I ignored the potential conflict of interest issues, I could work for Kace. The pay increase would change my life in more ways than I could count. I'd be able to afford a new car—a decent one that wasn't at risk of dying every time I started the engine.

If I did what was better for me rather than what was better for the company, my life would change.

I returned my copy of the employee's handbook to its drawer along with the rest of my personal employment papers and checked on the all-important toy shipment again.

Things would be so very different if only I put myself first for a change.

Instead of spending my time bailing out the CEO's useless, lazy son, I made certain I'd done all my work correctly, had no personal information on my computer, and otherwise prepared for quitting or being fired. Either served my needs. When I searched my office for anything I would need to take home, the lack of personal touches astonished me. Most people had trinkets and personal belongings tucked in every corner.

I had a puppy, her supplies, and a few pens I'd been given as gifts over the years. The pens went into my purse, and the puppy and her supplies would take less than five minutes to pack up. In a way, it helped with making the decision to leave. My office would be ready for someone else within half an hour.

Then, to test the waters, I sent Kace a text informing him I was going to be running a high chance of losing my job.

His immediate reply, consisting of an offer to pick me up from work, made me smile. I replied that unless I got them to fire me, I'd probably be stuck for two weeks unless I could afford a lawyer to punch holes in the employee handbook's recommendations to give employers two weeks while they enjoyed at-will removal of employees.

A few moments after sending the text, my cell phone rang, and the screen informed me Kace would rather talk than text. I answered. "I may be losing my mind."

"No, you're just smart and have new information to work with. You work for Chaplon's firm, right?"

"I do."

"I'll motivate him to cut you loose without a fight. That's easy. What tripped your trigger?"

I checked to make certain my office door was firmly closed. "His idiot son botched a huge shipment, and I haven't had time to fix it—and it's not my job to fix it. I just usually do, so the company doesn't pay for his idiocy. I'm still monitoring the other shipment. I don't have time to jump hoops to fix his shit."

"How large is the botched contract?"

If I logged into the system to check, I'd have to start the groundwork of fixing the problem to cover my trail. Sighing, I began with checking the notification emails that had alerted me to the problem. "I have five transports with issues."

"Entire transports of goods?"

"Yep."

"Five of them."

"He doesn't make wise choices of transporters. He sent an important shipment to the wrong part of the country earlier this week."

"Did you sign your copy of the employee handbook?"

Unlocking the drawer, I double-checked the binder for any evidence of a signature. When I'd been hired, I hadn't signed much documentation—only what was needed to confirm my Social Security number and employment agreement for my salary. I still had a copy of the original agreement with the employee handbook, which I checked as well. "No, I didn't sign it. There isn't anything in my original signing agreement for hire about the employee handbook, either."

"You can quit without giving them two weeks. Two weeks is only if you're feeling polite, and I can promise you, your next employer won't care if you're polite about leaving a workplace that's taking advantage of you. If they feel they're owed two weeks, I'll provide the lawyer myself as part of your hiring bonus."

"Since when do companies give hiring bonuses?"

"Since forever, Ginger. We've always given small hiring bonuses to all employees, usually to help them with the transition process. We generally give two weeks' pay at signing in the form of a check to make sure they're able to pay their bills before their official start date, which is usually two weeks unless we have an immediate opening, or we don't have a lot of prep work to do. I'm between secretaries right now, so you'd be able to start immediately. If you miss logistics, I can have some of our contracts bumped to your desk, but you'll find you'll be pretty busy working for me."

I liked being busy. Being busy kept me sane. Being busy made me feel useful and valued. "I didn't get a hiring bonus here."

"I figured as much. I could give you a two-week window before you start, but for some reason, I expect you'll resist that and want to work yourself to the bone doing too many jobs until Christmas is over."

"How did you guess?"

"You may as well have written it on your forehead, Ginger. You got as close as it gets to fainting last night without losing consciousness. Your stubborn pride is amazing, honestly. And I'm looking forward to yanking Michelle's chain when she gets back. I should pose you on my desk wearing a scandalously short skirt the first day she's back in the office while you're holding one of my file folders and ruling over my schedule."

I narrowed my eyes at that. "That sounds remarkably like the expression of a fantasy, Mr. Dannicks."

"It really is, and I'd get to lord it over your sister while shamelessly enjoying the situation."

"I have some bad news for you."

"What?"

"I don't own clothes like that." I stayed professional, and that usually meant slacks, as I didn't trust most men at the company to maintain their professionalism if I dared to wear a skirt.

"You have that one dress Wendy showed me. You could wear that. It's short."

It did count as scandalously short, but it wouldn't work for what he wanted. "You need the sexy secretary look for your goals, not the stripper on the prowl look."

"I will increase your hiring bonus to cover a professional wardrobe for working with me. In a private agreement, you'll get one outfit meant for revenge on your sister."

I was beginning to understand why Kace and Michelle worked so well together as partners in crime. Kace would test my limits if I let him, and it worried me that I wanted him to push my buttons to see what would happen. Michelle lived to test Kace's limits, and with them pushing at each other all the time, they likely found the best of both worlds and ran with it, turning dreams into reality. "How much of a scandal will it create when people find out your executive secretary is living with you?"

"None. Mitchel works at our company, too. Nobody cares. The only rule is that personal disputes aren't allowed in the office. All fighting has to be done at home or outside of the office."

That sounded simple, yet somehow challenging at the same time. "Okay. I can do that."

"Please don't take this the wrong way, but is your phone a company phone?"

I sighed. "You know my financial situation, Kace. It's a company phone. Well, I do have a cheap prepaid phone that barely works. I should get rid of it. Your number is on that phone."

"I'll be there in half an hour. I can make Chaplon a good proposal that will open him to using our firm for touchier logistics situations. In exchange, he'll have to cut you loose with all paid benefits and a severance."

"What do you mean by touchier logistics situations?"

"High-security transports. We also have clearance to transport some radioactive materials. That was your sister's idea. We're a fallback transporter for hospitals needing medical isotopes for cancer treatments. We can also stand in when a company needs medical equipment transported. It's not a huge part of our business, but it lets us use shipping equipment that might otherwise be waiting around."

"You have your own fleet?"

"Currently, we have a fleet of fifty planes, a hundred transports, and ten armored vehicles."

"Like for transferring money between banks? That kind of armored vehicle?"

"Yes. Exactly that."

I would've killed for access to armored vehicles for some contracts. "I'm not sure I want to be your secretary when you have a fleet of planes, transports, and armored vehicles."

"You can play with the fleet during lulls, and you can help with some of the high-security jobs once your background check clears. If we get a government job, you'll need clearance."

I squeaked. "Government jobs?"

Kace laughed. "Shipping for the government can be very lucrative when they need things moved in a hurry. Once your background check and security clearances go through, you'll be able to learn more details. I trust you don't have a record?"

"It squeaks when you rub it. I haven't even gotten a speeding ticket in my entire life."

"Was your car capable of exceeding the speed limit?"

Ouch. "I'm sure it could have if I tried to. But a tow truck took it out. I haven't dealt with the insurance company yet."

"Since you seem to be getting off work early today, we can deal with it then. I'm going to get off the phone with you to drive. I'll see you soon. Try not to worry too much."

I appreciated he didn't tell me not to worry. No matter what he said, I would worry. Kace hung up, and I took the time to delete my personal contacts from my work phone and wrote down the numbers and email addresses of my more important transporters, as my cheap phone had run out of charge again.

It took me less than ten minutes to erase my life from my work, and while I waited for Kace to arrive, I monitored the shipment of dolls destined to add extra mayhem to the holiday retail season.

I GATHERED VIRTUE'S SUPPLIES, and under the guise of taking her on her afternoon walk, I waited for Kace to arrive. He pulled up in a sporty car I hadn't seen before, and its engine rumbled when he parked it in one of the guest spots. The bright red drew the eye, and I bet he had cops sniffing at his tailpipe whenever he took it out for a spin.

Unless my guess was way off its mark, the car cost more than my new yearly salary.

Virtue wagged her tail when she spotted Kace, and she did a little dance and barked her head off to greet him.

"Your puppy likes me."

My puppy liked everybody. Laughing, I walked over and held up the bag of her supplies. "This is everything from my office."

To my amazement, the tiny car had a trunk, and Kace took the bag from me and stowed it for safekeeping. "Here's all you need to know about this, Ginger. If he tries to yank your chain, all you have to say is that you quit. At-will means just that. You can quit at any time for any reason, and he doesn't get to keep his at-will status while taking yours away. We have legal documentation at our company that removes at-will status; as the employer, we must give two weeks of notice if we're letting you go for anything other than an immediate firing offense. We have a list of immediate firing offenses. You'll be expected to sign off on the documentation. This makes it a better situation for you. We also have a list of reasons an employee may quit at will, including sexual harassment, a threat to your personal safety, and so on. You can also exercise at-will if someone in Human Resources signs off on it, but that process takes some time."

"That sounds fair."

"Michelle hates at-will, so we made our company policies to

have more protections for employees and employer. It's pretty balanced."

"Have you defended it in court before?"

"Yes. We won. The employee got an offer to start work immediately elsewhere and wanted at-will. He lost the case, which meant we weren't required to pay out extra benefits or his banked vacation pay."

"I'm not expecting to see anything like that anyway."

"Don't be surprised if you walk away the victor. Also, don't be surprised if you finish the large shipment for them for the holidays. I'll use that as part of my pitch. My job is to make you come out of this ahead of the game. Just follow my lead, and don't be surprised if Chaplon implies we're sleeping together."

"Which one?"

"Both. They're both womanizers, though they tend to keep their mitts off employees; it's too much of a risk for the company. Should he do that, I'll probably just tell him I fully intend on marrying you, and that you deserve better than a one-night stand, so I'm holding out until you agree."

My brows shot up. "That's not very professional."

"Neither is implying you're a whore because you're getting a better deal working with me. It's common knowledge we encourage couples in our firm. That's why we have counselors available if there are any marriage issues. It's been great for the business and better for the employees. Hopefully, he'll behave himself. I doubt it. Losing you will hurt him a lot."

"How do you even know that?"

"I have my sources, and I started poking my nose where it didn't belong the instant I saw your financials. I'm not the only one who thinks you deserve better."

Of the gossips at work, I could think of a few who would actually want good things for me. "Marianna?"

"She's one of them, yes. She knows who I am, so she got my

number and gave me a call. She may have tipped me off that I should hire you."

"She didn't!"

"She did. And should she lose her job because of doing that, I'll poach her, too."

Damn. Kace played dirty on the business front, and I'd have to keep an eye on his potential ruthlessness when I planned his schedule. "You're something else."

"You have no idea, Ginger, but you're about to learn."

Chapter Nine

THE INSTANT KACE stepped through the doors, his entire attitude and stance changed. His body language oozed confidence, his expression warned everyone he wasn't in the mood for any bullshit, and he marched like a man on a mission. He didn't need any guidance from me; he headed straight for the executive reception.

I suspected Kace had tipped Marianna off about his intentions. She was ready for him, and without missing a beat, she pressed a button on the intercom beside her. "Mr. Chaplon, Mr. Dannicks from K&H Enterprises is here to see you."

"Send him in," the CEO barked.

According to his tone, Mr. Chaplon wasn't pleased Kace had interrupted his day.

He'd like the interruption a lot less when he found out I was jumping ship for better waters—or at least for better pay.

"Good luck," Marianna said. I wasn't sure which one of us she was talking to. Kace headed for the elevator behind Marianna, which led to the top floor of the building. I found the security measure ridiculous; we didn't have much of a security team most days, and the night crew just kept an eye on the place for anything obvious.

Virtue stuck close, and I had to keep an eye on her so I wouldn't trip. Kace waited for us at the elevator, and to keep from looking like an idiot, I picked my puppy up.

"Relax, Ginger. Everything will be fine." Kace pressed the button for the top floor, and the doors slid closed.

"You're crazy if you think I can relax."

"I'll settle with you not throwing up on me."

"I'll try to avoid that," I muttered. Considering my track record of keeping control of my stomach, I worried I just might.

While Mr. Chaplon had a receptionist, she wasn't in the office, something that didn't seem to bother Kace at all. He crossed the reception to the hallway leading across the floor and past the various other manager offices. Fortunately, Mr. Chaplon had gone with a windowless design, which offered the illusion of privacy.

It wouldn't last. The instant I quit, was fired, or transferred to Kace's company, news would spread faster than a wildfire. The gossips would have me sleeping with Kace—likely with commentary they wanted to sleep with him, too. I couldn't blame them for that.

If he took his shirt off, I'd be sorely tested.

When we reached the end of the hallway, Kace knocked once before opening the door and sweeping into the CEO's office like he owned the place. Without any other realistic choice, I followed him in and closed the door. I longed to hide behind Kace, but I stood at his side, holding my puppy close to my chest. She wiggled in my arms and tried to lick my face.

"You're about to say something I won't like," Mr. Chaplon said, and he growled the words between clenched teeth. "Spit it out, Dannicks."

"I'm hiring your employee, and I thought I would offer you

a deal to make her transition as streamlined as possible. She's going to be my executive secretary, although she'll be doing some work in my logistics department. I want you to cut her loose immediately, with all owed vacation time and other owed benefits paid out. In exchange, I will notify my logistics department that you are to be added to our high-security list. You'll have to qualify each shipment, but you'll gain access to the fleet. You will have to negotiate the rates with my logistics department, but you'll have a foot in the door. If the arrangement works out for both of us, it can be a long-term deal. We'll do a limited test run to see if our companies work well together."

Mr. Chaplon, an aging man who'd seen a little too much stress and not enough sun, narrowed his eyes and regarded Kace with open suspicion. "Why?"

"Why else would a company hire someone? She's quality employee material, and I am making her a better offer. That's the nature of business. You know that as well as I."

"Or you just want easy access to your next lay."

If Kace hadn't warned me the CEO might play that card, I might've reacted. I just stared at him, refusing to let any of my emotions show. I did set Virtue on the floor and adjust my hold on her leash so she wouldn't escape.

While hoping my puppy would pee on his floor made me a bad person, I hoped for it all the same.

Virtue flopped on my feet and rested her chin on her paws.

"While the offer I issued does involve marriage, I'm hiring her for her work ethic, her intellect, and skills. All of these things are certainly a part of my interest in marrying her, but I plan on hiring her even if she rejects my marriage proposal. As I'm a gentleman, I'm giving her all the time she wants to consider my offer. And as I am a gentleman, I wouldn't dream of asking her for her company until after we exchange vows."

Kace's tone made it clear he meant business—and that he found Mr. Chaplon's comment unacceptable.

Mr. Chaplon's brows rose. "You want to marry her? You, a millionaire CEO of a large corporation, wish to marry someone like her? She barely makes over minimum wage, she doesn't work with sensitive materials, and she has no experience doing executive secretarial work."

"No, she just cleans up your son's messes when he makes childish mistakes on important shipments. The rumor mill never sleeps, and it's reached even me about how you've been underpaying a miracle worker in your company. I have no intentions of making the same mistakes."

"My son does not make mistakes."

I snorted a laugh. Did he really believe his son didn't make mistakes? I clapped a hand over my mouth to stop myself from cackling at the absurdity of his statement. While I didn't chortle outright, another snort burst out.

"Miss Harriet!"

"Why don't you tell Mr. Chaplon about his son's mismanagement of shipments, Ginger?"

"He sent a recent shipment to Denio instead of Des Moines, and he put five critical transport loads with an unreliable, slow freighter. The cargo won't arrive in time unless he detours them to the nearest airport and pays rush delivery fees; if it's the contract I think it is, I expect ten more transport loads will be delayed by the end of the day. This is a daily occurrence, Mr. Chaplon. I've been fixing these errors as I find them, and I have delay notifications sent to my inbox to streamline corrections. This usually costs me one to two hours a day. I have not done his corrections today because I was focusing on the more important emergency shipment. All goods in that shipment are on route to their final destinations now, and they should arrive within the next twenty-four hours, ahead of schedule. All goods reached the United States overnight, and this morning, they were successfully transferred to the next shippers."

I looked the old man in the eyes. "You will find, the instant I leave your employment, that your success rate for freighted goods will drop by a minimum of twenty percent, and most of the failures will originate from Mr. Chaplon's contracts. He does not have sufficient skills and qualifications for this work, nor does he have the patience and attention to detail required to work in logistics."

Kace watched me, one of his eyebrows creeping upwards. His mouth twitched, and after a few moments, he cleared his throat and covered his mouth, likely to hide a smile. "This is exactly why I am hiring her. When she sees problems, she quietly fixes them in the most efficient way possible without stirring up any unnecessary drama. This is a critical trait in my executive secretary. I loathe unnecessary drama."

"Yet you work with Mrs. Ollends."

"Mrs. Ollends also happens to be Miss Harriet's sister. I look forward to when my business partner returns from a business trip, so I can inform her of my latest accomplishment. Will you deal or not? I need to get back to the office, and I will be taking Miss Harriet with me one way or the other. Decide."

"No deal."

I recognized my cue, and already annoyed that the CEO had made a jab at my sister, I announced, "I quit."

Then, without waiting to see what either man had to say, I picked up my puppy and left.

Kace could deal with the fallout, and I needed some fresh air before I told Mr. Chaplon exactly what I thought about his incompetent child.

✦ ✦ ✦

MR. CHAPLON DIDN'T APPRECIATE me walking out of his office, and with his face red-splotched from fury, he tailed me all the way to Kace's car. A light snow began to fall, and I set my puppy at my feet, clutched her leash, and wondered how I'd deal with the man. Kace followed at a sedate pace, but his expression told a different story: He waited for Mr. Chaplon to make a move, and he meant to act. Something about the hardness in Kace's eyes promised he'd take things too far if they escalated.

We'd have to have a talk about that.

"You didn't want to deal," I informed my ex-boss, careful to keep my tone mild. "No deal means no deal. Delaware is an at-will state. I did not sign any paperwork waiving my rights to quit at-will, so I'm quitting, effective immediately. I'm sure your son can handle the critical shipments, as you seem to be of the opinion he's capable. My computer has been unlocked, so all of the files can be accessed, my work phone is on my desk, and as the firm has retained their right to fire at-will, I also have that right and will not be prevented from using it."

For the first time since my employment with the firm, Mr. Chaplon spluttered.

I counted that as my victory. "You would have to pay me four times what you do now for even a hope of keeping me, and you'd have to make a lot of changes to your operations to make even that worth my while. I'm tired of being stepped on. And while I fully expect to be stepped on in some regards at my new place of employment, at least I'll be paid well enough to make it worth my while. Barely getting by while doing backbone work for your business is no longer good enough. I will submit the final paperwork for my resignation today to HR, and I will expect to be paid my owed dues in a timely fashion."

"And should you not, my company will be providing the lawyer to take the situation to the labor department," Kace said, his soft-spoken words thinly veiling a threat to follow through if needed.

Mr. Chaplon took a single step towards me, and Virtue's

ears snapped back. She bared her teeth and issued a puppy growl.

I needed to give her a treat and a lot of love. While she wasn't all that big, Mr. Chaplon received the message and retreated out of her reach. "Have a good day, Mr. Chaplon."

"How dare you?" Mr. Chaplon asked, and the splotches on his face darkened.

"I dare because you're cheap, and I've been thoroughly educated on the error of my ways. I'm worth more than you're paying, and I see absolutely no reason to display any company loyalty to a company that isn't likewise loyal—or paying me a fair wage. I'll take the better pay and work environment, thank you. Beats being worked to death with nothing to show for it."

Kace unlocked his car, opened the passenger door for me, and waited, and the man smirked the kind of smirk that could easily result in the complete removal of my clothes.

I needed to take my libido out back, give her a trouncing, and restore myself to peaceful sanity.

Taking the hint it was time to leave, I got into Kace's car, patting my leg to encourage Virtue to join me. The puppy squeaked out another growl at Mr. Chaplon before scrambling inside with a little help from me. As soon as I had Virtue on my lap and both feet in the car, Kace closed the door. He then spoke with my ex-boss, but I couldn't hear a word of the conversation.

After a few minutes, Kace got into the car. To my surprise, unlike Kace's other car, the vehicle used a regular key, and the engine roared to life. "That man is an irredeemable asshole at times."

No kidding. "Does it make me a bad person that I felt that was very satisfying, and if given another chance, I'd do it again?"

"It's a symptom of an employee figuring out they've been taken advantage of. It's really common. We try to keep people happy and turnover low. It happens even to us, though. Just not that dramatically, typically. If he had been using a single brain cell, he would've opted to deal." Kace backed the car out of the spot, and he kept a close eye on the infuriated CEO. "Did you tell him you moved?"

"No."

"Keep it that way. I'll pay your next rent as part of your hiring bonus to give you proper time to get moved out, but I don't want you going to your apartment by yourself. Men like him do not appreciate when women like you get the advantage. And he's an old idiot. I don't trust him."

"Michelle told me you sometimes become an overprotective freak. Is this what she meant?" I asked, careful to keep my tone amused despite it being the truth.

"Yes."

Well, I could accept him openly admitting he could be overprotective. "Is it bad I was kind of hoping Virtue would pee on his floor?"

"I'd rather if Virtue had peed on him, truth be told. I'm very pleased your puppy has good common sense and recognized a bad man when she sees one. It's the first time I've heard her actually growl at someone outside of playing with tug-of-war toys."

"It was more of a squeak than a growl."

Kace kept an eye on his rearview mirror and eased the car onto the road, driving slower than usual, probably because of the snow. I hadn't checked the forecast, and snow would make a mess of everything, especially my evening job at the mall. I didn't even want to think about my weekend jobs that would send me skittering across the mall like a chicken with its head cut off. When I expected him to head to his house, he took the highway towards his office building instead.

I wasn't sure if I could handle being a professional anymore. "I'm a mess. I'm not sure you should take me to work with you."

"I have a meeting in twenty minutes, so you'll have to tag along. I'll give you to one of the nice ladies in HR. You can watch their heads explode when I tell them you're Michelle's sister, I'm keeping you, and that your residence is my house. It'll be fun. I'm sad I'll have to skip it because of the meeting, but I'll rescue you from HR as soon as I'm finished."

That didn't sound good. "I'm going to get eaten alive by HR."

"They won't eat you alive, but they're going to have questions. They'll want to know your Social Security number, where you live, your job skills, and so on. I'll have one of the ladies type up your resume on the fly. They'll probably forgive me when they find out you're going to be my executive secretary and solve so many of the problems currently plaguing them."

"Dare I ask?"

"There are about twenty people doing various tasks for me all over the company."

I had found my way directly into hell, but I would be paid good money to explore hell and make the most of my visit. "Why does this seem like a disaster in the making?"

"Ginger, your sister is my business partner. Were you really expecting anything different?"

"Okay, that's a fair statement, but out of familial obligation, I must protest your commentary about my sister. Yes, she's crazy, but you don't have to say it!"

"Someone has to say it, and my entire job revolves around turning her crazy into profit."

My eyes widened. "Does that mean my job would be to help you turn her crazy into profit?"

"Your job is to keep me from going crazy from trying to turn her crazy into profit."

"That's crazy."

"It really is."

"Am I going to go crazy, too?"

"It's entirely possible."

"That's not comforting," I muttered.

"You'll get used to it. Just don't run when we get to work. I'd have to chase you, and neither one of us is wearing good shoes for running in the snow."

Chapter Ten

AS I'D DONE my best to stay out of my sister's professional life, I'd never been inside the K&H Enterprises building before. Until I'd somehow gotten roped into working for Kace, I hadn't thought a building could intimidate me. I wanted to stay in his car with my puppy, hidden in the underground parking garage, until it was time to go to the mall.

I was already tired, and I hadn't been formally hired yet.

"I feel like I should be able to enjoy unemployment for more than ten minutes." I doubted my ploy would work, but I refused to remove my seat belt and pet my puppy.

"You'll probably survive. Get out of the car, Ginger. It's too late to get cold feet."

"It's never too late to get cold feet. It's December."

"And we're inside a heated parking garage. For now, we'll leave Virtue's stuff in the trunk; I need to go upstairs. I can't be late for my meeting. I'm also not leaving you in the car, so get a move on. I'll come down for Virtue's supplies once my meeting is over."

Damn it. I couldn't justify messing up Kace's work because I was having doubts about the situation. Sighing, I cooperated, got out of the car, and cradled my puppy so she wouldn't try to investigate every single car in the garage. "All right, but I think you've made a mistake."

"I haven't made a mistake. I've been watching you. Your work ethic is excessive, possibly insane, and your work quality is good. I've seen your paperwork."

"You mean randomly stuffed in a folder so I could try to make something from nothing for my bills?"

"Not exactly. You have an accounting ledger for your home. And it's filled out properly. As soon as I get your stuff moved into my house, I'm fully planning on poking my nose into wherever you keep your tax work so I can marvel at its beauty. I'm positive it's a thing of beauty."

It was, but it annoyed me he wanted to poke his nose into my private business. Then again, I couldn't justify becoming too upset with him. His nosiness had landed me a new job, one that would drive my sister to the brink of madness. If Kace took off his shirt, I would do more than drive her mad, but one of us would be happy. I would be the happy one. Michelle would feel betrayed, because me sleeping with her business partner belonged right at the top of her list of things I shouldn't do. Every time I talked to the damned man, the odds of me jumping him rose. The instant his shirt came off, jumping him would likely become my top priority.

I could be persuasive. He'd dived right over the interested into the obsessed category, and while I thought he needed to have his head examined, the possibility of being able to make an arrangement existed.

Kace led me to an elevator and pressed the up button. "Normally, I should be getting you a guest badge, but I'm going to take you to HR myself, and I'll make them issue you a badge. It would take thirty minutes, I'd have to deal with the whining, and I don't feel like dealing with more whining today. Unfortunately, I'm going to have to. Someone put that in my job description. That someone is your sister."

After having butted heads with my ex-boss, I didn't blame him. I could deal with the whining, but the stupidity of the situation boggled my mind. Kace had been offering a good arrangement, one with a streamlined resignation. "If you hiring me is payback against my sister, I might kill you myself."

"No, I'm hiring you because you're perfect for the job. I'm campaigning to marry you because you're perfect for me. That someone perfect for the job and perfect for me also happens to be the same person is just a bonus. It's not my fault your sister wasn't smart enough to realize you're perfect."

My sister liked to think she was the perfect one. In many ways, she was. She had the perfect job; being the co-ruler of a thriving company was the American dream in so many ways. Her co-ruler was easy on the eyes, and I was learning that he was too nice for my own good. Part of me wanted to believe his behavior was the ultimate trap, but my sister liked him.

For all of her faults, my sister didn't associate with mean people. I couldn't imagine her continuing a partnership with someone malicious. I could see her biting her tongue through arrangements with other businesses, but if given a chance, she'd find someone else to work with.

"Should I be taking you to the doctor? I'm concerned, Kace."

He heaved a sigh, and the elevator finally arrived, pinging before the doors opened. He pressed the button for the ground level. "Michelle didn't mention you had self-esteem issues."

"I don't have self-esteem issues. I'm just dirt poor and am not in the same class as you or Michelle. The only reason I have a puppy is because Santa gave me everything she needs for months, which is enough time to make sure I can keep feeding her. Being able to take her to work was a factor, too."

"You can still take her to work, but we'll have to get her properly trained. That won't be a problem. I'm planning on paying her training bill. She seems really smart, so I bet she'll train well. She's a husky, so you'll need to give her plenty of time to work off her excess energy, but if we give her jobs around the office, she'll be happy."

"What sort of jobs can you give a dog at the office?"

"They're couriers."

My mouth dropped open. "What? Couriers? Like delivering things to people?"

"That's exactly what I mean. Instead of running to Michelle's office, you can train Virtue to take what you need to her. The marketing floor has three courier dogs, and they're all owned by employees who didn't want to leave their dogs at home. We paid for the training, and the dogs get a paycheck."

"You pay the dogs?"

"Of course. They're working, so they get paid. They are paid with a salary and benefits."

The elevator arrived at the ground floor and swung open to the lobby level, which married marble and steel in what I thought was an elegant yet absurd combination. While I froze, trying to figure out how a dog could be paid a salary, Kace took hold of my elbow and guided me towards a second bank of elevators nearby. A quartet of security guards watched with interest.

"She's my new secretary and future wife, she's Michelle's sister, and she'll be getting a badge from HR. I have a meeting."

"Kace!" I choked out. Was his plan to just tell everyone he wanted to marry me until I fell in line?

I had to admit, it was a good plan with high odds of working if he put in any extra effort, kept being a nice person, and took off his shirt.

I needed to get control over myself and stop daydreaming

about him taking his shirt off. At the rate I was going, I'd get myself into trouble with no effort on his part.

Kace being Kace, he ignored my protest. "Oh, the puppy is a courier dog in training, and she'll need a badge. Her name is Virtue. She's a purebred husky. I'll have her license info for you this week, so please just put pending on her forms. She'll need an insurance policy, and I haven't spoken to our trainer yet, but she'll need to be booked."

"Mr. Dannicks," one of the security guards, the youngest of the batch, complained. The other guards looked to him for guidance despite his youthful appearance, which intrigued me.

"You can come scold me in my office in an hour and a half. It'll probably be more enjoyable than the meeting I'm about to step into. Don't let my new secretary escape. If she hasn't been badged by the time she has to take Virtue on a walk, keep her company and take her back to HR when she's done. If she's hungry, feed her. She can't escape. I just finished stealing her from another company." Kace reached into his pocket, pulled out a white card on a lanyard, and slapped it to a metal panel next to the elevator. "If you have to write something down in the guest ledger, just write she's Michelle's sister. That'll drive Michelle crazy later when she's back. Michelle will be back after Christmas, and I think she needs a new badge as penance for running off."

"Understood, Mr. Dannicks. I'll disable her badge immediately."

"Disable her pesky husband's badge, too. That'll serve them both right."

"Of course, sir."

My sister would lose her shit if she tried to go to work and discovered she couldn't access the building. "That was mean."

"I have my moments." An elevator pinged, and Kace dragged me to it, hauled me in, and pressed his badge to the interior panel before tapping the button for the sixth floor. "The sixth floor is for Human Resources, but the elevator is coded, so if my badge is used inside, it won't take any detours. There are only four badges with that privilege, and you'll be the fifth person to get one of them, but unless you're about to miss a critical meeting, you're not to use it."

"Okay." I adjusted my hold on Virtue and hugged my puppy. "Virtue really won't be a problem in the office?"

"She's fine. She'll just have to earn her keep. Huskies are work dogs, so they're happiest with a job to do anyway." When the elevator opened, Kace herded me out, and he aimed straight for the receptionist, a young woman with dark brown hair and bright blue eyes. "Theresa, this is Ginger. She's Michelle's sister, she's my new executive secretary, and if you could get together with the ladies and come up with a game plan on how I can convince her to marry me, that would be great."

I rolled my eyes. Unless I did something about him, he'd probably drag me to a courthouse next to start whatever the hell paperwork was required to actually marry me. "Only some of that is true. My name is Ginger, I am Michelle's sister, and he is hiring me to be his executive secretary."

"You already live with me. I refuse to lose this battle. I will make you mine." Kace checked his phone, cursed, and bolted for the elevator. "I have a meeting. Don't let her escape, Theresa."

Virtue wiggled in my arms, watched Kace disappear into the elevator, and whined over his departure. Even my puppy liked him, which didn't bode well for my future. Or it boded too well for my future. I needed time to acclimate to the idea of someone being insane enough to want to marry me. "I think he's lost his mind. I'm sorry."

"I think that depends on if the part about you living with him is true," the receptionist replied, and I recognized the moment she decided I was an interesting new entity worth paying attention to.

Double crap on a cracker with a cherry on top. "It is at least temporarily true due to an invasion of two nieces and a nephew and a microscopic apartment. Add in a very angry ex-boss, and Kace isn't inclined to drive me to my apartment. To add to the complications, I would drive myself, but a tow truck took my car out in a blaze of glory. Apparently, the engine had died, but icy roads decided the tow truck and my broken car were destined to form an intimate relationship. My car lost."

"Mrs. Ollends had mentioned a cursed sister, but we thought she was exaggerating. Honestly, we weren't even sure you actually existed."

"Michelle has issues. But I do actually exist." I would get my sister back for that. "I'm going to remind her I exist through strategic revenge decorating of her house."

"Please take pictures."

"Kace told the security people I wasn't allowed to escape. Is there a back window I can climb out of?"

Theresa laughed. "I'm afraid not. Mr. Dannicks takes building security seriously. Why don't you have a seat. Please feel free to let your puppy loose so she can stretch her legs. We have two courier cats—"

"Courier *cats*?" I blurted.

"They don't do a very good job, but Mr. Dannicks can't resist their charms. They're his cats, and like the dogs, they are given chores to do. Unlike the dogs, they don't do their chores unless they're asked to warm someone's lap. They were sickly strays found outside of the building last winter. One is partially blind, and the other is missing part of his tail and has a limp, because his paw was broken and it never healed quite right. Every week, they stay in a new office, and every few months, they go to a new floor. They spend the nights in Mr. Dannicks's office. When the office is closed, they go home with either Mr. Dannicks or Mrs. Jenkins, the head of the accounting department. On weekends, they typically go home with Mr. Dannicks, but these few weeks they've been going home with Mrs. Jenkins."

"That's probably my fault." I set Virtue down and unclipped her leash so she could stretch her legs. She decided the only place suitable for her was on my foot. As usual. On second thought, I should've named her Footsies, but it was too late to rename her. "I'm sorry."

"Don't be sorry, please. I, for one, am relieved Mr. Dannicks found someone he wants as his executive secretary. Let me call the head of the Human Resources department and get you sorted out. She'll have to contact Mr. Dannicks for specifics of your hiring agreement, and as he's in an important meeting, I expect he's going to want us to get your badge sorted out, make things up as usual, and otherwise have to guess what he actually wants until—"

Theresa's phone rang, and she picked it up. "K&H Enterprises, Theresa speaking." The woman's eyes widened, and then she laughed. "Yes, ma'am. She's with me, rather at a loss of what to do. You have the offer? Okay. I'll send her back. She looks like she could use a cup of tea or coffee and a few minutes of peace. Mr. Dannicks quite literally dragged her in here, and he was very vocal he didn't want her to escape. She has a puppy with her as well. Okay. I'll ask James to handle it."

Theresa hung up. "That was Mrs. Carre. She's one of the managers. Mr. Dannicks called her with the details and asked her to take care of you, as the head of our department is being called into this meeting over an issue, apparently. James is one of the assistants on his floor, and he's also one of our dog trainers, so she suggested your puppy stay with him while you're being sorted."

"Okay. That sounds good." It didn't, as I liked my puppy and didn't want someone I didn't know watching her, but there wasn't a lot I could do about the situation. While I wouldn't say anything, I concocted a long list of things I would do to James if he hurt my puppy.

I realized I had even more issues than Kace. Damn.

Theresa picked up her phone and dialed a number. "James, Mr. Dannicks's new executive secretary is here, and she has a puppy with her. Mrs. Carre asked for you to come watch the puppy and evaluate her for her trainability at Mr. Dannicks's request. Thank you."

"I don't think she'll be a training problem. She hasn't had any accidents inside since I got her. She's been very good. She's not nearly as hyperactive as I've been told huskies can be." I crouched and pet my puppy. "I'm worried she's not as hyper as I thought she'd be."

"Like people, dogs have their own personalities. She's still pretty young. It could just be she's had a really rough time and now feels safe, so she's sticking to you and being a good girl. But James is great with dogs, and if there's an issue, he can tell you and also tell you what to do about it."

A few moments later, a young man bounced through the door, caught sight of my puppy, and squealed. "She's fabulous. What is her name, what is her diet, how old is she, has she had all of her shots, is she licensed, and where are her supplies?"

With wide eyes, I stared at him, opening my mouth to reply but at a complete loss of what to say.

Theresa sighed. "It's okay, Ginger. I can call you Ginger, yes?"

"Please."

"James is rather energetic. It's part of his charm. You'll get used to him. If he tires you out, send him back to his office with a toy."

Professionalism, I decided, was a very odd beast at my sister's company. Then again, if Michelle had to behave to the standards of other professional companies, she would've been fired long ago. It made sense for the company of an eccentric pain in the ass to be staffed by eccentrics.

My work would be cut out for me.

I lifted my chin, deciding I wouldn't let anything crazy drive me away from a good job, better pay, and being able to keep my puppy at work. "Her name is Virtue, her supplies are in the trunk of Kace's car in the parking garage, she's about three months old, I feed her what Santa gave me, so please don't ask me about the brand—I don't really know anything about it, but Kace found it acceptable—she has had all of her shots, and she isn't licensed yet but will be soon."

"Keep her, Theresa. She answered all my questions without getting upset I asked. Also, could you repeat that part about Santa? I couldn't have heard you correctly."

"Santa gave me Virtue as an early Christmas present. She's a purebred."

"Santa really likes you. She looks like a great dog; her coloration is aces, she's the calmest puppy I've seen in a long time, and she looks healthy. Have you taken her to the vet since you got her?"

I shook my head, unwilling to admit I couldn't afford the vet visit—yet.

"And I know where I'm going in ten minutes, Theresa. I'll charge the company credit card and put it under the boss's name. I'll have our vet just do a checkup since her vaccinations are up to date, but Mr. Dannicks is strict about animals in the office; they get seen by our vet on his dime."

Well, I wouldn't look a gift horse in the mouth. "Okay. I don't have a good cell phone right now, so I guess call Kace if there are any issues. My battery is dead."

"They're living together," Theresa announced.

James whistled, looking me over with wide eyes, raised brows, and a disturbing amount of interest. "You mean I won't have to be his gopher now?"

Shaking her head, Theresa rose and headed for the glass doors leading deeper inside. "I wouldn't hold your breath, James. Come along, Ginger. Let's get you something warm to drink and get you settled. This will be long and tiring, but we'll take care of you."

Despite the feeling my life was about to become a chaotic mess, I left Virtue with James and followed Theresa.

Chapter Eleven

TWO HOURS, a mind-numbing amount of paperwork, and several coffees later, I had a new job as Kace's executive secretary, my dog had a salary, and I was worried I'd lost my mind. Losing my mind didn't seem like a bad thing when I considered all the perks my new employment offered. The first floor boasted a coffee shop, the executive floor had enough coffee machines to tame my sister's ravenous desire for caffeine, and there was even a gym with showers for those who wanted to get in some exercise during the day.

My sister would kill me when she found out.

For a chance at a good salary and decent work conditions, I'd deal with the risk of death at my sister's hands. Then again, I placed the blame for how things had turned out directly on her shoulders. If she hadn't wandered off, I wouldn't have needed to take care of her kids *or* rely on Kace. My car would still be alive, too. My luck hadn't soured until she'd wandered off and left me at the mercy of her children and her business partner.

I waited for Kace in HR's reception area, wondering how Virtue handled her adventure with James. I wanted to be the one to take her to the vet, but before Kace's takeover and decision to hire me, taking her in hadn't been an option at all. Instead of being upset for myself for not being a good puppy mother, I'd be grateful she was being taken care of.

I could handle it without crying *or* snapping at anyone.

The elevator opened, but instead of Kace, an older woman in a blazer and skirt strode into the room, and she wore a pair of knee-high boots I'd consider killing for. While I stared at her feet, wondering how a pair of simple black boots could possibly look so damned good, she strode to the reception desk. "Where is she, Theresa?"

I tore my attention from the woman's boots to the receptionist. To my dismay, the woman pointed at me. "Please try to return her in the same condition, or Mr. Dannicks will become upset. You'll also want to let him know when you're returning her to his residence or the office, or he'll become upset. He also messaged me asking to ensure you're taking her away from the building to feed her."

Narrowing my eyes, I considered how to make Kace pay for handing me off to a babysitter. "I wasn't planning on running off or anything."

Theresa laughed. "His meeting is running over, and your former employer is attempting to get you back. Mr. Dannicks isn't having any of that, so he asked Mrs. Carter for a favor, as you need some work-appropriate attire anyway." The receptionist picked up an envelope and handed it to the woman. "Here's a company credit card authorized for your use, Mrs. Carter. Mr. Dannicks says you're to use it at will. Her entire wardrobe needs to be overhauled."

"My wardrobe isn't that bad," I protested.

"What you're wearing is fine enough, but you need better, and I make better," Mrs. Carter announced. "I'm Juliette, and by the time we're done today, we're either going to be best friends, or you're going to hate me with every fiber of your being, but you'll put up with me because I'm good at what I do, and once you see what good clothes can do for you, you'll never want to go back to anything other than a properly fitted wardrobe."

Damn it. I stared down at my chest and plucked at my shirt. "That's fair. I've lost weight and hadn't picked up anything new yet. I'm hoping to regain some weight soon."

Assuming the chicken nuggets didn't rise up from their grave and try to kill me.

I'd find out about that soon enough.

Mrs. Carter frowned. "Stand up, please. You're Ginger, yes?"

"Yes, I'm Ginger, ma'am." I stood, and she twirled her finger. Taking the clue she wanted to get a closer look at what she had to work with, I turned in a slow circle.

"Juliette. I'm too old for that ma'am crap. The only one I want calling me ma'am is my son when he's gotten on my last damned nerve. He does his best to get on my last damned nerve at least once a week, but I haven't heard a ma'am out of him in years. I get a plaintive 'But, Moooooomm' instead. No one told me children never stopped whining, not even after they grew up and left the house. You're underweight, so I'll dress you in spares for today."

"I've been taking care of my nieces and nephew, and I can't say I've heard too much whining from any of them. Actually, they've been really behaved considering the circumstances."

"You're the aunt. They try not to whine too much to aunts. Aunts get them what they want, usually. My son didn't luck out in the aunt department; he has a few bastard uncles who don't let him get away with anything, but they're jackasses anyway, so we don't talk too much to them. We don't like jackasses in our household, so we don't bring them home with us. We only deal with jackasses at work."

"I have no idea who you are, but I can't imagine anyone not liking you," I admitted.

"That's because you're a sensible woman. You wouldn't put a neon-green skirt with a pumpkin-orange shirt, would you?"

I grimaced at the thought of that combination. "No. Why would anyone do that?"

"One of my clients. They were going to an ugly sweater party and wanted to be the ugliest in designer clothes. I've never been so disgusted with myself for going along with something in my life. The sweater redefined ugly, however, but I did demand the entire outfit be burned afterwards in a purification ceremony."

"Was the outfit burned?"

"I have a video. I demanded to witness the purification. I had my husband record it while I attempted to purify my soul in the heat of the outfit's flames."

I'd met someone crazier than my sister and Kace combined, and she'd be helping me pick my clothes. "I'll try not to make any requests that would require you to go through a trial by fire to purify yourself."

"That's the spirit! You're already one of my better clients. The best clients let me dress them and stand nicely for my designing amusement. Are you going to be one of my best clients?"

I did the math: if I went with the crazy designer and let her dress me, Kace had to pay for it with his company funds, and then my sister would murder me for the company spending money on my clothes. "I've never been so intimidated in my life, not even when I told my boss I quit a few hours ago and got kidnapped by Kace to become his secretary," I confessed. "My sister is going to kill me when she finds out Kace used a company card to buy me clothes."

Theresa laughed. "Don't worry about that, Ginger. Accounting will deduct the expenditures for your clothing acquisitions from his personal accounts when the bill comes in. While we do have a fund for clothing emergencies, he wanted to handle your purchases himself. As Mrs. Carter already has a company card with her name for instances like this, it's more efficient to do it this way until you have your own cards."

Only an idiot would issue a credit card to me, but I held my tongue. "Virtue is still with James."

"James will take care of her, and when they're back from the vet and meeting with the trainer, he'll bring your puppy to Mr. Dannicks, so please don't worry about her. She's probably having a great time. We try to make sure the animals don't develop anxiety from going to the vet, so they'll try to make it as fun for her as possible."

I'd stepped into a surreal world. Had I already fallen prey to the uncooked chicken nugget? "Thank you, Theresa."

"You'll be fine. Juliette will take care of you."

"Come with me, Ginger. Your current outfit fits well when you're the right weight?"

"I think it does."

"That'll do. I'll work some sorcery, figure out what size you should be, and I'll talk to that gremlin upstairs about making sure you're properly fed and maintaining a good weight. If you're anorexic, you may as well tell me now, as I have some therapist friends who specialize in helping women with weight-related mental health issues. I'm dressing the whole package, and I prefer when the packages are healthy."

I pressed the button for the elevator, and it opened. Once inside and the door was closed, I replied, "It was a money issue. That's been resolved."

"Well, considering you're the gremlin's executive secretary, I'd certainly say so. He's a hard boss, but he pays well. It's a downright pity he has so much trouble keeping someone around. Nobody meets his standards." Juliette pressed the button for the ground floor. "What's this about you being delivered to his house?"

Hiding the truth wouldn't do any good, and while I had a lot of problems, I'd gotten tired of sweeping it all under the rug. "My sister is his partner, and he's determined to marry me."

"Well, well, well. I'd wondered when he'd finally get off his lazy bum and try to win a woman. You must be something special to catch that gremlin's attention."

"Why do you call Kace a gremlin?"

"That's what he is. He loves shiny things. I'm convinced he lives in a little cave, and he only comes out when there's something shiny to chase."

"Wouldn't that make him a magpie?"

"Magpie, gremlin. Close enough. Calling him a gremlin gets better reactions. Your eyes bugged the first time I said it, then you got delightfully confused—probably because you can't figure out how he could possibly be something like a gremlin, right?"

I'd underestimated Juliette Carter, and if I wasn't careful, I'd like her and want to bring her home with me just so she could call Kace a gremlin to his face. "He's an overbearing jerk who does like chasing money, and money can be quite shiny. But he's a good person. When you add in the type of money that he has, I think it's harder to stay a good person. But he does, somehow."

"He's a good little gremlin, but he probably has a bathtub filled with gold he bathes in at his whim."

"Wouldn't that make him a leprechaun?"

"Leprechauns are just Irish gremlins who wear funny hats and lure people to the end of rainbows."

I'd never look at St. Patrick's Day the same ever again—and I'd have to look into Irish folklore to find out if leprechauns might truly be Irish gremlins who wore funny hats while luring people to the end of the rainbow. "Santa's elves?"

"Gremlins who stole the souls of women out for the blood of young children. Unfortunately, they forgot to check the mall rules, so their efforts prove in vain every year. The women who didn't have their souls temporarily stolen were likely lured in by some attractive mall Santa, and who can blame them for that? And the ones who weren't lured in by an attractive mall Santa like kids or need the money. It's a crazy world we live in."

It occurred to me I had heard of Juliette Carter before: on very rare occasions, the clothing boutique I worked in part-time got a few of her pieces.

They sold for thousands, and the store often had to run a raffle to keep shoppers from going insane. "You're *the* fashion designer, aren't you?"

"Sure am. Don't worry. I won't rob your future husband completely blind. He's a good customer, and everyone in upper management here has clothes I've designed; I have corporate lines open to some businesses, and yours is one of them. Usually, I just do the measurements, pick the best styles and colors for the employee in question, and have a set made. Since you're the gremlin's executive secretary and future bride, I'm afraid you're going to have to get some special treatment. It might take all night."

Oh no. "But I have work tonight. I need to do my shift at the boutique."

"Boutique?"

I grimaced, realizing I'd made an error. The elevator arriving on the bottom floor spared me. I almost ran directly into Kace while trying to dodge admitting I had two part-time jobs. "I thought you were in a meeting."

"I'm on a twenty-minute break before I succumb to the urge to murder your ex-boss. Apparently he's on his way over. Juliette, please keep her amused until I'm sure that asshole is out of here."

"Sure, little gremlin. When's the wedding date?"

Kace chuckled. "As soon as I convince her to go along with it."

"Add six months. That's how long you'll need to properly

plan and dress her appropriately. I'm claiming the right to make the dress, as she's far too pretty to be trusted with some amateur. I'll try to shower her with tales of your good side, but you're going to have to work hard to make up for your gremlin ways."

"Just because I got a good deal out of you for clothes doesn't mean I'm a gremlin, Juliette. I'm too handsome to be a gremlin."

"It doesn't matter if I think you're handsome. You don't disgrace my clothes, and that's all I care about. And you pay me promptly. I care about that, too. Now, I do care about if the lady here actually likes your attention. I will rescue her if she does not. I will meddle if she does. I'm very good at meddling, just ask everyone who knows me. I just hired a new employee, and she's single. I'm just biding my time until she's comfortable before putting an end to her unfortunate lack of a love life. I was just minding my own business, and the poor woman was telling my assistant how she'd struck out yet again. I haven't found a single man worthy of her yet, but I'm working on that. In the meantime, I'll just have to work with what I have."

Kace lifted a hand and pinched the bridge of his nose. "She's Michelle's sister, Juliette."

"I'm aware. This only makes it more amusing, as I do enjoy every opportunity to screw around with Michelle. She makes it so easy and entertaining, and she absolutely hates her sessions with me. If she didn't try to have opinions about clothes that were wretched and abhorrent on a good day, we wouldn't have issues."

"Please tell me my sister wasn't behind the awful sweater incident."

"Fortunately not. She comes in as a close second, however. She wanted to wear red, and your sister? She looks terrible in red. I finally pulled out a prototype, stuffed her in it, and forced her to look in the mirror until she acknowledged she resembled a tomato with jaundice."

I grimaced. "Tomato with jaundice doesn't seem like a good look for anybody."

"I then dragged her to the doctor myself to make certain she didn't actually have jaundice. Turns out she had a minor case of it due to an iron deficiency, which was fixed with a supplement. Even without the jaundice, she still doesn't wear red well. You might be able to get away with it, but I'd have to shove you into a prototype first to find out. I'm undecided what color is best."

"I wear black often."

"Black is an excellent, classic, and professional look, but it's boring, Ginger. I don't like boring."

Kace sighed. "If you're going to corrupt her, please at least return her smiling, Juliette?"

I gave up. The way I figured, I'd lose all of my self-respect by the end of the day anyway. I pointed at Juliette's boots. "Having a pair of boots like those would make me smile."

"My pesky employees keep telling me these boots are too plain and classic to sell well, so we don't have them in the line."

I'd dealt with a lot of bullshit during the day, but anyone thinking Juliette's boots were too plain and too classic topped the shit cake of my day. "Can you make an exception? I'd really like a pair of those boots."

"Would you be willing to model a pair of these boots for me on my quest to convince my pesky employees they're superstars?"

"I don't know how to be a model."

"You just have to walk back and forth without tripping over your feet, look straight ahead, and pretend you have no emotions."

"So, you want me to act like a corporate drone?"

"While dressed in humiliating attire, knowing everyone will be laughing at you. Okay, that part isn't true. I don't torture my models with design monstrosities. I know plenty of designers who do like to torture their models with monstrosities. I prefer having women model for me rather than sticks dressed in bubbles and toothpicks."

"Bubbles... and toothpicks?"

"The last fashion week in town was a weird one—even weirder than normal. One designer dressed a model in a toothpick dress, and he attached little bubbles of junk to the ends so she wouldn't get stabbed. It was a disaster. The woman could barely walk. Now, I give that model credit. She made it down the runway without a single grimace. If I had toothpicks crammed around my thighs and near where the sun don't shine, I'd be dancing a jig and begging for mercy."

"But why bubbles and toothpicks?!"

Juliette shrugged. "Fashion designers are insane. I'm insane, too, but I'm the sane sort of insane."

I had no idea what the sane sort of insane was, I wasn't sure I wanted to know, and I questioned everything about how my life had turned out. "Kace, are all fashion designers like this?"

"Juliette is a special breed among fashion designers, but she is, as she says, the sane sort of insane. Before I hired her, I went with a fashion designer who truly and genuinely believed codpieces were going to be coming back into fashion soon upon seeing another designer do an entire set themed around codpieces worn over the top of regular attire."

"Unless you're participating in a sport where a codpiece is recommended, please never do that. That sounds vomit inducing."

Juliette laughed. "It really is. I was at that show, and I had to leave before I died of laughter. It was the first time in my entire career I had to leave so I wouldn't humiliate another designer. It was a horror show. I almost missed my own damned segment because I was crying in the bathroom from laughing. My assistant had to come in and drag me backstage to make sure everything was okay with all the models. That incident only reinforced why I wouldn't torture any of my models."

Kace checked his watch. "Shit. I have to go back upstairs. If there's any issues, call me. Ginger, if you start feeling ill, make sure you tell Juliette right away. She'll make sure you get to the doctor and contact me. Unfortunately, if you're going to get sick, it'll probably hit you like a train or sneak up on you and then feel like it hit you like a train. Stay hydrated."

While tempted to roll my eyes at him, I fully expected my nugget to return from its grave prepared to take me out. "I'll try."

"I'll keep a close eye on her, so don't you worry any. She won't be left unattended. If she gets sick, I've a doctor friend who's willing to make calls and can take any blood tests required. Salmonella risk, you said?"

"Raw chicken nugget. It's rare, but it happens. I've already spoken to the manager at the restaurant, and they've preemptively agreed to cover any expenses associated with illness. They'll pay the medical bill and any time off associated with salmonella as long as a doctor can verify the cause of illness."

I raised my brows at that. "You got them to preemptively agree to that? But how?"

"I told them what I'd do if they didn't, and I made a reasonable request. I didn't ask for damages, just covering the expenses you owe and your paid time off while you recover. A lot of people go for damages in this situation, which leads to pricey lawsuits nobody wants. I brought a reasonable request to the table, and I've found when reasonable about something like this, they'll play ball. It doesn't hurt I have the money to take it to court if they didn't go with what I wanted. They offered free nuggets for a year, too."

"Please tell me you accepted that. Please."

Kace laughed. "As a matter of fact, I did. I warned them you had quite the appetite for nuggets, so they're issuing a gift card for the value of a twenty pack a day for an entire year, and it doesn't expire. I figured you'd like it, and they don't really care if you get other food there if you're tired of nuggets."

"Bring on the salmonella!" I could deal with being sick for a few days for a year of free nuggets. "I will never betray you like you betrayed me, nuggets."

Still laughing, Kace hit the button for the elevator, and the door opened. "Have fun with Juliette, Ginger. You could use a little fun, and Juliette's one of a kind." He stepped inside and tapped his pass to the panel, which warned me he hadn't been kidding about his schedule from hell for the day. "I'll see you tonight, and yes, I know I'm responsible for Virtue until you're done. She'll be fine."

"Introduce her to your cats so they can come home with us, too." To prevent any argument on it, I stepped away from the elevator and gave Juliette my full attention. "Do your worst. I'm woman enough to handle it."

"I love it when the clients talk dirty to me."

※※※

JULIETTE WORKED IN MANHATTAN, and her fashion design studio took up five entire floors. She gave me a full tour, and it amazed me how many seamstresses and tailors could share so much space in harmony. Hundreds of different outfits decorated mannequins along the wall, and three floors into the tour, I fell in love with a slinky black dress that covered all the important bits while still oozing elegance and sex appeal.

"Please tell me that dress is for sale," I whispered.

Juliette turned around, lifted two fingers to her lips, and let out a piercing whistle, which caught the attention of everyone nearby. She pointed to the dress I liked. "Which one of you hooligans is in charge of this project?"

One of the tailors raised his hand. "I am, Juliette. What can I do for you?"

"You, me, now. Look her over, see if we have a dress in her size, and if we don't, I want it on the list, Adam."

The tailor got up, looked me over, and narrowed his eyes. "I've got her size and a size up, too."

"Grab both; the size up will fit her when she gains weight. Actually, you better get two sizes up, as I'm not sure about her ideal weight yet. I'll meet you in the main studio in thirty minutes. If you need overtime, tell HR I've authorized it because I'm stomping on your day."

"You got it, Juliette. Want me to grab Carl? He's in charge of the boots and heels that'd best go with that dress."

"Drag him kicking and screaming if you must. What size shoe do you wear, Ginger?"

"A seven most of the time."

"You better grab Andrea. She's going to need some accessories for that dress." Juliette patted my back and gestured to the next mannequin in line. "See, Ginger? This can be fun. You're supposed to fall in love with clothes, and if the dress doesn't suit you, we'll figure out a dress that does, which you can fall in love with instead. And sometimes, it's okay to have a dress that doesn't suit you just because you love it. These clothes are about you."

"Kace's wallet will not appreciate the price tag of that dress, will it?"

"It won't, but should the dress suit you, and I can convince you to walk the runway in it, you get the dress for free; I always give my models the clothes they wear down the runway. In exchange, they tell people who designed it."

"How does this work? Do you design all the clothes here?"

"I help design everything that falls under my brand, but everyone is assigned a project. I designed that dress from top to bottom, and I assigned the project to Adam because he has an excellent eye for women's shapes; he will alter the base design to make the dress work for women of as many shapes and sizes as possible."

Juliette took her time strolling along, peeking over her employee's shoulders. Every now and then, she paused to make a comment, and while she criticized, she offered solutions or suggestions, and the few times she had neither a solution nor a suggestion, she told the employee to swing by her office at the end of the day so they could put together a game plan to resolve the problem.

I found several casual outfits I adored, which were added to the list of things for me to try on, and one blazer and skirt set I thought would make me look like a professional.

Juliette snorted at my selection. "Other colors than black and white exist, Ginger."

"But I like black and white."

"Other colors exist. I will find you other colors you like, and I'll prove it to you. You just haven't met the right cut in the right color yet. But you will."

"As I said earlier, do your worst. I figure there's a finite time you can dress me up, as I have part-time work tonight."

"You do? Where at?"

Resigned to my situation, I told her the name of the boutique I was scheduled to work for. "I usually work at the candy store in the same mall, but I do shifts there on my days off from the candy store."

"I know the manager there." Juliette pulled out her phone and tapped at the screen. "Theo, darling. It's Juliette. You have a young lady named Ginger working for you tonight, right? Excellent. I have a favor to ask you. I need to play with her tonight. I'm stealing her for modeling purposes, and she's one of my client's employees. I'm going to send one of my minions to fill in for her. I'll handle my minion's pay, so just pay Ginger for her shift as usual. I'm sure you won't have problems, and if you do, my minion can handle anything. Sound good?

"Also, if I have my way, I'll have a slinky black dress available soon, and Ginger will be modeling it for me. I'll do the reveal at your store, but you'll have to pay out half of my appearance fee to the model. If you want two outfits, we can talk shop, but I'm only using Ginger for the reveal, so you'll have to deal with whatever I pick that works best with her. Talk to your boss and get back to me. I'll bring a prototype for auction, and the proceeds will go to charity. That should draw in some new customers for you. We'll make a party out of it. Ping me if there are any issues. If I don't hear from you, my minion will appear in time for Ginger's shift. As I'm a true asshole, I will have my minion wearing my clothes, and your boss will be begging me to provide rack stock." Juliette hung up, giggled, and returned her phone to her bag. "I love my job."

"I feel like I've missed a lot."

"I know most boutique owners and managers. It's part of the gig here; while I have sales teams and negotiators, I make a point of forming relationships with any boutique that sells clothes in the price range I sell at. It happens I've sold clothes through your boutique before, and it worked well enough I'd try again. A prototype auction will draw in a lot of people, especially when it's announced that all proceeds will go to charity. I'll probably have the food retailers in the mall provide catering. People love the dichotomy of a brand name bash with cheap but tasty and unhealthy food. I'll probably have a raffle for a second prototype for charity with a base entry fee of five dollars. That lets just about everyone have a chance.

"The second raffle will be for a surprise prototype that'll fit the winner, where the first raffle for charity will be for a specific outfit in a specific size. If I can convince the evil marketing minions to go for it, I'll make your boutique the only place to get that dress for six months as an advance sale. I make so much money on those, as people love having a limited edition. But I'll have to sweet-talk my marketing minions."

No wonder Kace thought Juliette was the sane sort of insane. With one simple but strange idea, she opened her reveal to everyone, even though most couldn't afford her clothing. "That sounds *amazing*."

Juliette laughed. "I do try. My marketing minions typically don't like my raffles because I'm writing off those specific outfits for at least a month. I don't like the outfits being sold for at least that long to draw in more money for charity. The boutique agrees to host the raffles because they want the people attending to buy other clothes. The main line on these events is twenty percent to the store, twenty percent to me, thirty percent to the craftsmen, seamstresses, and tailors that made the clothes, and the rest goes to manufacturing, materials, salaries, and so on. Those percentages can change if a product has a higher cost to manufacture. Sometimes, the percentage to me is split between my business and the models.

"The boutiques don't get to set the price of the dresses, and I don't allow discounts on my clothes in boutiques. Everyone pays the same amount for the dress. I will only run a sale on clothes that haven't sold within five years, and I haven't had enough to run a sale in ages. Which is exactly what I want. I limit how many of each outfit is produced, but if someone has purchased a dress and it's worn to death, I will have a replacement dress made at manufacturing cost, craftsman cost, plus ten percent as my fee for the replacement. The outfit has to be at least five years old to be eligible."

"That is also amazing. You really replace at cost with just a small profit?"

"They already bought the outfit, and it's a limited-release item. They don't get to keep the worn dress, although they will have the option for something to be made for them out of the old outfit if it's in acceptable condition. I charge the craftsman cost and my ten percent for that; I have a bunch of designs already on hand for that. Since those are only made from recycled goods, they're extremely rare."

"That is *insane*."

"I told you I was the sanest insane designer ever. People like when their money goes the extra mile, and with my brand, they're buying quality, the name, and longevity. I'll even change the size of the dress if it's worn out and doesn't fit well after the five years, on the same terms."

"Do I want to know how much the slinky dress will cost?"

Juliette chuckled. "Ten thousand dollars."

The shock of the dress's value removed my general ability to comprehend how life worked. My legs decided they no longer needed to function, and I sat down hard. I stared up at the woman while every drop of blood fled the general vicinity of my head. "Ten thousand dollars?"

Juliette leaned over and patted my head. "It's okay, Ginger. The gremlin can afford it, and you're worth every penny of the investment. And anyway, he's not even going to be paying for it, because I do believe you and that dress are a match made in heaven. It'll work out, and by the time the reveal is done, you'll have earned that dress and then some."

I hugged my knees and bowed my head. "I'm a poor nobody, and I fell in love with a ten-thousand-dollar dress. I couldn't even afford a thousand-dollar puppy, but I got one anyway. I don't even know what's going on anymore, or why."

I wanted to cry, but if I started, I wouldn't stop.

Juliette patted my back. "It's okay, Ginger. You're not a nobody. The gremlin likes you, and while he's a snooty little gremlin, he's an excellent judge of character. For him to want to marry you, that means you're the exact opposite of a nobody. You're a somebody he loves being with. I can't fix your self-esteem problem, but I can make you feel like you're worth a million bucks. And you are. I have a list of people who are worthless assholes, and you're most definitely not on that list. Get to your feet, and let me show you just how beautiful you are. But mark my words, Ginger. If I can't convince you you're worthwhile, the gremlin will, and he's an aggressive little monkey when he has a point to prove."

The thought of a designer calling Kace an aggressive little monkey made me laugh. "I just haven't earned it, Juliette."

"You will. View this as a modeling job interview, and you have to wear the clothes to model. I just pay in boutique bonuses and the clothes you model. If I have to make you model every piece of clothing you're buying today, so be it. How tragic, having such a pretty woman wearing my clothes at reveal events. We'll make a fortune, you and I."

"But ten thousand dollars?"

"Darling, my boutique appearance fee is thirty thousand dollars on average, half of which goes to me, half of which goes to the model. I try to only take one model with me, but if I have to bring two or more, the boutique appearance fee is raised, and I take a lower percentage to make up for it. The boutiques will easily make their money back from sales for the day, as me showing up gives the boutique a nod, and the boutiques wisely showcase accessories and outfits that complement what is being revealed.

"Since the craftsmen, who are all my employees, get a cut of every sale, it's paid out in bonuses or in company stock—their choice. The cut to me will also go to employee salaries if the general manufacturing budget doesn't cover it. I rarely have to dip into my share to pay the employee bills, but it happens sometimes. I only take home specific profit if everyone else is paid first. Of course, I'm paid in stock, and I have a salary, too, but my salary is comparable with upper management. It encourages us all to work harder. Now, come, come. We have a lot to do and only a little time to do it, so let's make every minute count."

Chapter Twelve

HELL BEGAN with a headache behind my eyes, which I blamed on the studio lights and the dizzying bustle of activity involving me being measured, remeasured, stripped out of most of my clothes, and put on display. Juliette shook her head and clucked her tongue over my mismatched bra and panties.

"First, I commend you for having a properly sized bra. Most women don't know how to pick their bra size to save their life. No gap, no spillover. It doesn't look like your straps are digging in, either. Bend over and give your breasts a good shake, please. I want to see how well you move in the bra. A good bra is critical for wearing clothing properly."

I'd gotten accustomed to men and women alike scrutinizing me within a few minutes of the measurements beginning. Someone also measured my removed clothes to determine what my regular size should be, which was approximately a size and half from what my measurements claimed I should be wearing.

I bent over and gave my chest a good shaking. My bra and breasts stayed put.

"Yep. That bra is the right size. Good. Turn."

I straightened and turned, and Juliette checked my bra's

tag. She gave the measurement to one of her minions, who skittered off to do the designer's bidding. "I bought three new bras when I lost weight," I confessed.

"Hurt your back from your breasts bouncing every which way at their whim?"

"Yeah."

"We'll get you some transitional bras until you're back to the weight you're supposed to be. We make a line of cheap but good bras just for this reason. My clients suffering from eating disorders tend to be very sensitive about those issues, so we try to accommodate them as they get back to healthy weights. It's hard enough for them to overcome their challenges without their clothing fitting poorly. I have special exchange programs for them, too; I have generic outfits in a range of half sizes that everyone can use as they need. It's a special line of clothes, since they're used and switch hands often, but it really helps them on the clothing front. They pay a monthly subscription fee, and they come in for sessions to get remeasured and work with their therapists. Some are in more often than others."

"Dare I ask how much that costs?"

"A hundred a month, and the therapy is included. We use training therapists partnered with experienced ones, and it works great. I sometimes make arrangements with medical schools to make sure we get my clients the help they need at a price they can afford, and most insurance companies will play ball with us, too, so some folks don't even have a bill. The clothes belong to the company, and they're required to buy anything they don't return, but we put them on a payment plan. It hasn't happened yet. Once the therapist is confident the patient isn't going to backwards slide, the second stage of our program begins."

"What's the second stage?"

"They become models at a healthy weight. I will do a series of reveals centered around a new wardrobe designed with him or her in mind. I do a two-week tour with the model in a city at various boutiques. They get the model fee for doing the reveals, which builds their model resume at a healthy weight. It helps end the stigma that models must be tall twigs, too. I won't use traditional models for my projects. This makes me an insane designer in the industry."

"The sanest insane designer. Because you're doing sane things in an insane way."

Juliette grinned. "Exactly so."

Juliette's minion returned with her arms piled with lingerie boxes, and Juliette plucked one off and handed it to me. "The bathroom is over there, so get changed into that and see how it fits. We'll match the bras to the type of clothes you'll be wearing. I'll try to do the clothes in sets to minimize the number of times you'll have to change your underwear."

I did as told, and by the time I emerged, my headache had spread to the entirety of my skull. Juliette's eyes narrowed. "You have a headache."

Not a question, but a statement. As lying wouldn't do any good, I nodded.

"Probably the start of salmonella poisoning. I've had it before, and the headache was unbelievable. We'll keep going until you're done, and then we'll call in the doctor and go from there. Just let me know when it becomes unbearable. Adam? Fetch Ginger a case of ginger ale, antacids, Pepto, and raid my office for my ibuprofen. I doubt she'll keep anything down in a few hours, but we'll do what we can. We'll do your dress as soon as you're back, as I want to make sure that one is done at the minimum."

"I'll call Dr. Ramone while I'm getting everything," the tailor promised. "Want me to relay to your assistant?"

"Don't tell her I suggested this, but have her order soup for us. Have her put a general dinner call out, and make sure everyone turns in their delivery receipts to accounting. Ask for some volunteers to help Ginger while she's sick and miserable. We'll want to dress her up as much as she can handle. Distractions are good, will tire her out, and help make sure she can sleep despite feeling like hell. And when you call Dr. Ramone, ask him what I should be feeding her. I'm assuming soup, but if I'm wrong, tell my minion whatever he recommends. Also, make sure he knows I'll need a diagnosis letter to give to the gremlin for her file."

"You got it," Adam replied before shuffling off.

"I have no interest in torturing you when you're sick, so once you don't feel up for this, we stop, okay? Also, If you start incessantly throwing up, I'm taking you to the hospital myself."

"It's the revenge of the chicken nugget."

"Chicken nuggets are a delicious peril, aren't they? I sigh sadly often when we pass fast food joints. They're so good but so bad for me. I'm not supposed to have any deep fried food at all. It's bad for me, or so says the doctor who wants me to live forever. Unbeknownst to him, I sneak some at least once a month. Life was meant to be enjoyed."

"Is Dr. Ramone that doctor?"

"He sure is. If I annoy you, snitch on my nugget habit. I'm woman enough to handle it."

"The headache sucks, but I can live with it."

"When did you have the nuggets?"

"Two or three days ago. It's a bit of a blur. I've been busy."

"And this is the first headache you've had?"

I thought about it. "Honestly, I've been so tired I don't even know anymore."

Juliette checked her phone. "A little late for it to be starting, but still within the right window. Apparently it has to be tested with a stool sample rather than blood, but if it has gotten into your blood, it has to be treated specially. Yuck. That's not going to be fun for you."

"Or anyone," I muttered.

"It'll be all right. We'll try to make this as painless as possible. While we wait for Adam, let's try on some of the corporate drone outfits you'll love and I'll hate. May as well make the most of every minute."

JULIETTE WAS RIGHT; I adored the corporate drone outfits she hated, but we compromised somewhat. As long as she gave me black blazers and skirts, I'd wear just about whatever shirt she wanted. She even talked me into some colorful jackets and skirts to make her happy. To her horror and my delight, I accomplished what my sister failed to do: I rocked red. I rocked red so hard I made the designer cry from a mix of joy and horror.

"Of all the colors, you just had to work red. I'm going to have to get out my collection of red dresses. Do you know how hard it is to find a model that actually works well with red? I've tried six reds on you, and they all worked. This is cruel and unusual punishment. How is it your sister looks like a disaster in red, but you? You are anything but a disaster."

"I am not a vampire afraid of the sun. I go out in the sun as often as possible, really. I like the outdoors. It's called a tan. I have one. Michelle doesn't. Michelle believes the sun will reduce her to a pile of ash."

"Despite your beliefs, I've seen Michelle go into the sun. She did not immediately burn away into a pile of steaming ash. She did make warding gestures against evil, but she didn't incinerate. She didn't even get a sunburn. She stopped whining after I suggested she put on her shades. She's a strange but entertaining woman. But she's a strange and entertaining woman who should never wear red."

"I will tolerate standing here and being dressed whenever I'm not throwing up as long as I get to strut in front of my sister wearing red. I will wear red every day for a month once she's back home as punishment for saddling me with her kids while she globe-trotted with Mitchel. If you have any other suggestions to torture her, I'm listening."

It only took ten minutes after the headache hit for the nausea to kick in at full force, and I'd already interrupted the measurements and modeling twice being sick. I expected it to get worse before it got better. I guzzled ginger ale at Juliette's suggestion, which helped some. According to Alan, the doctor and soup would arrive within an hour.

I never thought I'd be happy to see a doctor.

Dr. Ramone took one look at me, checked my temperature, snorted, and proclaimed if I didn't have salmonella poisoning, he'd eat his PhD for dinner along with a side dish of eternal shame and self-loathing. If I never had to acquire another stool sample in my life, I'd die happy. I survived the experience, but I destroyed an entire bottle of hand sanitizer convincing myself my hands were clean.

According to the doctor, it would be up to four days for the sample to be tested and confirmed, but my symptoms, while starting a little later than generally expected, were classic of salmonella, and he would file the initial doctor's report. He took a blood sample, too, just to be sure. To limit the number of times I'd have to see him, he prescribed an antibiotic and recommended anti-nausea medication, but I wasn't to take anything unless my symptoms worsened or the bloodwork came back positive for salmonella in my blood stream.

He'd have the labs for the blood test done by the end of the day, and he would text me with an update.

Juliette waited until the doctor left to hold her hand out for the prescription, which I gave her. She, in turn, handed it to one of her minions. "Get that filled through the online pharmacy, and if Ramone calls crying about it, I'll deal with him myself. Get the anti-nausea medication, and if she throws up two more times tonight, she's taking it, and I'll fight him myself about it. She's too thin to deal with not being able to hold anything down. After that's done, run to the store and get those sick-people shakes. If she can't keep the soup down, maybe she'll be able to keep those down."

Juliette's minion took the prescription slip and ran off with it.

"I thought I needed to be there to fill the prescription."

"Online pharmacies are great. If she needs any information from you, including your insurance or driver's license number, she'll ask me for it. I'll relay the info she needs, and it'll be delivered in a few hours. There's one right down the street, and we use them all the time. They'll call if there are any issues. Now, about your plan to torment your sister."

"She needs to suffer for running off without a word."

Juliette chuckled. "So you want to wear red and taunt her with it?"

"I'm even going to let Kace try to convince me to marry him the entire time I wear red. It'll be like those animals that use bright plumage to attract a partner. Do you think it'll work? He's crazy to like someone like me, Juliette."

"News flash for you, woman. You're pretty, you're nice, and you're dealing with being sick and a fitting because you have a strong sense of ethics and responsibility. You're aware that I'm dressing you for work, and you don't want to disappoint your new boss. Who you've just said you were planning on enticing with pretty clothes like it was plumage. You don't have to dress to impress, Ginger. You've already impressed. Just get to know him. If you like him, keep him."

"You make that sound deceptively simple."

"No matter how you look at it, relationships are work. Go in ready and willing to make it work, and you'll do all right. There's nothing wrong with being in a relationship with your boss, either—as long as you keep work and business separate. I don't think you'll have a problem with that. You're ethical."

"How do you even know that?"

"I've been in this business a long time, dressing people for success, love, and life. I have clients who quit the instant things aren't sunshine and roses. They're not willing to put in a little work. You're here, a rather uncharming shade of green, putting in the work because you believe it's necessary. Apply that to your love life, and you'll be just fine. And for all I tease the gremlin, he's the same exact way. The perfect woman for him is the one willing to work through thick and thin. And you? You're all that and more. I think you're the kind who needs a challenge, and trust me on this one. Gremlins are challenging. It doesn't hurt he's easy on the eyes. It's always nice when the good ones are easy on the eyes, isn't it?"

"He must have some sort of serious flaw. He's still single."

Juliette chuckled. "Or he saw the woman he wanted and bided his time until he could have her. That's you, for the record. How long have you known him?"

I shrugged. "Since he partnered with my sister to start their company, I guess. I told my sister she'd picked well in the looks department, but she'd be screwed if he lacked brains. She usually sticks to decent people, so I couldn't nail him on that."

"So, you challenged him right out of the gate."

"With jealousy he was stealing my sister and more than a little disgust he's prettier than I am."

"It pains me to admit he really is pretty. I won't tell the gremlin if you don't tell my husband."

"Deal. Any ideas on how to get appropriate payback on my sister? She deserves some payback for Christmas."

Juliette cackled and rubbed her hands together. "As a matter of fact, I do think I can help you with your little problem. I do enjoy a good prank, especially when I get to tweak a client's nose with zero fear of consequences. First, dressing in red to taunt your sister is a good one. She wants to wear red, and I won't let her wear red in any of my clothes. She looks awful. I'll get someone to dig out the reds, and we'll start there. The next step would involve the gremlin."

"What would we have the gremlin do?"

"He will follow you around like a lovesick puppy."

"He's already doing that, Juliette."

"I never said it would be a difficult plan to implement. We just need to make certain the gremlin does it whenever she sees him so she believes he's lost his mind. Then we bring in other employees. They will all pretend everything is absolutely normal."

"That's going to fuck with my sister's head so hard. I just want to point out that will drive her crazy. At the end of the first work day, she will go insane."

Juliette grinned. "This is only the beginning."

"What do you mean?"

"Unless he's talking to you in an official capacity, you will pretend he doesn't exist."

"I already do that."

"I never said it would be a difficult plan to implement. But pretending he's invisible unless he's being official will drive her crazy. He can work while sitting on the edge of your desk, and you will have to ignore your desk ornament. Just don't acknowledge he's there at all."

I giggled. "That's so evil yet so simple."

"The best plans are often evil yet simple. When does Michelle return?"

"Christmas."

"That's not a lot of time to put together a plan. When do the offices reopen?"

"I don't actually know."

"Probably the third of January. He likes giving staff off between Christmas and the New Year. If I pull in staff over the holidays on overtime pay, I think I can pull together something that will drive Michelle insane."

"What?"

"I'll dress the entire staff in red. Except her. Some of the ladies can't wear red well, but I can get away with accents, purses, accessories, and things like that. Red coats might work, and it's been a while since I've done a line of red coats. I can do two cuts of the same coat, one for this prank and one for the public; I'll change the liners to differentiate them."

"How long does it take to make a jacket?"

"It depends on if we already have the materials in our warehouse. Let's find out." Juliette grabbed the wall-mounted phone and stabbed at the buttons. "Patty, darling, I need you to find out if we have enough red material, any type, to make fitted coats for everyone at K&H Enterprises. I will have overtime hours available for any craftsmen willing to work over the holidays to fill an order. If we can't do a set of matching coats for everyone except Michelle, I'll come up with something else. We'll need a men's coat and a design for the ladies. If we don't have a spare classic design, I'll do the drawings and the mock coats tonight in shit fabric at home."

Juliette broke into laughter. "Sweeter words have not been heard in a long time. That's brilliant. Call the gremlin and pitch him on the costs for the materials and the craftsman fee, and the staff hours. He gets this at cost; I'm passing on my fee. I get to screw with Michelle, and I will take a personal loss for a chance to screw with Michelle. What? You're not going to let me? Damn it, Patty! I want to screw with Michelle. How about five percent? No, he's paying the staff. I just said that. Ugh. Fine. Ten percent, but I'm doing this under protest. Make a jacket for Michelle, but hold it back. She doesn't get hers until her sister is safely married to her business partner."

She hung up. "We just got our leather batches for the next three months in. I have enough leather in our warehouse to make whatever I want. If I can get in my leatherworkers and make them do an assembly line based on sizes, we can have everything done on time. We have a deep red that should be friendly for most that we can use."

I worried for Kace's bank account. "This sounds expensive."

"Don't worry about it. The gremlin has been begging for matching office jackets for a while. I'm sure he'll approve, especially as it'll be a badge of pride among corporate gatherings. It's one of those status symbol things men tend to enjoy. It'll drive your sister crazy when everyone at the company has a jacket and she doesn't."

"Just how many employees do you need to have jackets made for?"

"I'll just do the main headquarters, which is eight hundred and ten employees, including you. Oh. I should have jackets made for the courier dogs and cats." Juliette snatched up the phone. "Patty, the animals need matching vests, too. Confirm with the gremlin how many pets we need to make vests for, and make sure they have pockets for documents and folders. For the cats, just include pouches to add catnip or something. They're adorably useless couriers."

My life had turned crazy. "Kace is never going to forgive me for bankrupting his company."

Juliette stared at me. "You really have no idea how much K&H Enterprises is worth, do you?"

"Why would I?"

"Well, your sister does own half of the company."

"Yeah, I try to forget she's super rich and I'm kinda not. Actually, I was facing eviction because I didn't have enough money to take care of Michelle's kids, so I was coerced into moving in with Kace. And a tow truck ate my car."

"A... tow truck ate your car?"

"The engine died, then the truck slid on ice and crunched my car."

Juliette checked her watch. "Well, that changes plans. Nothing distracts better than car shopping, and we're going to torment your sister with a complete makeover, and I'll make the gremlin pay the bill." Picking up the phone yet again, Juliette dialed a number. "Hello, you devil of a gremlin. I'm stealing your woman, and we're going car shopping. I heard about the tow truck. Also, she's sick, just as expected, she's already seen Dr. Ramone, and I've taken care of it. I'm going to distract her with car shopping and a complete makeover. When she's too sick to handle it, I will return her to your home or take her home with me. I may just take her home with me."

My eyes widened.

"No, I'm not letting you decide. You gave her to me to care for, and I'm definitely more qualified to care for her than you are, you devil of a gremlin. I'll return her another day. Also, you're buying everyone in your company a custom leather coat, one line for the ladies, one for the gentlemen, and you're going to like it. They're going to be red. And everyone will receive one except Michelle. I'll give Michelle hers after you convince the lady to marry you. Not a moment before. Yeah, I figured you wouldn't mind that part. You're getting them at cost plus ten percent. You can thank me later. Just tell Patty you agree. Let me know if invoicing before the end of the year works better for you than at the beginning of the year. I'm good either way. Yes, I plan on picking a vehicle that will make Michelle cry herself to sleep, and yes, you're paying for it. It will be your wedding present to your future wife."

There was only one thing I could say. "You're really insane, aren't you?"

"It's good to be rich and crazy. Sorry, little gremlin. Ginger asked me a question. Yes, I'll make sure she's taken care of. She's not that sick yet, but she won't be working anywhere tomorrow, so if she has part-time work to attend to, she'll need someone to cover her. She mentioned something about working at a candy store? I'm covering her boutique work. I've already cut a deal with her boss. I could use a day at home to do design work anyway, so it works well for everyone. I'll keep you in the loop. I'm going to feed her some soup, finish up here, and figure out what her dream car is, which we will acquire specifically to screw with her sister.

"Also, you're to follow Ginger around like a puppy in the office, but she's going to pretend you don't exist. It'll be fun. Please tell me the third is your first workday after the holidays? It is? Excellent. Tell everyone to arrive an hour early so they can claim their jackets, and nobody can tell Michelle. Otherwise, the surprise would be ruined. Have a good night. Fine, I'll have her call you before she goes to bed if you're feeling that lonely." Juliette returned the phone to its hook. "There. You're coming home with me tonight, and I'll start getting you on the mend. He'll take care of the kids and your puppy and birds."

I sighed and shook my head. "When did my life become so weird?"

"You're Michelle's sister, so I'm going to suggest it was weird from the day you were born."

"Good point."

Chapter Thirteen

I'D NEVER PUT any thought into what kind a car I'd buy if money no longer mattered. I'd always picked my vehicles to get me to and from work in one piece. My sister had a nice-looking car, sportier than I liked. It didn't take me long to figure out I wanted anything other than sporty and easy to crunch in a wreck.

Juliette's first choice of dealership involved sporty little cars destined to crunch in a wreck.

She scratched her head. "You're a truck girl."

"I'm a what?"

"You're a truck girl. You like big trucks."

"I do?"

"You're looking at all these cars like they will kill you if you attempt to drive them."

"Well, they certainly don't look durable in a crash."

Juliette pointed across the lot at the SUVs. "What do those look like to you?"

"Moderately safer than the sporty cars that'll crush like a tin can. But aren't they a flipping hazard?"

"How about a larger family car?"

"I have a husky. Will she fit? Also, would it fit Kace's ego? I have to account for Kace's ego. It barely fits into his sporty little car. His sporty little car is comfortable, but it's so tiny. He barely fits. I barely fit. Can I trash his car for Christmas? It's too small. He'd get crunched like a tin can in an accident, and while he's an annoying gremlin, I seem to like him."

"Just tell him you're concerned he's not safe in the vehicle and you'd like him in something a bit more robust. There are sportier models of cars with more body." Juliette pointed across the lot. "You could get a muscle car. They're big and mighty."

"Muscle cars?"

Juliette linked her arm with mine and marched to the dealership's used lot, and she pointed to a hulky car that looked like it would plow through anything that crossed its path while moving at high speed. "This is a muscle car."

Well, it wouldn't break into a billion pieces if it hit something. "It looks big enough to drive yet small enough to fit into parking spaces," I admitted.

Juliette turned to the salesman following us around. "What's the best muscle car you have on the lot, what makes it special, and why should we buy it?"

"We have a Chevrolet Camaro with three thousand miles on it. The owner drove it across the country, decided he didn't like it, and sold it. It's fully loaded, and it's pretty durable. It's not a convertible, and it'll fly if you put it on a track. It's a V8, and it lives to be driven. It's red. The owner decided red didn't actually make it perform better. It's in pristine condition, but since it's so new, it's not cheap. It's certified, but you're welcome to have a mechanic look it over. No accidents, and while the owner drove it across the country, he took good care of it."

"So, you're saying it's new," I replied.

"Essentially."

"And it's red?"

"It's a cherry red. The color will raise your insurance premiums."

"Having a nice car will raise my insurance premiums, so why not? How does it handle?"

"Well, it doesn't corner like it's on rails, if that's what you're worried about," he replied. "You won't be spinning wheels around a dime in it, but it corners well enough. Would you like to take it on a test drive?"

I stared at Juliette, unsure if my stomach would cooperate with any attempts to test drive a new car. The woman smiled and patted my back. "She's not feeling so well, so let's just sign some paperwork and take it home. I'll make my husband come pick up my vehicle, and we'll drive this one off the lot. Let's be quick about it, though."

The salesman's mouth dropped open. "Aren't you going to ask how much it is?"

"Nope." Juliette checked her watch. "I want to be out of here in an hour. We'll call the insurance company while you fill out the paperwork. If she doesn't like it, we'll just sell it and buy something else."

Rich people were insane. "Who just buys a car like that?"

"Me."

Right. Of course. "This is insanity."

"I warned you I was the sanest insane person on earth. It's not my fault you didn't listen. I'm hungry, I want to go home, and I want you to eat something else. You barely sipped at your soup at the office, and you need to eat. So, I want to be out of here. If you don't want the Camaro, point at the first car you like that's new, and we'll take that one. The gremlin will be happy you're spending his money. That's how gremlins show off their plumage for interesting people they wish to wed. I'll tell him it's his wedding gift to you purchased in advance, and that will make everyone happy. And gremlins don't want wedding presents. They want pretty things to unwrap and enjoy after their offerings have been accepted. I just decided this. Just roll with it. I want to spend money that's not mine for a change."

I surrendered. "Can I look at the Camaro first?"

The salesman smiled and gestured across the parking lot towards the main dealership. "It's inside as a showcase car, ma'am. Please follow me. If you like it, I'll get the manager to sign off on the sale, and we'll get the glass doors open so the car can be driven off the lot tonight. I do believe we can keep to your hour timetable as long as we can get your insurance policy number."

"You'll have a policy number," Juliette swore.

The salesman led us inside where a red car with black trim and chrome waited, and it delivered on being muscular and robust while also sending a clear message it wanted to hit the roads where it could fly. I doubted I'd ever understand Juliette's impulsiveness, but I couldn't deny my interest in the vehicle. It wouldn't crunch like a tin can in an accident as long as I stuck to the speed limits. "Manual or automatic?"

"It has an eight-speed paddle automatic transmission with a 6.2-liter supercharged V8 engine. I think you'll find it has plenty under the hood for your driving pleasure."

"I'm translating that to mean it goes when you tell it to go."

"That would be a correct translation."

"It's pretty, it goes when it's told to go, and it works. All of my base requirements have been met. Pretty isn't a base requirement, but I upped my standards for a change."

"We'll take it before she second-guesses herself." Juliette took out her phone. "I'm going to deal with my insurance company and have them hook you up, Ginger. They'll play ball with me, and they'll give you a decent rate; I have an employee plan for insurance with them, and they don't like rocking my boat. Be a dear and hand me your driver's license."

I did as asked. "Thank you. I don't like dealing with insurance companies."

"Nobody does. I like quick and painless. Go have a seat and start filling out forms while I take care of this." Juliette targeted a different employee and beelined for him. "Hey, you. I need information on that car so the insurance company can laugh at me. Make, model, and anything else they'll need to start laughing at me, please."

I turned to the salesman. "I'm so sorry for the trouble, sir."

He humored me with a smile. "It's not the first time Mrs. Carter has come in here on a mission. I'm just glad she didn't make me march over to the dealership next door to get a new car this time. There's nothing quite like a cage match between two salesmen, and she loves putting us on the spot."

Wow. I'd underestimated the woman's ruthlessness. "Please don't tell me how much this car is. Just cover the numbers where I can't see them. I'm not sure I can handle seeing the price tag right now."

"I think I can manage that much, ma'am. If you'll please come with me, I'll make this as painless for you as possible."

Painless worked—or as painless as I could get with my body protesting my love of chicken nuggets. "Let's get this show on the road, then. I don't think I want to know what she'll do if we're not done in an hour."

"Turn the entire dealership upside down, possibly buy a new vehicle for herself to justify the time spent here, and then realize she bought something and have to sell her other vehicle, which her husband and son would have to bring over, which would result in a screaming match in the showroom."

My brows rose. "How often does that happen?"

"Once every three months or so, usually when she's determined to help a friend or client get a new vehicle at a price they can afford. We keep good used vehicles we got at excellent deals reserved for her just in case she knows someone. We have her on speed dial. If we're not done in forty minutes, I'll be very surprised."

"Forty minutes sounds better than an hour. Let's try for that."

※ ※ ※

THIRTY-TWO MINUTES after we started signing papers, I had a new insurance policy number, and my monthly premium shocked me, as I'd only pay thirty dollars more a month for a Camaro over what I'd paid for my piece-of-shit junker. Then, in what had to count as unfair business dealings, Juliette crossed the street, dragged over a Chevrolet salesman, and demanded replacement insurance on the barely used car.

The resulting scuffle, which involved the manager of the Chevrolet dealership, the manager of the whatever-the-hell-brand dealership we'd gone to, and four salesmen, needed to become a reality television show. I'd watch the hell out of it daily without ever tiring.

Juliette really wanted replacement insurance.

"It's not like I'm asking for free replacement insurance, Doug! I'm wanting to pay for the insurance. The car has fewer than five thousand miles on it. So what if it was purchased at a different dealership? It's your brand, you said yourself you could pull up the serial, and the previous owner had replacement insurance. It's not like Chevrolet got a refund on the prior insurance. Just give me what I want already so I can get out of here tonight."

Two men strolled into the showroom, and I pegged them as father and son, and the father had aged well enough that whoever married the son would be in for one hell of a ride later in life.

Damn.

"Juliette, what on earth are you doing?" the older man replied.

"Getting replacement insurance on Ginger's Camaro."

"I can't help but notice we're in the used-car showroom," he countered.

"We are, indeed, in the used-car showroom, but the Camaro has fewer than five thousand miles, and Ginger deserves replacement insurance through a dealership."

Both men sighed, and the younger one rolled his eyes. "Mom, you're a mess. While you fight with the dealership, I'll take Ginger home." He gestured to me. "You're Ginger?"

"I'm Ginger."

"You look like hell. My wife is in Mom's kitchen baking cookies and making soup for you. Why don't I take you to the house?"

"You can't steal her, Julian. I forbid it. I'm driving her home in her newly insured Camaro."

"She's sick, you're going overboard, and you could just get replacement insurance from your insurance company for a few bucks extra."

Juliette scowled. "I could, yes. But then I'd lose this argument, and that's unacceptable. Also, there's a new Mercedes SUV on the lot. It's in silver, just like Chloe wants. You could talk me into buying it today."

"I'm not talking you into buying Chloe a second SUV. She's already got one. I already have one. We're out of parking spots in the driveway, and we keep having to juggle vehicles as it is. Stop buying us cars. We don't need a new one. Her other one isn't even a year old."

"The baby needs a new car."

"The baby is eighteen years too young to need a car."

"You need to drive her car around for her."

"You can't last a year before you need to get a new car. Any car you 'buy for the baby' would be replaced numerous times before the baby is capable of babbling coherently. Also, she's asleep, and Chloe says if anyone wakes her up stomping into the house like elephants, she will plead guilty to multiple counts of murder."

"But it's my house."

"Not right now it's not. It's Candice's house, and Candice is sleeping. Murdered, Mom. Candice is peacefully sleeping, and Chloe is enjoying the first moment of peace and quiet she's gotten since the baby came home."

There was only one way to end the misery. I turned to the manager of the Chevrolet dealership and said, "Give her full replacement insurance on the vehicle, and if Chevrolet won't bite, exchange my slightly used car for a brand-new one, but make Juliette model a new line of clothes on the car. Chevrolet wins, and I get to go be sick somewhere other than in the lobby of a car dealership."

Everyone stared at me as though I'd grown a second head.

"I'll bite. I'll provide the car, new, *and* provide the replacement insurance policy on your current one, but I get an entire line with the models posing with my showroom vehicles."

I turned to Juliette, narrowed my eyes, and braced my hands on my hips. "I will tolerate you dressing me up in an entire red line. I want my second new car in a really nice shade of blue, and I'll give it to the gremlin as a counter wedding present."

"Sold," Juliette announced.

"Can we leave now?"

The Chevrolet manager grinned. "I'll draw up the contracts in the morning and send them to your email, Juliette."

"I've been goosed by a model. Also, the standard appearance fee applies, because I can't get out of that. My employees would murder me, and then there'd be no deal."

"Corporate will pay it. They've been asking managers to find gimmicks to draw in new customers. I think this will work nicely."

"I've been wanting to expand our men's line, too. This gives me a good excuse and extra clothes to draw tomorrow. Call my office, ask for Patty, and tell her to get you a summer timeline. That's your best season, correct?"

"Summer works. I'll talk them into a bonus if you can get in during our peak weeks."

"We can discuss that." Juliette glanced at the manager of the lot we'd taken over. "I'll give you a slot for next year for putting up with your turf being a negotiation point, but the terms will be similar. If you can negotiate with Chevrolet for a joint deal, I'll do two lines back to back, which should draw customers to both lots."

"Corporate is going to have kittens," the Chevrolet dealer predicted.

"But they'll bite because they'll get a line during their peak weeks. Just tell them the only reason they're getting a chance at a deal is because of their competitor. May the best dealership win."

"You're crazy, Mom. I hope both dealerships find a way to goose you. This is not how the world is supposed to work."

"Just because these managers have more sense than average doesn't mean this isn't how the world is supposed to work. I just know how much my work is worth, and I know a good idea when I hear one. Also, I better tell the gremlin he needs to make his new executive secretary and future wife his chief problem solver, because she did that without batting an eyelash while suffering from food poisoning. No wonder he wants her so much."

I gave up. "I'm starving, and I know I'm just going to throw everything up in ten minutes. I'll try to eat something, though. I make no promises I won't wake the baby."

"Chloe would never murder someone sick for waking the baby. It's the rest of the hooligans she's worried about," Julian replied.

"I'm probably one of a million people who has asked this,

but did your mother seriously name you Julian when she's Juliette?"

"She wished she'd been born a boy, so she pretends to live through me," he replied.

Juliette sighed, and the older version of Julian laughed.

"I'd say that's weird, but honestly, that's the sanest thing this woman has done today, so okay."

"That didn't take you long to figure out." Julian grinned. "Will it scare you off if I admit Dad and I are lawyers?"

"No, but I now know if I'm up shit creek without a paddle, Juliette can recommend lawyers."

Juliette tossed her head back and laughed. "I love this woman. The gremlin warned me, but I love it when they've snapped and are ready to take on the world even when sick. Tomorrow is going to be a great day." Still laughing, she held out her hand to the salesman, who'd done the paperwork in record time. "Keys, please. I've a world to conquer, clothes to plan, and a grandbaby to visit."

Chapter Fourteen

JULIETTE CARTER LIVED in a modest townhouse in Hell's Kitchen, and even with a new used Camaro available for my use, I wondered how I'd get back to Delaware alive. My home state seemed so much saner than New York. I needed to thank Kace for living somewhere sane. Delaware, despite its status as a "blink and miss it" state, had its perks—and barely enough skyscrapers to support Kace's company.

I'd have to make sure the company never moved to New York. I'd go crazy, too.

I wondered if Hell's Kitchen had been named because a prophet had anticipated Juliette Carter moving into the neighborhood.

To my relief, everyone tiptoed into the townhouse to keep from waking the baby only to discover the baby was already awake and cooing at her blonde-haired beauty of a mother from a baby carrier on a granite countertop. "That didn't take nearly as long as I was expecting. Did you cuff your poor mother, Julian?"

"Why is she my poor mother? She was at a car dealership."

"You just answered your own question. She was at a car dealership."

"Just because you have learned you hate car shopping does not mean Mom hates car shopping." Julian joined his wife in the kitchen, kissed her cheek, and waggled his fingers for the baby girl, who reached for them. "And how is my baby girl doing?"

"Never again, Julian. She peed in my hair."

Juliette giggled. "I warned you, Chloe."

"You did, but I didn't think she'd actually aim for my face." Chloe heaved a sigh. "There's baby pee in my hair."

Smiling at his wife's misfortune, Julian kissed her cheek again with no evidence he cared their baby had peed on her. "Beats an ice cream cone to the cleavage. Are you done with the cookies? I'll take you home and help you shower that out."

"I've finished, and the soup's ready, too." Chloe sighed. "I dumped hand sanitizer on my head, and it didn't help. I feel so dirty right now."

Julian smirked. "I'll fix that as soon as we're home."

I didn't want to know. I hid behind Juliette and hoped nobody would draw attention to me while the couple flirted. "Is that what the future looks like? Flirting as a consequence of baby pee?"

"With the volume of pee a baby produces, it's either live with it or be miserable, and well, if she can find a silver lining in having the baby pee on her, more power to her. She'll be an old hand at this in a month, but then she'll only have to deal with the really nasty surprises."

"We've already had two poopsplosions, and I'm resigned to many more in the future. You're Ginger, right? Let me tell you something, Ginger, there is nothing as terrible as a baby poopsplosion, and there's nothing more amazing than a man willing to deal with it."

"Add this to Kace's list of minimum requirements, Juliette.

I'm not sure I can deal with such a thing alone. I can't even deal with food poisoning alone."

"Poor thing. I'm sure the gremlin is perfectly capable of assisting in such matters. Julian can help train him."

Julian's brows rose. "You're dating Kace? Kace Dannicks? Mom has a pretty short list of people she calls gremlins. But I'm having a hard time believing Kace is dating. No offense meant."

"It's a hostage situation, really."

Chloe giggled. "Hostage situations can really work if marriage is the goal. I kidnapped Julian and waited until he surrendered and begged me to marry him. His mother helped."

"I provided the outfit and the general kidnapping equipment, and I made sure her friend had a good vehicle for the kidnapping," Juliette announced, stepping into the kitchen and heading for her granddaughter. Julian and Chloe made space for the older woman.

"That doesn't sound legal."

"I had no problems with my kidnapping. It was a lot of fun, and I got exactly what I wanted most for Christmas last year. The baby is a bonus."

"An unexpected surprise courtesy of a broken condom and my inability to take birth control," Chloe explained. "I vomit. Excessively."

"You should tell your husband he should stop breaking the condoms."

"He says it's my fault I'm so beautiful, and he's okay with at least six more, as our daughter charmed him from her first blood-chilling shriek at birth."

"She has very healthy lungs," Julian reported. "I'm concerned about when she's a little older. She's going to be as beautiful as her mother, and I'm not sure I'm going to be able to beat off the suitors sufficiently alone. I'm going to have to recruit help."

"She's a baby, Julian. You don't have to worry about that

until her age ends with 'teen.'" Chloe shook her head, abandoned the kitchen, and began restoring her baby bag to rights. "I'd shake your hand or offer a hug, Ginger, but I'm covered in baby pee, and you're not feeling well. I'd rather you not get a whiff and get sick. Food poisoning, I heard?"

"A chicken nugget has zombified inside of me and seeks revenge."

"A chicken nugget *what*?"

"Zombified. It didn't get cooked when we ordered a mass batch, and I bit into it. It looked cooked on the outside, but I guess it must have gotten stuck on top of the batch in the deep fryer and didn't get submerged in the oil. That's the only thing I can think of." Considering I hadn't put much thought into it, I thought my theory was a damned good one. "It's okay. It's been bad, but not as bad as I thought it would be so far. The headache is wicked, though."

"After the first few hours, she stopped throwing up. The anti-nausea medication has something to do with that, though. Dr. Ramone is on the case, and the gremlin got the restaurant to play ball for the medical bills. He even got a gift card out of them for her favorite food. Personally, I'd never touch another damned chicken nugget again after that, but I'm pretty sure she's already eager to have more."

"I could go for a six-pack, but I'll take some soup. It smells really good."

"Juliette's recipe. She's convinced it will cure everything. She kept texting me to tell me exactly how to make it. I think she was just bored."

"She was dressing me up as a doll and sighing every time I interrupted being a doll for her due to my stomach declaring war on the rest of my body."

"Juliette, you're something else."

"What? I couldn't continue dressing her while she was being sick or when Dr. Ramone was checking her over, so I checked in with you to help with the soup. Admit it, you're glad I helped you with directions."

"Well, I know where Julian inherited his ego from."

"His father. I was born reclusive, shy, and completely lacking in ambition. I required extensive training."

Julian's father sighed. "I hate that it's true. I'm the egotistical bastard responsible for all of your problems, Chloe."

"Well, shit. I can't even get mad at you. You're too nice. Where did your egotistical bastard tendencies go again?"

"I left them at work. I find lawyering is an excellent outlet for my egotistical bastard tendencies."

"Right. Lawyers." Chloe sighed. "I work for a bunch of lawyers during the day, then I come home to a lawyer, and my father-in-law is a lawyer. How did I become so thoroughly entangled with a bunch of land sharks?"

"Carefully. Did you leave the other car seat in the house?"

"I did. She'd scream if we left it in the car with it being this cold. You know Candice doesn't like getting cold."

"Neither does her mother, I've noticed. I particularly notice when I wake up without any blankets," Julian replied wryly.

"It's your fault you're so handsome when naked."

"If you'd like a second child, Chloe, please address that at home. While I love encouraging such behaviors, let's not embarrass Ginger too much, especially when the gremlin has not yet convinced her to marry him," Juliette announced, making shooing gestures in the direction of her front door. "And no drooling over Ginger's Camaro. It's the gremlin's present to her, except he had no idea he was buying her a Camaro today. Oh, Ginger. When I spoke to the gremlin during your doctor's appointment, I was notified that your insurance company is cutting you a pitiful check for your deceased car. What on earth were you driving to get a pittance for it?"

I should have been more ashamed of my situation than I

was. I blamed the food poisoning. "It was more rust than car. It was what I could afford."

"The tow truck did you a favor, then. Make sure the gremlin makes space for your Camaro in his garage."

"Will my Camaro even fit my dog?"

"It has two front seats, so yes."

"But then no one else can fit in my car."

"They can if your dog sits on your passenger's lap. If they're unwilling to hold your dog, they don't deserve to ride in your Camaro. Also, it technically does have back seats, but it's a tight fit."

"She's a husky."

"Irrelevant. Huskies are oversized lap dogs with egos almost as large as mine."

Chloe giggled. "You got a husky?"

"Santa gave me a husky and two lovebirds for Christmas. They're staying with Kace right now."

Julian chuckled and helped his wife pack their baby's supplies. "Kace must be in hog heaven. He loves animals. He's hesitated getting a dog because he has his office courier cats, and one of them has special needs."

"Virtue will be required to love Kace's courier cats. I told Kace he had to start bringing his cats home with him at night."

"If you need any help making plans to capture Kace, ask. We're glad to help. It's obvious you're good for him."

"You barely know me."

"You've met my mother-in-law, you just hid behind her, and you're not running in terror despite having been used as a living doll while sick. I've learned my mother-in-law is an excellent judge of character, and if you can work with her, you've got patience, intellect, and display base levels of ethics. She hates working with unethical layabouts. She works hard for the money, and she expects others to work hard for the money, too."

"Except she keeps trying to give stuff away."

"But only to people who have tried their best to work hard for the money and their life's circumstances didn't make ends meet. You'll get used to it," Julian promised. "And once she's decided you worked hard for the money and life didn't treat you fairly, she'll never stop. Insist she gets her fair percentage and stand your ground, but honor whatever the hell deal she bargained with you this time. She won that fair and square."

"She's just making Kace pay for everything, and I have to model for the stuff I want to earn and can't pay for myself basically."

Both Chloe and Julian looked me over, their expressions surprised.

"She wants you to model?" Julian asked. "She has Chloe model sometimes, but casually—not for any actual hardcore work. She's picky, and Chloe's typically too pretty for the lines. Don't kill me, Chloe, but Ginger's just as pretty as you are."

"We have a strict 'look but don't touch' policy in place. You're looking. Touch, and I'm taking your hand off," Chloe replied with a smile.

"She wears red well, she's not as pretty as Chloe—no offense intended, Ginger—and Ginger fits the appearance of an average American blonde-haired woman. She's a little underweight right now, but after I plump her up, she'll be a good model for petite but healthy women. Chloe, you just don't fit the 'petite but healthy women' model line. It's really hard to find healthy women of small build suitable for the runway."

"So, you're saying I'm a pretty enough twig to model but not too pretty of a twig?" I laughed. "I can work with that. I've never been all that pretty in my opinion, and I'm okay with that. If I'm representative of a lot of women in my shoes, then that's great. I'll model for that."

"Chloe's in a league of her own. That makes her wrong for my reveals but perfect for wearing in casual settings and events.

And that's fine, so neither of you feel bad for that. I want to open a line for average women."

"Average women pay no more than a hundred bucks for a dress," I muttered.

"I'm planning on doing a tour with reveals in every city and major town I can, and I'll have local women sign up to receive a set of clothes. I'll profit, they'll get clothes, and I'll become more accessible for everyone. If a reveal series does well enough, I'll begin an internship line to train new seamstresses, tailors, and leatherworkers. Everyone wins, and I still produce quality clothes with a price tag closer to a hundred dollars. I'll force my pesky minions to accept a lower profit margin on those lines."

"Juliette refuses to use international manufacturing workshops, so everything is done in America unless the materials legitimately cannot be sourced in the United States. That raises her manufacturing costs substantially," Julian explained. "How many employees in the United States are you up to?"

"Ten thousand, mostly craftsmen, marketers, and warehouse workers. Business has been going well, but I have a huge bottom line to maintain, so I have to keep things fresh and on the move."

"Ten thousand employees?" I whispered. "But you only had a few floors at your offices."

"Oh, that entire building is mine, Ginger. I just hadn't warned anyone I'd be bringing someone in, and I don't like springing that on folks. The floors I showed you have guests in all the time, so they're used to surprise visits. I give the other floors a week of notice so the introverts can relocate for the visit. I have some very, very shy employees."

"She also has employees with various disabilities, and they get embarrassed," Julian admitted. "She tries to make their work environment as pleasant as possible. They're amazing workers, but public scrutiny really bothers them. She has several floors dedicated to employees with special needs."

I had a new idol in my life, and she was as crazy as she was generous. "Wow."

"Everyone deserves a chance, and I make as many chances as possible. You know that jacket job? I'll have to turn people away or add in another project because a lot of my employees don't have any family, or they have debt, or life just wasn't kind to them, and they find purpose when they come to work. I'll probably find another project for the extras, because the company can afford it, even if I have a line that sits and stews for a while because I didn't plan on it in any releases. I was actually about to start pulling my hair because business has been so smooth lately, and I didn't have a holidays project yet."

"That's incredible. I didn't know people like you could even exist."

Juliette smiled at me, but something about her expression seemed sad. "That's why I do it."

HELL HAD A NAME: salmonella poisoning.

My sister would pay for my misery. If she hadn't gone running off without a trace, I wouldn't have been put in the line of fire, I wouldn't have had to take up extra retail work near the holidays, and Kace Dannicks wouldn't have barged into my life holding nugget temptation in his hand.

Despite feeling like death warmed over, I really wanted a nugget. Nuggets would make me feel better. Why did my favorite food have to rise up and attempt to kill me? Sometime between one of my countless trips to the bathroom down the hall, I fell into a coma-like state to wake up with my puppy snuggling against me and trying to insert her tongue into my ear.

Yuck.

Moving took too much effort, and while I should've stopped

Virtue from cleaning my ears and washing my face, I dealt with it.

"How is she doing?" Kace asked.

"Someone is going to have to run down the street and get the poor woman some nuggets at some point today. The poor thing keeps crying about her favorite food rising up in defiance, and she wants to put those nuggets in their place. Their place, apparently, is in her stomach. I've got to give her credit. She doesn't go down without a fight," Juliette replied. "She'll be fine. I'm making sure she drinks water, broth, and whatever else she'll accept, not that she's had much luck keeping anything down. The only food that is guaranteed to stay down are the nuggets. She is holding a grudge against them right now for some reason. Dr. Ramone came in and checked on her the first night, and he brought an antibiotic. She's unlucky. The bacteria was in her bloodstream from the start. He thinks her immune system is compromised from stress. Also, I told you this yesterday. While I'm amazing, I do not have the ability to travel back in time."

"I just wanted to make certain. I'll make sure her schedule is cleared for the next few days."

"Once again, we've gone over this multiple times. Are you feeling all right? I lost count of the times I told you I'm taking care of her one part-time job."

I appreciated Kace's forgetfulness; it helped me figure out what the hell was going on.

"I've got the other job covered. Saul went to her other part-time job and spoke with her manager, then her manager spoke to her boss; he's taking over her shifts until her contract is over. Saul is barely old enough to take on part-time work, so it's his first job, and he's frighteningly excited about it. I may have bribed him."

"With what?"

"If he earned the money, I would take him shopping for a

used car and battle his mother with him about having a vehicle of his own, and I promised I'd take him on some practice drives. He has provisional license, but his mother and father don't have a lot of extra time to drive him with him."

"That's a good bribe. I did similar with Julian when he was that age. It's good to get them used to responsibility early. How do you want me to handle Ginger?"

"Let her sleep it off. It'll be quieter for her here, but I am expecting you to return her when she's able to put up a fight."

My stomach informed me it was empty and needed something in it, likely so it could torture me later. "If she brings me nuggets, she can kidnap me and keep me forever. Kace, my puppy is eating my ear. Make her stop. It's too much work to stop her myself."

I whined, but I lacked the energy to care I sounded like a child who'd dropped her lollipop in the dirt.

Kace laughed, and a moment later, my puppy no longer assaulted my ear. A few moments later, Kace relocated her into my arms, and I cuddled her close. "Keep your owner company, Virtue, and try not to lick her face off. Ginger, if you get cold, just give a shout. I'll be here for a few hours discussing business with Juliette."

"Did you hear from my asshole sister?"

"Another letter showed up. I opened it. It was a taunt with some safari pictures. I figured I'd save that train wreck for when you're feeling better. I think it's safe to say she's fine."

"Won't be soon." I debated my current status as an invalid, decided I wasn't going to die if I got up for a while, and lurched upright, setting my puppy on my lap. "We need to torture her for Christmas. I've been tortured, so she gets tortured, too."

"What do you have in mind?"

"I'm going to wear red, look amazing, and talk about how I have this great new job that pays decently, but my boss is an absolute jerk of a man, I hate him passionately, and then emphasize the passionately repeatedly."

"When you're sick, you're vicious. And vindictive," he observed. "Am I really a jerk of a man you hate passionately? I'm not sure how to interpret that, honestly."

"I will be testing my acting skills."

"Okay. What do you want me to do to help your scheme?"

"Agree with everything I say, then start lamenting about your horrible luck with women and executive secretaries."

"I do that normally."

"Exactly. Act normal."

"I don't see how this equates to revenge, Ginger."

"When she comes back to work, she'll first find her badge doesn't operate. I'll go in with her that day. Concoct some sort of damned excuse."

"I'll offer to help train your puppy at Christmas."

"This is a good excuse. You're also hiding my Camaro at your house so she doesn't know I have it."

"Done. I'll have you stay at your sister's place on Christmas Eve, and you can claim you moved in because you were being evicted anyway. I'll get the kids and a truck, and we'll put your stuff in her house to maintain appearances. I'll tell a few fibs and pick a fight with Michelle over not having signed up to rescue her sister from certain death due to stress and plague. We'll come clean on that after she realizes she's been had."

Juliette snickered. "I'll show up on Christmas with some of your new clothes. I have prototypes in your current size that aren't doing me any good residing in my closet. I'll make sure there's an obscene amount of red in it. And I'll bring presents for everyone but her. That'll teach her. Expect me to play Santa at noon; my husband and son will be here cooking dinner, as that's their day to shine. I handle Thanksgiving. They'll appreciate me being out of the house for even a few minutes. Chloe will be at her home napping while the men watch the baby. That is her Christmas present."

"That's a good present," I admitted. Yawning, I rubbed my eyes. "Do I want to know what day it is?"

"You've been reenacting various death scenes from Hamlet for almost three days," Juliette announced.

"Did I do a good job?"

"Thank you for being coherent enough to make use of my bathroom. You had one incident in the kitchen, but you miraculously made it to the trash can, and you cried, promising to clean it up. I had to draw lines because I wouldn't let you take the trash out. It was snowing, and you were in your pajamas. That triggered more crying, and my husband was forced to console you with chicken nuggets. For the record, it's the only thing you've kept down since you've gotten sick. You cut open every nugget to make sure it wouldn't rise up from its grave and eat you again, and then you attacked them with horrifying enthusiasm."

"I'm so sorry. I've been a menace!"

"You've been sick, I kidnapped you, and I keep refusing to let the gremlin take you home with him, so he's been over here whenever possible. You're an excellent hostage, by the way. You only tried to go home with the gremlin once, and he used your puppy to attempt it. He's not a very good kidnapper, so if you want to ever kidnap someone, don't use him as an accomplice. Use me instead. I'm far superior."

"Okay. I'm a hostage, then?"

"You are."

"That means you're responsible for feeding me?"

"I am."

"I'm hungry, and I have to get some revenge on more nuggets."

"If you go home with me, I'll buy you all the nuggets you want," Kace announced.

"Go home, you damned gremlin! She's mine. You can't have her until she's better and she's dressed up in my clothing. She has to look over sketches and see what she likes. I refuse to let her out of my house until we've gone over the sketches. I have hundreds of sketches now, as I've had to stay home and defend my turf from you. If I leave to go to work, you'll sneak over here and steal my hostage. Out, you filthy gremlin!"

Kace laughed. "I'll go out to buy nuggets, but I'm not leaving without her."

"No, you may not live in my house."

"I'm not leaving without her. You've had her for three days, and I want her back."

"She is not a possession for your amusement."

"Says you, who won't let her leave!"

"She's in no condition to leave. When she puts up a fight and sincerely attempts to escape me, then she can go home with you. But she has to put in a serious attempt to escape. I will allow you to return with her nuggets, but you will not be living in my home. Go live in your own home. You have three kids to take care of. Go take care of them."

"But they're not Ginger."

"Are you a child?"

"If it lets me hang around, yes."

"No. Go get nuggets, come back with them, and then go to work where you belong. Stop skipping your lunch to come over here, damn it."

"Has anyone ever told you that you're mean, Juliette?"

"Daily."

Kace sighed. "Fine. I'll be back in a few minutes, and I'll go back to work, but I won't like it."

After he left, I raised a brow at Juliette. "What did I miss?"

"A lot of whining, posturing, and complaining. You needed someone to keep an eye on you, and without Michelle around, the gremlin needed to know someone was taking care of you. I can work from home, and the minions bring over whatever I need if necessary. I get to do a lot of design work, which means more business for the company, and everyone's happy. I have hundreds of new sketches for future lines, and I'm really happy with some of them. I've even started putting together some test pieces with material I've had on hand. It's working out well, so don't you worry about a thing. If you're feeling up for it, go take a shower while the gremlin gets your nuggets. Sending him out to feed you will make him feel better. He doesn't feel like he's doing enough. Also, feel free to take the puppy into the shower with you. Dealing with a wet dog will give him something to do, and she loves water."

"Virtue loves water?"

"She lives for your next shower or bath. I have no idea what you're going to do when you want to take a soak and your husky wants to join you. You're going to need a large tub and fur traps. It could be worse."

"How could it possibly be worse?"

"She could roll in mud and hate baths."

Juliette presented a good point. "Okay. What am I going to wear?"

"I've got clothes for you. I'll bring them to the bathroom for you. The gremlin brought over your bathroom kit, by the way, but you're welcome to try out anything in there you'd like."

"Thanks, Juliette."

"Anytime. Honestly, I'm loving this. It's been too long since I've gotten to baby someone, as my husband and child refuse to get sick and hate when I overly pamper them. You, on the other hand, soak up attention like a sponge. Just don't get this sick often, please."

"Trust me, I'll try not to."

"Thus your new habit of checking every nugget before you attack it seeking revenge."

"The brethren of the zombie nugget deserve to perish at my hands for my culinary enjoyment."

"That they do. Once you're done, we'll go over sketches and talk about our plan to torture your sister. Christmas is just around the corner, and there's nothing I love more than a good prank — and trust me, Michelle deserves everything you toss her way."

"She's going to hate us for this, isn't she?"

"I wouldn't worry too much about it. She's a grown woman; she can handle a little misery and suffering. The hard part will be making sure all actors in this prank remember their lines. Feel free to ham it up. The more you ham it up, the more your sister will absolutely freak out, as there's no way you, her hard-working, luckless sister, could be brought so low as to give up and admit failure."

"Well, I know one thing for sure. This is going to be a memorable Christmas."

Chapter Fifteen

JULIETTE MEANT every single word of her threat to hold me hostage until I freed myself from her clutches. For a freakish stalker of a designer, I couldn't help myself: I liked her too much for my own good. I liked her too much for Kace's good. How could I begrudge Juliette's enjoyment of caring for an invalid?

I snapped like one of my favorite cookies on Christmas Eve after a ridiculous time holed up in her home serving as a living doll for her enjoyment. At two in the morning, I stole my favorite outfit from the ones she'd foisted on me, put on my new favorite pair of black leather boots, and climbed out the window, which I'd begged to be left cracked open. Concocting a lie had helped my cause. Upon admitting the last vestiges of my fever were having its way with me, she'd left the window cracked open. I'd had the brains and wisdom to warn my doctor there was nothing wrong with me anymore, and that if he could play along with my escape attempt, I'd be forever grateful.

He'd offered to be my getaway driver.

Dr. Ramone picked me up a block away from Juliette's

house, and I dove into his SUV to freedom. "You are a lifesaver. Literally."

"Well, I can't say this is normally a part of my job description, but if I'm going to be up at this hour anyway, at least it's for something fun. Got the keys for the house?"

I held up my sister's house keys. "I had to leave my wallet and everything else in her clutches, as she was 'holding on to them for safekeeping.' That's just a convenient way to keep her hostage where she wants, I've learned."

"Juliette takes her caretaker duties seriously. I'll do another blood test just to make sure you're in the clear when I drop you off. I brought the kit with me."

"I will submit to being poked, as I'm utterly grateful you're rescuing me."

"Just so you know, Juliette requested I check on Mr. Dannicks and your nieces and nephew. I actually came over here from over there, as they were out late due to the boy's late work hours."

"That's my fault. He took over my part-time job."

"So I heard. That's fine. They're in good health, although I suggested that Mr. Dannicks be treated for separation anxiety. Your puppy is better behaved than he is."

"I have the best puppy, and I have the best birds, too."

Kace had found a way to bring the lovebirds over for visits, too, and it involved wrapping their cage in a blanket so they wouldn't get cold. I'd found his efforts to ensure I saw my pets ridiculous and endearing.

"They're lovely animals. You're feeling better, I presume?"

"Tired, but you said to expect that. The other symptoms are all gone. I'm constantly hungry, though."

"That's normal. Let me guess: you want nuggets, don't you?"

"I have something to prove to every chicken nugget on this planet, but Juliette is holding my wallet hostage."

"I'll bill her for your nuggets plus a patient transportation fee. I'll have fun with it."

"You're the best, Dr. Ramone."

He chuckled, plugged my sister's address into his car navigation system, and headed towards Delaware. "I have been asked by Mr. Dannicks and your nieces and nephew to pass on a few requests and bits of news."

"Uh-oh. When are they expecting you to deliver this news?"

"In the morning, I presume. First, all the decorations for your sister's house are in the living room. You can do whatever you want with them. Your nieces are responsible for the 'adult-oriented' surprises, although Mr. Dannicks is the one who went into the adult stores to acquire them. That is part of why I was so late leaving from Mr. Dannicks's residence. He asked me to make certain all three of them knew the horrors of pregnancy and childbirth. I did so. I provided a video. One of my patients had her birth recorded and gave me permission to share it with young men and women interested in intercourse. It was most entertaining. They are now fully educated on condoms, birth control methods, and sexually transmitted diseases. They asked me if you needed any of these things to deal with Mr. Dannicks. I thought you'd appreciate knowing."

"He doesn't get to touch this package until after I officially agree to marry him, so it's generally a moot discussion point."

"Be prepared for much sighing in your future."

"I expect he won't have to sigh long. I'll likely officially agree to marry him about five minutes after I see him with his shirt off."

"There is an open pharmacy next door to the McDonald's I'm planning on taking you to, and I will bill Juliette for all of your purchases."

"Actually, that would be really appreciated. My sister's house has nothing in it—or didn't the last time I checked."

"Mr. Dannicks hired a maid service to do the entire home,

and he had the fridge stocked by someone sane who understands how cooking works. You'll probably need your bathroom supplies, a toothbrush, and the basics, however."

"Thanks. I really do appreciate it."

"You're welcome. Get whatever you want at the pharmacy. Juliette can afford it."

"How about the Christmas presents I haven't gotten yet?"

"Go to town, Ginger. Whatever makes you happy."

***

EVERYONE WAS GETTING bath and body products for Christmas, and to my utter delight, I located a bag of charcoal for my wicked sister. I acquired the gaudiest wrapping paper money could buy, and I got clashing ribbons to make my presents count as the devil's work.

I would have a grand time wrapping presents on Christmas Eve.

My sister's home had been cleaned to even my standards, and as warned, decorations cluttered the living room. I appreciated the warning about the nature of some of the decorations. My nieces had made Kace buy a horrific selection of adult toys. A handwritten note begged me to hang them on the tree or anywhere I could find, but if I could put "The Fist" in a present and wrap it to look nice, and to address it to their father, they would appreciate it.

Upon a brief search, I located the Fist, which was made of black rubber and depicted a hand balled into a fist.

The Fist was twice the size of my hand, and I stared at in shock.

I went to my sister's home phone, amazed she still had a landline, and I called Kace's cell number, grateful I'd memorized it.

"Mmmm?" he answered.

"Why did my nieces, my sweet, innocent little nieces, have you buy the Fist? This thing is a nightmare, Kace!"

Kace barked a laugh. "I see you escaped Juliette. How are you feeling?"

"Fine. The fever was a lie to get an open window so I could escape. Dr. Ramone picked me up and drove me to my sister's house. What the hell is this thing? Who would use it? Why? I have questions."

"Trust me, I have questions, too. They asked me to get as much as I could with their earned allowance. They were willing to spend every penny they'd earned on their prank. Also, your sister is a skinflint. They had five hundred between the two of them, and they've been saving for years."

"And they spent it all on adult... things."

"Sex toys."

"Yes, sex toys. A lot of them. This is only five hundred dollars?"

"I told the kids to keep their money, and they could come over and help with chores for six weekends to repay me for making the purchases on their behalf. I spent fifteen hundred on sex toys."

"That's ridiculous."

"Personally, I think the Fist is worth it. I bought them some real presents, which are under the tree. I was planning on heading over after work, but before that I have to pick up Saul and then help wrap things."

"Offer accepted. I'll decorate with the rest of it. Juliette's really coming at noon on Christmas?"

"With the start of your wardrobe plus some other presents."

"She's insane."

"She likes you, and she tries to do something for everyone she likes. It is unusual she's dropping over for Christmas, but when there is a prank to be played, Juliette is usually the first to volunteer. She does like Michelle, so a prank against Michelle is right up her alley."

"Does Juliette know everyone?"

"She knows everyone who matters. If you want to see who is a decent person in this town, you watch Juliette. People of all types wear her clothes, but she only keeps company with interesting people with ethics. You have all that. And she really means it when she says she does her best to reward people who work hard but spin their wheels."

"I don't think we deserve Juliette."

"We really don't. Do you want me to come over?"

I thought about it. "As a matter of fact, I do. I miss my puppy and my birds."

"I'll ask the kids if they want to head over, too. They'll probably appreciate their own beds for a change. I expect we'll be over shortly. Saul will pass right out, and he might not even comprehend we're heading over. I think he's developed a serious case of admiration for you. He asked me how you were able to do it. I reminded him you were on the brink of collapse and got sick. He's really mad at his mother now, so expect fireworks tomorrow. School and one part-time job is exhausting him, but at least he's off school for the rest of the year."

"Poor kid. Will he be okay?"

"It's only a week longer, apparently."

"They're keeping him beyond Christmas?"

"He works hard and does a good job, so yeah. He'll likely work right up to the end of the year. I told him he should decide if he wants to keep working part time after he's experienced it for a week."

"It's hard work."

"He's starting to figure that out. So, there's a turkey thawing in the refrigerator. It will be ready for Christmas morning. My chef friend is highly offended I wanted a frozen bird, but then I reminded him someone other than him had to cook it. So, he spatchcocked it, spiced it, and froze it himself, so it's now thawing in the refrigerator. It should be ready to pop into the oven on Christmas morning. The directions are in the drawer next to the refrigerator in case I forget. I'll get the kids ready and be over soon. Don't run away."

"I ran away to here, Kace. Why would I run away elsewhere?"

"You're slippery."

"If you say so."

"I do say so. Don't go anywhere. We'll be there soon."

※

I STOLE my sister's entire stash of duct tape, which consisted of six rolls. As I hated my sister, I used all six rolls, various sized boxes, and sacrificed one of her towels to wrap the Fist. Mitchel would need a knife, a lot of patience, and brute force to bust into the present addressed to him, and knowing how the man ticked, he'd have my wicked sister help him unwrap it.

They'd hate me by the time they found out what their daughters had purchased—hopefully enough to keep from being too mad at their daughters for securing some payback.

I was working on the fourth layer when Kace barged in through the front door with three kids in tow. "Good. You're still here."

"Where else would I be? I am not walking out in that cold mess when I can sit in here and decorate with utterly inappropriate things for anyone of any age. Also, you girls are evil."

My nieces grinned. "Feeling better?" they chorused.

I nodded and resumed my war against the towel and the duct tape.

Amelia cleared her throat. "Hey, Aunt Ginger?"

"Yes?"

"Is that one of Mom's good towels?"

"It sure is."

"Ouch. I thought we were giving her a present, not a heart attack."

I smiled. "If she hadn't run off, she'd still have one of her good towels. For Christmas, she is getting an odd number of good towels."

"Evil," the girl replied. "That is pure evil and brilliance. What else do you have in mind?"

To give the girl a chance to figure out the extent of my evils, I tossed her both empty rolls of duct tape. "Many boxes, even more duct tape, and if I can get my hands on enough glue, a layer of that. I haven't figured out where she keeps the glue."

"Rubber cement, white, or super?" Amelia asked. "We can make gunk, too."

"Gunk?"

"Water, flour, newspapers. You know, that gunk."

"Papier-mâché." I went with a full French accent because I could. "All of the above, please. I'll even clean up after you if you use more of your mother's good towels for this, but make certain you keep the spared towels to an odd number."

The twins darted off to do my bidding while Saul gaped at me.

"This is a very important lesson of life to learn now," Kace announced. "Never upset a lady. The lady will find some way to secure revenge, and the lengths she will go for revenge directly correspond to the severity of the sin."

Saul raised a brow, reminding me of his mother at her worst. "You upset Aunt Ginger all the time."

"I have a death wish and a desire to marry her. She doesn't seem to respond well to subtle hints. I tried that. She just ignored me. I got better results annoying her."

"Why are you giving me advice you can't follow yourself?"

"I'm just saying you should go into this with your eyes wide open. When you upset a lady, you will pay the price for it in some fashion or another. Right now, your mother is paying for upsetting the lady in her good towels."

"What about our father?"

I regarded the box I wrapped and shrugged. "He's getting the Fist. That seems like punishment enough, honestly. Add in the rest of the items your sisters made Kace purchase, and I think his share of this will be paid in full. If he doesn't seem horrified enough, I will put extra paperwork on his desk for a month. I'm sure I can, using Kace as my scapegoat, find extra work to do."

"Damn, Aunt Ginger. There's mean, then there's *mean*, and that's just *mean*."

"Then they shouldn't have run off without telling you kids what the deal was, when they'd actually be back, and put us all through hell. This is only the beginning. When I'm done with them, they're going to be bowed at your feet begging for forgiveness."

"Not at your feet?"

"No. They hurt you more. I'm just going to steal her business partner and keep him for myself. It will be a very lengthy punishment for all parties involved."

"I just feel like I need to state that I do not feel your theft of my person is a punishment. It's a reward."

I turned my attention back to my wrapping. "That is because you're brain damaged, Kace."

"I would be hurt, but if being brain damaged wins me the lady, I will cheerfully accept my new status as mentally impaired due to blunt force trauma, but if we could avoid the blunt force trauma, I would be appreciative."

"Get me chicken nuggets, and I'll think about it."

Saul stared at me in horror. "The nuggets tried to kill you, Aunt Ginger!"

"And now I am on a quest for revenge. Nuggets, Kace. I require nuggets to deal with this mess. Better get me a twenty-piece just to be sure I have enough fuel to make it through the night. I have a lot of work to do."

"Anything else you'd like?"

"Actually, yes. My sanity back. I seem to have misplaced it somewhere."

"I think you'll be fine without it. You get me as a consolation prize."

"Don't you mean punishment?"

Saul's eyes widened, and he looked up to Kace. "Juliette returned Aunt Ginger in a mood, Kace. What are we going to do?"

"I'm going to buy her nuggets and hope we don't unleash the apocalypse by feeding her after midnight."

✶👤✶

IT TOOK me until eight in the morning to finish my preparations. Kace needed to attend to business, but he worked from my sister's home so he could keep an eye on everyone. I picked the couch as my base of operations, so I could, whenever I woke up thanks to unfamiliar noises and surroundings, admire the scenery. The sex toys hanging from the banisters, ceiling, and everywhere else I could dangle them set a certain mood, especially as Kace had gone casual while tapping away at his laptop and handling calls on his cell phone.

I couldn't decide if I liked him better in a suit or in a partially unbuttoned shirt. The rest of the buttons needed to stay in place, or I really would toss my self-restraint out the nearest window.

Working with him would be a peril, but marrying him would open up some interesting evening activities for our general enjoyment, which would make the frustrations developed during the day much easier to bear. If he insisted on going around with his buttons partially undone, I wouldn't last until our wedding day.

We'd both enjoy it. Maybe I'd give myself an extra special Christmas present in the form of my sister's business partner, but I'd have to make some conditions, including a marriage date and an outing to pick wedding and engagement bands.

I could work with test-driving a relationship with benefits to make sure everything worked before we made the ultimate commitment.

Sometime after noon, I crawled off the couch to attend to important matters, such as lunch and taking a cold shower. Kace chuckled at my inability to function. "Do you need some help?"

I narrowed my eyes. "Where are the brats?"

"You were passed out when Juliette came over and secured all three of them. She'll return them tomorrow. She needs to go to the mall to discuss business with your employer anyway, so she's handling ferrying Saul to and from work."

"She needs a raise."

"She'd have to get paid to get a raise, Ginger."

"Well, shit. How are we supposed to pay her?"

"We don't have to pay her."

"But I can't give her a raise for taking the kids if we're not paying her."

Kace laughed. "I see your brain has not yet engaged this morning. Go take your shower. You look like you need it."

I sniffed at my armpit. Yep. I definitely needed a shower. As I'd already abandoned my self-respect and dignity, I decided I'd attempt to give myself a very early Christmas present. "If you unbutton your shirt a little more, it would be indecent and considered a mating dance if we were in the wild."

Kace set his laptop aside, braced his elbow on the arm of his chair, and propped his chin in his palm. "Is that so?"

"I know, for a fact, that my sister has a really big shower in her bedroom. It's the kind where it rains from the ceiling. I've been told it's the ideal place for adults to take leave of their common senses. Unfortunately, as I haven't been on a date in forever, I'm not on birth control, and this, frankly, is a problem right now."

"A responsible man keeps condoms handy in case they're needed. I may be a lot of things, but I'm a responsible man."

"You'll have to scrub my back. It seems like too much work to scrub it myself."

"I'm sure I can handle such an arduous task. I'll enjoy it, too."

I bet he would. "I also demand you leer at my sister and compliment her on her shower, but only when the kids aren't around."

He snickered, hopped to his feet, and rubbed his hands together. "I think there's still two of her good towels left in this house. We can defile those while we're at it, and I'll include some choice commentary on the quality of her towels while I'm at it."

"She's going to want to burn her entire house down by the time we're done with it."

"Only her bathroom. Should we decide we want some additional exercise, I shall drive us to a better location. We wouldn't want to make my bed jealous, soon to be our bed, should I have my way."

Who was I kidding? He would. I'd just put up a fight first to enjoy the chase. "I'm still requiring you to follow me around like a lovesick puppy in need of attention. Also, where is my puppy?"

"Juliette has her, and she also took the birds. They'll be fine."

"But I miss my puppy," I whined.

"We'll go visit your puppy after I'm finished with you, assuming you have the energy. I plan on doing my best to make certain the only thing you have energy for is curling up in my bed and taking a nap."

"I need to be back here for Christmas morning, sans you," I reminded him.

"Negotiable. We can fight about it in bed. It'd be good to see how an argument plays out."

Whatever. Some plans always failed, and I'd accept defeat early on—and just hope my sister and her husband returned sometime after I made my way back to their house on Christmas morning.

Chapter Sixteen

THE WEEK MUST HAVE BEEN as hard on Kace as it had been on me. While we managed to get through the shower portion of our plan, we got dressed, grabbed a bite to eat, and made it back downstairs before we both lost interest in doing anything at all.

My sister's couch needed to die, as did the armchair Kace had claimed for himself. The next thing either of us knew, it was the wee hours of the morning, and my asshole sister and her husband were attempting to tiptoe through their own damned living room.

Unfortunately for them, I hadn't clued in to who they were before grabbing the nearest thing to use as a weapon and flinging it at the source of my fright. The television remote crashed into my sister's face, and she yelped.

On second thought, I refused to be sorry for assaulting my bitch of a sister. I grabbed a cushion, and I flung it in her direction. I should've done something more than growl incoherent curses their way and fling cushions, but I needed more sleep and possibly another shower with Kace.

Kace stretched, yawned, and rubbed his eyes. "The assholes return."

"What are you doing here, Kace?"

"Your sister's been bordering on hospitalization ill, and it's my turn to take care of her. Your children are with a friend, and they'll be returned in the morning."

"Bordering on hospitalization ill?" my sister demanded. "What's going on? Ginger?"

"Zombie chicken nugget," I announced. Sometime after passing out, someone had retrieved my sister's favorite duvet from her bed along with her pillows. I flopped, burrowed into the blanket, and made myself comfortable. "My plague germs are now all over your blanket, so I'm claiming it as mine."

"But that's my favorite duvet."

"It's now my favorite duvet."

"Don't ask what happened to your main bathroom," Kace added. "I recommend you remodel the entire thing. It's the only way to be sure."

"What in the hell is going on here? Zombie chicken nugget?"

"I fed your sister chicken nuggets. One of them was raw. She got a severe case of salmonella poisoning. She's getting better, but I decided to keep an eye on her just to be sure. The kids weren't equipped to handle someone that ill, so I stepped in and made some arrangements. You may as well sit down, since you two have been so thoroughly busted."

"We were hoping to sneak in and not bother you when we saw you were sleeping in our living room," Michelle admitted.

My brother-in-law sighed. "She peeked through the window like some rotten little thief. I told her it's our house, and if we hadn't wanted people in it, we wouldn't have given them the keys and codes for the alarm system. Are you all right, Ginger?"

"Your duvet is really covered in my sick germs, so I'm claiming it as compensation."

"I think that's fair," he replied.

"Don't ask what happened to your good towels. It was ugly." I'd let them make assumptions. I enjoyed my new memories involving those towels. In fact, I'd demanded Kace relocate them to his trunk, as they were now our towels, and I'd fight my sister for them.

My sister groaned. "Those were special made."

"You'll just have to get some new special-made towels. I'd be sorry, except I'm really, really not. I'm making it my mission in life to make you pay for wandering off and leaving your children alone. I had three upset children in tears in my apartment. They tried to clean, Michelle. My apartment. They needed me to teach them how to clean, as you seem to have neglected to teach them how to clean. Also, you committed sins in your kitchen, and I'm never forgiving you for that."

I peeked out from my duvet nest in time to watch my sister grimace. "I forgot to load the dishwasher. I'm sorry."

"You left a toxic wasteland in your kitchen. Some pots and pans were too far gone to salvage. Deal with it," I announced.

"I'm really sorry about that. I got caught up in getting ready to go."

"You had things growing on your counters."

"Really sorry isn't going to cut it, is it?"

"A tow truck took out my car, a zombie chicken nugget tried to kill me, and I had to ask Kace for help because a tow truck killed my car. Then a mall Santa gave me a puppy and lovebirds for Christmas, but they were petnapped, and I haven't had a chance to rescue them yet. I miss my puppy and my birds. I haven't even named my birds yet, but they're so cute."

"What on earth has been going on here?" my sister blurted.

"I hired a new executive secretary while you weren't around to criticize my choices. If you don't like my choice of executive secretary, you should have been here to stop me."

The way Kace spoke led me to believe he'd been fighting

with my sister over his choice of executive secretary. Michelle's sigh confirmed I'd missed something.

"What's the issue with your executive secretary?" I asked.

"He has shit taste in skillsets for an executive secretary, so they always wash out. He wants someone who can do everything, and such a person doesn't exist. He refuses to delegate certain tasks, and it causes problems. He's a stupid idiot, that's what. He's a stupid idiot who overworks his secretaries, and then he gets mad they leave. We'd agreed I would pick your next executive secretary, damn it."

"I couldn't do your job, my job, and my executive secretary's job, so I hired an executive secretary. You're going to deal with it, because if you hadn't run off without a trace and invoked the damned missing-persons clause, I wouldn't have needed one. But I needed one. There's also a new courier dog to go with my new executive secretary."

"Another one?!"

"My executive secretary will have a courier dog to help with her duties. She'll need it."

"Damn it, Kace! We agreed we'd have same-gender executive secretaries to prevent office problems."

"My new executive secretary has all of the qualifications for the position, and I don't care about her gender."

Like hell he didn't, the sneaky little liar. I had a very good idea of what he had in mind for his new executive secretary, and if we hadn't fallen prey to needing rest, I would've been over at his house rather than my sister's house.

Then again, it worked out—had we gone to his house, we never would've been back in time to intercept my idiot sister and her husband.

"How qualified is she?" Michelle demanded.

"Call HR and ask. I'm sure you'll be forgiven if you convince them you're alive. The paperwork has already been signed."

"It'll wait until we go back to work on the third. I'm not going to bother anyone on Christmas morning."

"You're bothering me on Christmas morning," Kace complained.

"Well, if you hadn't fallen asleep in *my* living room, I wouldn't be bothering you right now."

She had a point, I had to admit.

"I was keeping an eye on your sister, and she picked the couch as her favorite place to sleep. I tried to talk her into one of the guest bedrooms, but I guess the couch was the only place that wasn't making her feel worse. She had a brief stay with a friend."

"Which friend would you trust with my sister?"

"I would say it was less trust with her and more she was kidnapped right out from under my nose. I brought her to the office to keep an eye on her. My friend showed up at the office and ran away with her, I'm afraid. It took a while to retrieve her successfully."

I snorted at that. "I had to crawl out a damned window and run away."

"You have to be shitting me."

"The friend is coming over, as the friend currently has your children and your sister's pets hostage."

Michelle sucked in a breath. "Are you serious?"

"A friend, Michelle. Not a serial killer." Kace rolled his eyes, unwrapped himself from one of my sister's spare blankets, and showed off his chest, which lacked a shirt.

"Are you half naked in my house?"

I never expected Kace to take egotistical male to the extreme, but he peeked under the blanket. "Does wearing boxers count as half naked?"

"That's closer to fully naked."

I had no memory of Kace getting out of his clothes, much to my dismay. I burrowed into my sister's duvet so I wouldn't be caught drooling. "Damn it, put some clothes on," I complained.

He laughed, probably because he had an intimate understanding of what he did to me when he removed his clothes. "You were passed out, and I was too hot to wear a damned suit. I wasn't expecting anyone until after eight in the morning. I would've gotten dressed again then. It's not like I wouldn't have taken off my clothes had I been in a bedroom."

"But that's my chair," Michelle wailed.

Damn. Kace was out for my sister's head, and he was winning the war against his partner. "It is your chair. That's part of why I claimed it. I have spent days establishing dominance over it. I've weakened your sister's resistances and forced her into a position of subservience, too."

"Like hell you did. Sick people aren't subservient, you asshole!"

"True. She mostly just slept and threw up most of the time," Kace admitted.

While somewhat accurate, I enjoyed his taunting of my sister too much to correct him on some of the points—like my supposed subservience. I preferred to think we had taken turns in the shower.

The next week would test me until we managed to pull the wool over my sister's eyes. That also led to the problem of where I'd stay until our ruse was exposed.

"What have you actually been doing with my sister? You're such a creep!"

"I haven't been a creep to your sister, although I have forced her to move into your house. Thanks to your stunt, she got served an eviction notice. She prioritized the kids first, and you seem to have forgotten that three kids are lethal to wallets in general, and her employer is, and forever will be, an asshole who never paid her anywhere near what she's worth."

My sister spewed curses, and once she exhausted her selection in English, she switched to other languages.

"My wife says she's very sorry, Ginger," Mitchel said. "She will do her best to make it up to you, and we're more than happy for you to stay here until you're situated."

Wow. My brother-in-law had returned from his vacation a changed man—and a generous one. "What happened to the Mitchel who can't stand freeloaders?"

"It's not freeloading if you were put in the situation because you put our children over yourself."

"I don't know what vacation did to Mitchel, but I like this Mitchel, Kace. Don't let him get away. You might want to chain him to prevent future escapes."

My brother-in-law sighed. "I'd be upset, but that's quite possibly the nicest thing you've ever said to me, Ginger."

"I've said nice things to you before."

"But this is the first time you've thought I should stay around."

"That's also not true. I just tell you if you're being an asshole."

Kace snickered. "You can't win this one, I'm afraid."

I scowled. "Which one of us can't win? Because I'm in a mood and want to win every single argument to cross my path today. It can be a Christmas present for me."

"Not you, Ginger. Your sister. I dealt with you being sick for a week because she bailed town."

"I didn't make her sick!"

"If you hadn't left town, she wouldn't have gotten the nuggets, and she wouldn't have gotten sick. This is entirely your fault."

"That's entirely unfair, Kace."

I laughed at my sister's whining tone. "Deal with it, Michelle. Welcome home, but go away. I want to go back to sleep without listening to you yell at your business partner."

"My business partner should go to his own home."

"If I return to my own home, I'm taking your sister with me."

"You will do no such thing. She's fine where she's at."

"I don't agree."

I rolled my eyes at the insanity in my sister's living room. "Go to bed, Michelle. Leave Kace where he's at, or nobody will get any sleep ever again."

Mitchel cleared his throat. "Before we do that, why are there penises hanging from the ceiling?"

"Your daughters believe you pulled a dick move and wanted a visual representation of your status as dickheads," Kace announced. "They offered me a substantial sum to make the purchases on their behalf. As you dickheads left them alone for weeks, you deserve having dicks hanging from your banisters."

Mitchel sighed. "We've created monsters, babe. What is Saul's contribution to this mess?"

"He didn't have time to contribute. He has been working a part-time job because your sister was too sick to work, so he asked her employer if he could take her place. My friend made sure he went to work last night, which is why he's not here. Ginger needed a chance to get some rest, and three kids are pretty exhausting when you're sick. I've just been supervising and working."

"I'm really sorry," my sister mumbled.

"The dicks stay the entire day," I declared. "And after you grovel sufficiently to your children, I might even forgive you… sometime next week. I might even hold out until sometime in January. But I'll probably forgive you, should you grovel sufficiently."

"I'll make sure my groveling meets your standards," my sister promised. "I'm going to go to bed and catch a nap. It was a long and unfortunately eventful flight."

Ugh. The last words I wanted to hear was that her flight had been eventful. "How eventful?"

"The plane broke halfway home and emergency landed. We got home sooner since there was a flight headed this way from the airport we landed at, so it worked out. It wasn't a bad landing."

I decided I didn't want to know. "Thank you for not dying during the crash, but you're still in the doghouse. But you don't get to be in the doghouse with my puppy, because that would be a reward. In fact, I'm not sure you've been good enough to meet my puppy yet. I'll think about it."

"Damn, Ginger. You're ruthless," my sister complained.

"Maybe that'll teach you to leave your kids alone without a word. Go to bed so I can get some sleep."

My sister and brother-in-law fled upstairs.

"I can't wait until they see the Fist," Kace whispered once they were gone.

"I can't wait until they see what 'your friend' has done. My sister is going to lose her shit, and I plan to record every moment of it."

"Has anyone ever told you that you're a delightfully evil woman?"

"As a matter of fact, no."

"You're delightfully evil, and I can't wait to see what you do next."

※ ※ ※

KACE STAYED AWAKE, and I caught naps between shameless sessions of admiring his naked chest. Sometime after my sister and brother-in-law retreated upstairs, he'd put his pants on, and his choice of slacks implied he'd be wearing a suit when he got around to adding a shirt to the ensemble. I noticed his tendency to work when unsupervised, but after having interrupted so much of his schedule, I decided I'd leave it be.

If the man wanted to work on Christmas day, he could—until it was time for Juliette to come over.

At ten in the morning, he called her, told her she needed to bring an outfit suitable for me, and that my menace of a sister and brother-in-law had safely returned and were still sleeping upstairs after a long and eventful flight.

He even warned her about the penis-themed decorations.

At eleven, I got up to prepare the turkey, and I wandered around in clothes I'd been wearing for too damned long. I'd need another shower, but as I wasn't brazen enough to drag Kace along while my pesky sister and her husband were home, I hoped pilfered deodorant would do the trick.

Kace occupied the kitchen entry, observing me work at figuring out how to cook the turkey butchered by a chef upset he had to freeze his fancy bird. It seemed simple enough. I checked the oven to make certain it was usable to discover someone had recently cleaned it from top to bottom. I preheated it, waited for it to announce it was ready for the turkey, and stuffed the bird in as directed on the instructions. "I like how your friend gave very specific step-by-step instructions. With pictures."

"I think he was expecting the kids to help."

"I do not mind being treated like a child when the turkey has been butchered creatively."

"Spatchcocking is not all that creative."

"What kind of cock is in my house now?" my sister wailed, pushing Kace out of her way so she could step into the kitchen. "My house has too many cocks in it as it is."

I pointed at the oven. "The turkey."

"Oh. That kind of cock is okay. Why is the plagued one handling the cooking?"

"I don't have the plague. Food poisoning is not the plague.

Kace was busy working, so I handled the turkey. He provided the turkey, though."

"Thank you for getting a turkey. However, it's Christmas. We don't work on Christmas."

"I was preparing some things for my new executive secretary. I didn't want her to come in when our offices open and discover hell waiting for her, so I'm getting caught up on things now so she has a pleasant introduction to work. I'm easing her in."

"Who are you, and when did you start playing nice with your executive secretaries?"

"She is a singular entity."

"You have been a living devil to your other executive secretaries."

"Most of them exaggerated on their resumes and couldn't handle the work they claimed they could handle. They only have their male egos to blame on not being able to handle the work I gave them. I was always careful to assign work that was listed as a skill on their resume. You know this."

"However much I hate to admit it, you're right. Do you think this woman will work out?"

"I do."

As turkey, or more specifically, only turkey, would upset a few people in the house, I went through the refrigerator to determine what I could make for the rest of the meal. "Kace, are there any potatoes? I'm going to be sad if there are no potatoes."

Kace pointed at a stand near the back door. "That's the onion and potato box. There's garlic and scallions in there, too. I got bread, but it might be too fresh for stuffing, though I did tear open the bags last night. I went with baguettes. They're in the pantry."

"Cranberry sauce?"

"Fresh cranberries are in the vegetable drawer, as I had no

idea where to put it. Oranges are in the fruit drawer, and I grabbed a bunch of other things I saw on some recipes, as I had no idea how you wanted to do it."

"Unlike my sister, you are not a useless human being, so you'll survive through today," I announced.

"Wow, Ginger. I get you're pissed at me, but that was just harsh."

"You'll probably survive until I've forgiven you. Probably. Despite current appearances, I do love my sister."

"I'm going to stage a retreat. Try not to be murdered by my sister, Kace. I need you at work when we go back."

"Gee, your concern for me is heartening."

"Our profit margin would nosedive if my sister killed you."

I snorted at my sister's callous commentary, and she swept out of her kitchen with her head held high.

"She's mad about the dicks hanging from her ceiling," Kace announced, raising his voice loud enough everyone in the house could hear him.

"Damn straight I'm mad about the damned dicks! It's Christmas, not Dickmas! And don't get me started. If I wanted dick, I'd ask Mitchel."

"Is that all I'm here for?" my brother-in-law complained.

"Yes," my sister replied.

My brother-in-law cackled and poked his head into the kitchen. "Don't mind her, Ginger. We're jet-lagged to hell, and she wants to see our babies. What time is your friend coming, Kace?"

"Noon and not a minute before. Possibly a few minutes after, but I expect she'll pull into the driveway at exactly noon."

"Are you sure we can't hide the dicks?"

"Positive. Your daughters would cry."

"They're ruthless. I produced ruthless children."

"Michelle helped." Kace chuckled. "But if you hadn't

worried them, they wouldn't have sought out revenge upon finding out you were just being assholes."

"I tried to tell Michelle she was taking her desire to get away for a while a little too far."

"You went with it."

"Can you imagine her left unattended? She'd end the world."

Kace grimaced. "Or try to rule it while collecting sporks."

"She's currently into chopsticks. She saw a cute set in the airport and now wants to collect all the cute chopsticks she can get her hands on."

"I refuse to start a line of chopsticks."

"I told her you would say that. Would it matter if they were cute chopsticks?"

"The answer is no, and I will ban her from ever entering the building again if she tries to pursue a line of luxury but cute chopsticks."

Poor Kace. Working with my sister had to test his patience daily. "Tell her you'll consider a limited-edition chopstick, but only included with a premier item you're selling. That way, the damage is limited to a high-ticket item. She gets her chopsticks, and you don't lose a lot of money on it. Chopsticks can't be that expensive to produce."

"They are when they're made of silver," Mitchel muttered.

"She does not get silver chopsticks," I said. "Silver conducts heat, and that is how you burn your fucking fingers. Have you ever tried to eat soup with silver? No. Tell her to go to a fucking psychologist and get some medication for her insanity."

Kace's brows shot up. "Wow, Ginger. That was harsh."

"I've barely gotten started yet. Now, fetch me some potatoes, Kace. I've decided you're my kitchen slave until my puppy and birds arrive."

Chapter Seventeen

WITH KACE'S HELP, I had our exceptionally early dinner ready before Juliette brought the kids over. I expected a single vehicle. Instead, three SUVs, all of similar model, pulled into the driveway. I peeked out the window, frowning at the congregation. Juliette, her husband, and her son proved to be the drivers, and three kids and my puppy escaped Juliette's SUV and bolted for the front door. I believed my puppy followed Saul on her leash because she found the teen the sanest of the lot.

I'd missed my puppy, and I wanted her to love me and only me.

The kids would plow their parents over, and I grinned as Kace held the door open so they could charge in. I waited to intercept Virtue, and when the kids piled through the door, I snagged her leash, made my lap available, and basked while she showered my face with sloppy puppy kisses.

The kids aimed for their mother, and all three crashed into my sister. She shrieked and fell to the bottom of the people pile.

"You deserve the cold shoulder, but a pancaking will suffice." I shook my head, picked up my puppy, and headed for the kitchen. She'd grown in the past week, adding on enough pounds I worried I wouldn't be able to carry her by the end of the year. I double-checked on the kitchen, cuddling with Virtue while I still could. Everything was as I'd left it, with the mashed potatoes, stuffing, and other sides safely contained in their dishes and the turkey ready to be ferried to the dining room for immediate consumption.

Juliette and her cohorts followed, carrying armloads of presents, which they deposited near the tree. It took them six trips to get everything, and that was with Kace and Mitchel's help.

"You brought too much stuff," I informed the fashion designer, and as Virtue had started growing up on me, I set her down and unclipped her leash so she could bounce around and play. She ran around my legs, jumped, and squeaked her excitement before barreling across the living room to join the people pile and offer kisses to everyone.

"We don't say such blasphemous things on Christmas." Juliette grabbed my arm, snagged one of the clothing bags she'd brought in, and dragged me off. "Hey, gremlin, where is the nearest bathroom?"

Kace pointed. "We're about to eat, and I'm sure she made enough if you three wish to stay."

"The baby will cry if Julian doesn't get home. By that, I mean Chloe might kill him if she's left babysitting the cooking for too long. We couldn't make everything fit in two vehicles, so I had to borrow him. Now I have to pay penance."

"It's about time someone made you pay penance."

"You are such an awful little gremlin. Why did I get you anything for Christmas?"

"You secretly love me, and I authorize payments to dress my employees."

"Foul play." Juliette dragged me into the bathroom, shut the door, and wasted no time shucking me out of my clothes and dressing me to her liking. The red lingerie, lacier than I considered buying for myself, would either die a terrible death at Kace's hands or become my favorite—or both. The dress would make my sister cry, and even without makeup and with messy hair, it worked miracles.

"Okay. You're obviously a goddess."

"Red is your friend. All I did was pick a cut that would flatter you. You did the rest. You'll have to unwrap your presents to find your new shoes. I really do have to dash, or Chloe really will kill us all."

"Thank you for taking care of my puppy and the kids."

"You needed the break, and from what I hear, you got to have some quiet time with the gremlin. I'm glad to help. Remember, for your plan to work, you can't follow him home tonight. You can't follow him home until after your first day at work. And at work, you have to treat him like he's a boot scraping so he can drool all over you helplessly to piss your sister off."

"Got it." I saluted. "This dress is amazing. Also, how much would it be for more lingerie?"

"I have anticipated your lingerie needs, and you will find one of the boxes loaded with extra sets in several styles. Each set is wrapped in tissue to keep them from tangling, but you'll be good on lingerie for a while, even if someone gets overenthusiastic."

Kace would become overenthusiastic, but I refused to acknowledge my new status as a thoroughly appreciated and pleased woman. "I have no idea what you're talking about."

Juliette leered at me. "I'm sure you don't." Opening the bathroom door, she herded me out. "Michelle, *this* is why I refuse to sell you a red dress. If you didn't look like a tomato in its death throes, maybe I'd consider. Your sister? She does not look like a tomato in its death throes. She looks like she's worth more than your entire company and then some."

My sister stared at me, and her mouth dropped open.

As I was a mature adult, I restrained myself and didn't stick my tongue out at her. Virtue bounded over and sat on my feet, and I crouched to reward her, scratching behind her ears and accepting more of her puppy kisses.

"This is entirely unfair." My sister bowed her head. "Why does *she* get one of your red dresses?"

"One?" Juliette snickered. "She's sweet, she works hard, and she makes my red dresses beautiful, just like you make my blue dresses beautiful. But red is not your friend. Red is her friend. I'm doing you a favor."

"How is giving her red dresses doing me a favor?"

"You're hopeless, Michelle. Just for that, I'm going to give her and the gremlin—and even your husband—something in red while you have to watch them and cry because you don't have something of mine in red."

Michelle scowled. "That's just cruel."

"I helped care for your sick sister because you ran off like a hooligan. Maybe if you beg, I will relent. Maybe. You need to take lessons from your sister on how to be charming." Smirking, Juliette strolled off, linked her arm with her husband, and headed for the door. "Don't linger too long, Julian. Chloe really might kill you this time."

Julian shook his head, rolled his eyes, and followed his mother to the door. "Kace, I'll call you. We'll talk about your problem."

Kace chuckled. "You got it. How does tomorrow sound?"

"I promised she'd get to sleep in tomorrow to make up for helping ferry things over. I think I'll be making that same offer for the rest of the week. Candice has been pretty quiet, so it's possible I might get away for a while, but I won't be able to for long."

"I'll work around your schedule."

"Sounds good. Try not to get into too much trouble with your business partner."

"Too late for that," my sister grumbled.

"Good luck, Kace. You're going to need it."

Julian wisely fled with his parents. To keep my sister and Kace from killing each other, I pointed in the direction of the dining room. "I cooked food, and I expect people to eat it."

"You've gotten bossy," my sister complained.

"I'm in the red dress, and the red dress says I can be bossy. Do you know what happened while you were gone?"

"What happened?"

I got in her face, looked her in the eyes, and announced, "Ginger snapped."

She backed off and held up her hands in surrender. "The dress is absolutely stunning on you, I'm sorry I've been a bad person, and I bet dinner will be absolutely delicious. I'm going to go eat everything offered to me, even the stuff I don't actually like."

As my sister valued her life and had listened to my blunt warning, I nodded. "Wise move."

Mitchel stared at Kace. "I don't know what you did to Ginger, but stop it. I've never been so scared of a woman in my life."

"You should've reined your woman in. Really, Mitchel? You two ran away for how long?"

Amelia and Wendy grabbed my hands and dragged me towards the kitchen. "Please don't kill our mom or dad, we need them," Wendy begged. "Even if they deserved it this time."

"You're so lucky your kids still love you, Michelle."

"I will spend the next year attempting to appease you, I promise! It won't happen again."

As that was the promise I was looking for, I allowed the twins to drag me off so I could address the important job of appeasing my hungry stomach and figure out how to pretend I wanted nothing to do with Kace until my first real day as his executive secretary, and my sister and brother-in-law learned a few important life lessons.

THE FIST RENDERED my sister speechless, and for the first time in my life, I witnessed a man faint. My nieces rolled on the carpet, laughing so hard at their father they sobbed. Saul refused to look at any of us, opting to sift through the piles of unopened presents and console himself with a gift.

Virtue observed the fuss before returning to her new collection of toys, which would require several trips to ferry over to Kace's house if we used his dinky little sports car. I suspected my puppy had been responsible for the need for an entire third SUV to haul everything over.

I debated if we needed my brother-in-law, or if we could just leave him on the floor, the Fist still clutched in one hand.

After half a second of thought, I took pictures with the new phone that had miraculously appeared in my new Carter purse, a delightful red tote I could use anytime with most of my new red dresses. She'd even given me a matching black one for the days I didn't take Delaware by storm in red.

"That thing is horrible," my sister finally said, her eyes wide. "Why would anyone buy *that*?"

"Ask your daughters," Kace replied.

"Revenge," the twins choked out between sobbed laughter.

My sister nudged her husband with her toe. "He fainted. He really fainted."

Kace crouched beside my brother-in-law and poked at the big black fist. "I'd faint, too, if anyone threatened to use that on me."

I would, too, but only after screaming from terror.

"I'm afraid to open the package you got me," Michelle whispered. "It took him almost two hours to break into that. And you ruined yet another one of my good towels. And there's two towels still missing. I have one towel left. What did my towels ever do to you?"

"I put them out of their misery." Michelle would kill us once she learned we'd stolen the towels, but it would be worth it. "I got you a lot of coal, and I spent a great deal of time wrapping it individually. There is some bath stuff mixed in with your coal, because I couldn't be so cruel as to get you nothing. I'll let you off the hook on unwrapping your coal for today, but only because Mitchel fainted, and honestly, that's a lot funnier than you unwrapping coal."

"You're ruthless."

"I held one full-time job and two part-time jobs while cleaning up your messes. You deserve far worse than coal."

Wendy giggled. "It's true, Mom. She worked so hard, and then the money math didn't add up, and that made her mad, so she tried to work harder. It didn't work out, so Kace made her move in with him, then she got evicted again to here. Which is probably for the best. They'd kill each other if they were forced to see each other all the time."

I foresaw the little brat becoming an actress when she grew up.

Amelia joined in, heaving a sigh. "It was awful, Mom. I worried there'd be a murder in the middle of the night. So much tension."

I loved how Amelia toed the line of the truth. There was still a lot of tension, but it was of the exact opposite type Amelia presented. Considering what the girls had made Kace purchase, they understood I fought an inevitable battle against Kace's charms.

"I'm so sorry for my sister, Kace. I don't know why she hates you so much."

"I'm an egotistical bastard," he replied with his best smirk. "That has something to do with it. I'm devastatingly handsome, smart, rich, and know my worth." He inspected his nails and blew on them, his expression so cocky I wanted to throttle him or drag him upstairs to my sister's shower. "She looks at me and wants to smack the smug expression off my handsome face. It's only natural. It's easy to hate perfection. She looks at me and gets angry because she knows I'm perfection."

Damn, he played me well, which annoyed me into scowling at him.

Cocky, self-assured, deliciously handsome bastard of a man.

I really wanted to take him upstairs to my sister's bathroom for a repeat session in the shower.

Judging from his sly smirk, he knew it.

My sister snorted. "That's bad even for you. But you would, as you love nothing more than annoying my sister. I'm sorry, Ginger. I don't know what his problem is."

I'd figured out his problem. He'd lost his mind and had fallen in love with me. Somewhere along the way, I'd lost my mind and had fallen in love with him, too. His naked chest had just sealed the deal a little faster.

Until after we returned to work and we got our final bit of payback on her, I needed to play the game properly. "He's an egotistical bastard. He told you that himself. He does get to add honest as his only redeeming quality."

"That's harsh even for you, Ginger." My sister sighed. "Is it really too much to ask you to get along with my business partner?"

"Considering you've never invited me to your workplace, yes. You told me yourself we would do nothing but fight and containing us in the same office building might result in the loss of the entire building. You need that building to keep the company alive."

"I'm sorry. You can come to the office with me. How about on the first day everyone's back? We're all going to be in vacation mode anyway. I'll give you a grand tour and everything."

Well, as I needed to go to work anyway, relying on my sister for transportation would make things a little less complicated. "Okay. That can be part of your penance package."

"Deal. The existence of a penance package is better than being on your shit list for the entirety of the upcoming year. I'll really try to do better. And you're right, I should've at least brought you in for a tour."

"For all I know, you could work in a closet, and you three have just been claiming you're super-rich smarty business types. You're probably all mooching off that egotistical bastard. He probably has a trust fund."

Kace laughed. "I blew what I had of a trust fund on your sister's harebrained ideas."

"They're not harebrained if they worked, and they worked. There's a reason you got a slightly higher profit share than me."

"And now we have equal profit share because the company sustained itself and repaid my investment money threefold, as per our initial loaning agreement." Kace took over my sister's armchair with a smug smile. "Was that a Christmas present, Michelle? You know how much I enjoy when you bring that subject up."

"It's more of a Christmas present to my sister, as she gets to witness you lord over me. Justifiably."

"I can accept that. After dealing with a zombie chicken nugget, she deserves many Christmas presents from you."

My sister sighed. "I'll take you car shopping next week, Ginger, and in the meantime, I'll drive you around as you need. When do you go back to work?"

Hmm. As I hadn't told her about my change in employment, I'd have to tell my first true lie—although it wouldn't be a lie, as I didn't expect to get anything done on my first official day on the job. "I believe it's the day after you go back. It's been a blur."

"It's the day after we head back to work," Kace confirmed.

"I wrote it down on your behalf, as you were quite ill at the time you found out your schedule."

"Wow. That was generous. That bastard of a boss of yours doesn't even like giving you time off for Christmas. Although I expect having the plague helped convince him to keep you out of the office. It wouldn't do for the rest of his slaves to get ill."

"I don't think food poisoning is contagious, Michelle."

Kace laughed. "Typically not, but there are ways to transfer the bacteria. Fortunately for everyone involved, you're an immaculate human being. The conditions required for spreading weren't met, so it should be fine."

I decided I didn't want to know. "Should we wake Mitchel up?"

Michelle smiled at her husband. "He's tired, so you may as well let him sleep it off. I want to see how he reacts to waking up with that thing clutched in his hand, though. I bet it will be amazing."

I bet it would be amazing, too. "I'm not a nice enough person today to prevent Mitchel's humiliation when he wakes up with that thing in his hand."

"I should feel worse about this than I do," Michelle admitted.

Shrugging, I took yet another picture of my brother-in-law. "This is just a gift that keeps on giving—and excellent blackmail material. I shall rule over this house with the evidence on my new phone. I don't know who gave me this phone, but it's amazing."

Kace shrugged. "Santa."

"No, Santa gave me a puppy and a pair of lovebirds, and he's the best Santa. I love my puppy very much."

My puppy ignored me, as she'd been gifted a mountain of new toys, all of which needed her immediate attention.

"Well, she loves her new toys. I'm sure she'll love you again tomorrow," my new boss and future husband replied. "You're just going to have to deal with being a second-string dog owner today."

"My birds still love me."

"Your birds would rather they be left alone in their cage, and you haven't figured out how to win your way into their good graces yet."

Kace would pay for telling the truth somehow. "You're an entity of pure evil."

He did as always, directing his best smirk in my direction without saying a word.

Yep. The man was pure, sexy evil, and I had no hope against his charms. To play my part, I crossed my fingers to ward him away.

My sister sighed. "Can't you two get along for five minutes?"

Kace and I stared at each other before redirecting our attention to my sister. "No," we answered in unison.

I loved we'd gotten onto the same page despite the show we were putting on for my sister. It would only make the next week of my life even sweeter, assuming I managed to survive without Kace showering me with his affection.

I'd gotten used to him showing up and trying to make my world a better place—and he did.

Life never failed to catch me by surprise, but for a rare change, I liked the changes life had brought to my door.

Chapter Eighteen

BEING aware that my Camaro waited for me in Kace's garage transformed my time stuck with my sister into a living hell.

She really, really, *really* wanted to buy me a new car. She dragged me from dealership to dealership as part of her quest to spend her money and pay penance for her crimes. I feared showing interest in any vehicle.

Any interest might result in me owning two cars instead of one. What would I do with *two* cars? I could only drive one car at a time.

"You were never the sports car type," my sister announced three days into dealership hunting. "I'm obviously an idiot. I've been taking you to places with sports cars. You're the truck type. You want a tank that's safe in an accident. I've been showing you teeny weeny itsy bitsy cars. No wonder you've been bored out of your mind and generally unimpressed."

I'd been very impressed with the Lamborghini she'd shown me—until I'd learned it cost almost twenty thousand for its basic maintenance bill. Still, I could appease her through it. Even she had agreed the maintenance bill was too far outside of anyone's budget, even if she paid for the vehicle.

"That Lamborghini, though."

We both sighed, as did Mitchel and the kids.

"We could go test drive it. On a race track." Michelle wrinkled her nose and checked her watch. "Do you think they'd let us test drive it?"

"Not without handing over your soul and your wallet first, alas." I eyed the cars on the lot. "I'll cut a deal with you."

Michelle perked up. "What deal?"

"I will consider a sporty car under one condition."

"What condition?"

"You have to buy Saul the same model."

I'd just won every best aunt award on the planet with my statement, and the twins stared at me with their mouths hanging open. Considering they'd all seen my shiny new Camaro, which would have another shiny new Camaro friend to keep it company soon enough, their reaction made a lot of sense.

Kace's garage—my future garage—had three spots total, and I had plans to look for something sturdy in truck size for the snowy days I didn't want anything sporty on the road.

"I know an SUV dealership," she announced.

I pointed across the lot where the overpriced SUVs resided. "There happen to be some of those on this lot."

"They're flip hazards, and I will not have Saul driving a flip hazard. They're also expensive flip hazards."

"I thought all SUVs were flip hazards?"

"No, not all of them. It depends on the design. Some are very stable. Actually, most are stable now that the cause for their flipping has been identified. Modern engineering is a marvel. How does an SUV sound?"

"I said I would consider a sporty *car*."

"SUVs can be sporty. Porsche makes a very nice sporty SUV. SUVs are like cars that got knocked up by a truck and had a baby. Some people even call them trucks, and the good ones can tow just about anything you might want. Like a boat."

"I want a boat?"

"You totally want a boat. You're the boat kind."

I was? My sister had lost her mind—or had left it somewhere in Africa. "What are you talking about?"

"I'm a terrible person, and I want to buy you something!" she wailed.

My sister had lost her mind, and if I didn't find some way to distract her, I'd really end up with a second vehicle. I was already having trouble coming to terms with my Camaro, paid for by Kace and his crazy company credit card. I liked my Camaro, and I fully planned on requiring Kace to pose in it, beside it, and possibly on it while in various states of undress.

I bet he'd turn my car into a thing of dreams while wearing a suit with his shirt partially unbuttoned.

My sister waved her hand in front of my face. "Earth to Ginger."

"I don't think you could afford the Lamborghini."

"Nobody with sense can afford that Lamborghini. I hadn't expected the maintenance bill to be *that* bad. We could go check out the Audi you liked. It's not a sports car, but it's definitely a luxury vehicle. I could be talked into buying one for Saul, but only if Saul were to sell his soul to the devil, maintain his grades to my standards rather than his, and agree to pursue college. In good news, I'm a considerate parent, and I will allow Saul to emerge from college unscathed."

By unscathed, I assumed she meant without student loan debt, a demon I still fought and would until my dying day, as I swore my payments did absolutely jack shit to lower the amount I actually owed. "I've changed my mind. Just pay for their college and I'll deal with the car shopping."

"You're still paying off your student loan debt, aren't you?"

"That was the only money number I didn't fuck up thanks to your stunt."

Amelia sighed. "It's true. She took care of our bills first, her student loan second, and everything else in order of importance afterwards. We'd watch her when she didn't think we were around. It's really impressive. She could do your job better than you do, Dad."

My brother-in-law grunted. "I don't want to get into that sort of competition with Ginger. She might win, and should she win, I'd never hear the end of it."

Mitchel would blow a gasket when he found out I'd be helping handle logistics as a part of my new job as Kace's executive secretary. "Logistics is the art of making the numbers work while also making a bunch of people do what I want, when I want, how I want, on the schedule I want. It is a battle."

I'd enjoy working the logistics circuit for Kace. He would actually listen when shit went wrong, and without fail, shit would go wrong.

"I made the mistake of criticizing your logistics work once. I will not make that mistake again," my brother-in-law swore. "I do feel a little bad we have good logistics folks at our company, whereas you're the only good logistics person they have at yours."

"I wouldn't say I'm the only good logistics person at my company."

Amelia snorted, Wendy shook her head, and even Saul joined in, rolling his eyes.

Damned brats.

"I know the asshole you work for. You're the only good logistics person there, because the rest would have quit out of frustration because he wouldn't know how to treat a good employee even if Michelle walked in and lectured him on the subject."

"I would really prefer if no one walked in on my boss and lectured him about anything. I value my job." I admired how well I told so many lies using only the truth. I'd have to text

Kace about it later, as we'd gone to covert communications to maintain the ruse that we hated each other.

Thanks to my sister's determination to take me car shopping, he held my puppy hostage.

It worked out well, as he took advantage of the time to begin training her, something I would appreciate later. Once my home life settled—and I pulled a fast one or three on my sister—I'd learn how to train her, too.

While it didn't help much, my birds had warmed up to me, and they'd perch on my finger and accept treats of seeds. The guide Santa had given me wanted them to eat special pellets, which they accepted with minimal fuss, but I offered them seeds and some fruits and vegetables as bribes for their affection.

My ploy mostly worked, although I'd learned from bitter experience birds could fly and wouldn't return to their cage without encouragement—or even more treats.

Saving their favorites for when they returned to their cage helped with that.

To begin mitigating the car shopping, I pointed at something red and shiny across the lot. "There's a red one. Let's go look at the red one."

"Seriously, Ginger? You're going to just randomly point at a red car and ask to look at it?"

"It seems more productive than standing here while the salespeople think we're nuts."

Saul grabbed my hand and pulled me in the direction of my chosen vehicle. "Aunt Ginger wants to see the red car, so we're going to see the red car."

The red car made Kace's seem rather monstrous in size in comparison, and only its position near the showroom allowed it to be visible at all among the larger, sturdier vehicles. I bent over for a close look and determined it had fewer than six inches of space between its undercarriage and the road. "I have questions, Michelle."

"Is the first one how anyone could possibly fit in it?"

"Yes."

"Is the second one how you don't lose pieces of the car on speed bumps?"

"It is now."

"You can't buy this car. It's an even worse accident waiting to happen than Kace's car."

I considered my options. "We could go back to the Lamborghini dealership. If I'm going to drive an accident waiting to happen, I'd rather drive that accident waiting to happen."

Michelle frowned. "You've already suckered me out of making sure my brats are fully paid through college, although that had been my plan already. That car is roughly of equivalent value." She turned to her husband and stared.

My brother-in-law sighed. "It's a fortune to maintain, Michelle, and she'd be terrified to drive it. The Audi is a better idea, and it's right down the street. She'll like a family car better."

"I will?"

"Low flip risk, practical while stylish and a good vehicle, sporty without being terrifying for you, and plenty of space for Virtue and her mountains of toys. As you'll freak when the weather gets bad, they handle surprisingly well in the snow. We'll just make sure you have proper snow tires and rustproofing. Just don't get it in red. It'll crank your premiums up."

I'd have to talk to Juliette to get another car added to my policy number, and she would laugh at me for being unable to tell my brother-in-law and sister no. "That's a really good sales pitch. Can I have it in red anyway? Is black trim an option?"

"If you really want it in red, I'm sure they can give it to you in red."

I pointed at a red car similar in shade to my Camaro. "That kind of red."

"We can discuss that at the Audi dealership," he promised.

"An Audi will work!" Michelle clapped her hands and hurried towards her car, which she'd parked on the exact other end of the lot. "Hurry up. I want to get this ordered so she can drive us to work."

"Wait, what happened to you driving *me* around?"

"Admit it, Ginger. You totally want to hold me hostage for a day."

I shook my head and followed my sister, wondering where I'd gone wrong in a past life to deserve my family.

* * *

MY SISTER BOUGHT ME AN AUDI, and she used her company card. The accounting department would laugh at her at the same time they robbed her and Kace blind spoiling me with vehicles. A better woman would've confessed.

I liked the Camaro more than the Audi, but the Audi matched, it came a close second, and it would do everything Mitchel had promised and then some. I even got my black trim.

It had taken a little work, but I'd gotten the vehicle added to my policy on the sly without revealing I was now the not-so-proud owner of an expensive monthly bill just to keep the damned cars legal. My sister had insisted on replacement insurance, too, but it hadn't done more than add a few minutes of aggravation to the shopping process.

I drove my new car to my sister's house, and Kace waited in the driveway next to a blue Camaro while my puppy played in the snow. I parked, and the instant I got out of the vehicle, he said, "She really made you buy a new car."

"I'm boring and can only drive a family car, apparently."

"Well, it'll look nice in my garage, I will say that much. Will you share?"

"Get rid of the tiny steel accident waiting to happen, and then my answer will be yes."

"I traded it. Apparently, my new car is blue, as you can see here, and I'm going to have to watch you pose in scanty outfits on it—and other cars—at that dealership. Juliette dragged me over by my ear yesterday to sign paperwork. The car was already ready, so I figured I may as well just drive the Camaro everywhere."

I snorted. "I have to drive my Audi to work tomorrow. And ferry the runaways. She paid with her company card."

Kace laughed at that. "I know. I got a call about it when the transaction went through, as it pinged the head accountant's alarms for big spending. Good job on taking your sister for a fortune."

"I like the Camaro better."

He smiled at that.

Before I could get myself in trouble and make some suggestions about other things I'd like, which involved him unbuttoning his shirt and posing with his Camaro, my sister pulled in. She stormed out of her car and pointed at Kace's new vehicle. "What is that?"

"It's a Camaro. It's mine."

"But why did you get that? Kace! That's not fair. It's shinier than her Audi."

Kace smirked. "I sold someone into slavery to get it, too."

My sister's eyes widened. "You wouldn't."

"I did. I'm under oath to tell you no details on who I sold into slavery, why they were sold into slavery, and what terrible things they'll have to do while enslaved." Kace ran his fingers through his hair and displayed his best smirk. "Well, that's not quite true. I'm the slaver, and I'm very much enjoying my time as the master. The car is just payment for loaning my slave to someone for a brief period of time."

I wanted to know what sort of benefits I got for playing as

his slave. Rather than admit interest in his ploy, I snatched Virtue's leash out of his hand and hurried to greet my puppy, who offered me kisses as always. "You're such a good little girl. Don't you let that mean man corrupt you."

My puppy, after confirming I still loved her, decided she wanted to roll in the snow and make a mess of her fur.

"You do not have a slave. Why did you get a new car?"

"I got yelled at about the old one, and I decided it was maybe time to trade up to something a little sturdier."

"Ginger." My sister crossed her arms and glared at me. "What did you do to Kace?"

"I didn't do anything to Kace. If I'd done something to Kace, he'd be in the snow curled in the fetal position, crying. Does he look like a hurt man to you?"

"He looks like he's having a midlife crisis, honestly."

"And what does that have to do with me?"

"That's a good point. Kace, has work been too hard on you lately?"

"Surprisingly, no. My acquisition of my new executive secretary has made me very happy with my work lately. I'm really looking forward to going to work tomorrow. Work tomorrow is going to be the highlight of my year. Part of this is because you will be forced to accept my choice of executive secretary. You will have to swallow your complaints and admit I have made the absolute best choice of executive secretary."

"I'm concerned you've lost your mind."

"Tomorrow, you will realize how wrong you are. I am not having a midlife crisis. I am claiming my rightful place as king of the world."

I snorted at that. "Don't you mean your rightful place as a deluded idiot?"

"I'd be hurt, but that was a well-aimed fastball right for my heart," Kace complained.

I widened my eyes and clapped my hands to my mouth. "You have a heart?"

"And Ginger just won that one for the rest of all eternity. Thank you for watching Virtue for us while we handled the car affair," my sister said, sweeping in to claim a hug from Kace. "I think you've lost your mind and are on a collision course for a midlife crisis, but I suppose I'll find out tomorrow."

That she would.

Chapter Nineteen

I WORE one of my new red dresses to work, along with the matching kitten heels Juliette suggested would break Kace's brain and do wonderful things for my legs. I picked my black purse for contrast and did as ordered, driving my sister and brother-in-law to work. My new pass was hidden in my purse, and Kace promised he'd have Virtue's work vest waiting inside to keep our targets in the dark for as long as possible.

Kace, to help with my ploy, made sure my sister's parking pass still worked, although security would give her a difficult time once inside, which would buy me enough time to go upstairs and join the rest of the employees inside wearing our new red jackets. I parked in the spot usually reserved for my sister, and the security guard raised a brow. He wore a red leather coat, a deep, rich color I would love wearing every minute possible. The lapel proudly boasted the company's logo. My sister bounced out of my Audi and struck a pose before presenting my car for the guard's admiration. "I bought this for my sister. This is her. Her name is Ginger, and I've been a very bad sister, so I have to give her the entire tour today."

"Yes. About that. There's been a technical glitch with your security badges, so they need to be reissued, ma'am."

My sister groaned and bowed her head. "Why does this always happen to us, babe?"

"Do you really think there was a technical glitch? Kace had our badges yanked because we inconvenienced him again. You should know this is how it works."

The security guard grinned. "I've been asked to send Miss Harriet to the top floor. Mr. Dannicks will handle her until your pass is fixed. There's some other paperwork we need to attend to as part of the new year anyway. Mr. Dannicks came in earlier and handled his share of the work."

"Of course he did. He's a shameless workaholic." My sister grabbed her purse out of my car, and I released Virtue from her seatbelt leash and clipped her work leash onto her collar. Virtue sat beside me, wagging her tail. "Oh! Where'd you get that jacket? It's gorgeous."

The security guard must have won some special draw to be the one to break my sister's heart, and he grinned. "Mrs. Carter brought them over this morning. It was Mr. Dannicks's Christmas present to the staff for exceeding goals this year. We all received one."

I would not laugh. Under no circumstances would I laugh. I would, however, add a few low blows to the jacket drama. "It's such a wonderful shade of red!"

My sister looked ready to cry, and I took out my phone and snapped a photo of her expression.

The guard's grin widened. "Isn't it, Miss Harriet? If you'll come with me, I'll get you headed upstairs while I deal with the issue of their nonfunctional badges."

"That sounds lovely, thank you." Once certain everyone had everything out of my car, I locked it and pocketed my keys. Once upstairs, the security guard unlocked the elevator for me and pressed the button for the top floor before making off with my sister and brother-in-law.

I managed to contain my laughter long enough for the elevator to reach the second floor. I cackled without any care if anyone saw me. By the time the elevator reached the top floor, I was crying, and I wiped away my tears as the door pinged. Kace waited for me in the reception area, and he grinned when he spotted me. "How is phase one going?"

"Michelle looked ready to cry when she realized the security guy in the garage had a red Carter jacket."

"We've done the office shuffle, and your new office is right next to mine. The previous owner of your office, upon learning who was occupying the space and why, laughed all the way to his new office, which is on the other side of the floor. That part is less than pleasant for him, as he needs to talk to me often, but he figured I'd be more efficient if you were close to me. I also bribed him with a promise of a raise."

"I like that I have an office. Is it a nice office?"

"It's the VP's former office, so yes. There's a connecting door between our offices, which will make us both more efficient. Juliette is waiting for us, as she is planning on changing your clothes, as your current dress won't match your new jacket."

The receptionist cracked up laughing. "It's been chaos since we all came in this morning. We started two hours early just to make sure we have our jackets ready."

My sister was going to freak, and it would be glorious. "Let's get this show on the road, then. Thank you for making sure the parking pass worked. I would've had a meltdown if we'd gotten stuck at the gate to get into the garage."

"I would've made them suffer through it if they'd been driving their car, but I figured you'd be stressed enough. How does the Audi handle?"

"Really nicely. I like it. I'm going to like the Camaro more."

Kace smirked. "Of course. You suckered me out of that car beautifully with Juliette's help. You should be proud."

"You're in a mood today."

"I finally have you back."

Oh boy. "Remember, I have to ignore you all day today."

"I get to take you home with me tonight, so ignore me all you want." Kace wrinkled his nose and sighed. "I really don't want you to ignore me. Please don't ignore me?"

It would be a long day, and I went to the receptionist's desk to introduce myself. "Should I apologize for him now? I'm Ginger."

"I'm Susan," the receptionist replied, rising to her feet and holding out her hand. "It's a pleasure to meet you. Thank you for agreeing to put up with him. I think you'll bring some very good changes to our floor."

"He's told everyone he's stalking me, hasn't he?"

"Juliette helped," she admitted. "We've also been informed she will require six months to appropriately plan the wedding."

"Has she already picked a date for us?"

"I believe so."

Kace snickered. "I said she could pick a date if she would restrain herself for once in her life. She spent an entire hour arguing with herself over it. I figured you wouldn't mind, as I've heard tales about how you hate having to pick dates for anything outside of work."

My sister would pay for opening her big mouth, and I'd establish dominance over the pesky fashion designer in the one way I knew how. "Take whatever date she picks, and make it one week earlier."

"That is pure evil, and I love it. Are you ready to get settled in for your first day of work?"

"That depends. Will I actually get a chance to get any work done?"

"No, but your ex-boss begged me to have another meeting

with him today, and I'm planning to making it clear he won't be getting you back. Also, I need to propose to you properly, but I'm afraid if I spring that on you without warning, you might kill me."

"Give me a ring, I will start wearing it, and wait for my sister to start asking questions."

Kace headed for Susan's desk, picked up her phone, and pressed a few buttons. "Juliette, please tell me you brought some rings with you so we can get one on Ginger's finger strictly for the purpose of tormenting Michelle and driving away an annoying ex-boss determined to hire Ginger back. Thank you, and I owe you a favor, but you can't steal my wife."

"I'm really not going to throw away such a nice job offer and return to destitution. I'm just saying there's zero chance I'm going to willingly return to destitution. That's where I was at before you hired me. Also, I'm not your wife yet."

"You're marrying me, Ginger. There's no way you'd be returning to any state of destitution. You might have to deal with being spoiled and pampered. I'm just going to start calling you my wife now to make it clear I will defeat all competition."

I hoped being spoiled and pampered happened in a shower. Or his bedroom. Actually, I didn't care where it happened as long as it was somewhere private. "You should propose to me in front of my sister while I'm working so I can just show you the ring and pretend like someone else had beaten you to the chase."

"You're evil, and I love it."

"I'm not evil, I'm just really mad my sister ran off and left her kids to fend for themselves."

"They didn't have to fend for themselves. They had you, and they had me, too."

"Maybe we should adopt them. We'd possibly be better parents. We could just steal them. Would they notice?"

Kace laughed. "Probably. Despite this incident, they do love their children dearly. I wouldn't be surprised if they'd talked to the kids about their disappearing trick before heading off. They didn't waste any time going to your place."

That was true. I frowned. "That makes it sounds like she was planning to bankrupt me and force me to live in her house."

"Knowing your sister, she was likely expecting my house, hoping we might resolve our differences."

The receptionist heaved a sigh. "That is something they would do. If you decide to elope with your executive secretary, Mr. Dannicks, please do so over the weekend when it is least disruptive for business operations."

Well, at least someone at the company understood basic responsibilities. "Does he ever get time off?"

"Unless ill or for a family matter, we prefer forty-eight hours of notice."

"It is a family matter," Kace announced. "I'm forming a family with Ginger. That should count."

"New York has a waiting period on marriage licenses, sir. You can't run away and get married today. At best, you could get the license issued today and get married tomorrow."

According to Kace's expression, he'd received earth-shatteringly bad news. Retrieving my new phone from my pocket, I checked the list of states that required neither a blood test nor a waiting period for marriages to be performed. "Rhode Island doesn't have a waiting period, blood-test requirement, or residency requirement," I announced. "Neither does Connecticut, Virginia, Ohio, or a lot of other states. We could fly to Vegas. I've never been on a plane before."

"Susan, I'm leaving for the day, and I will be back tomorrow. I will return happily married. Distract Michelle for me."

Juliette stepped into the reception. "What's this about you leaving today and returning happily married?"

"Connecticut doesn't have a waiting period for marriage, and I'm concerned someone will steal my wife. Like you. I'm also considering Vegas, as Ginger needs to experience the joys of flight, but that would be rough on her, as it's a long flight. I'm willing, but I don't want her to get sick again."

"Kace, what has gotten into you? I'm going to dress her in pretty clothes and pose her with cars, not marry her. I'm already married." Juliette dug out her phone from her jacket pocket and checked it. "No matter how you look at it, it's a three-hour drive to get to a state that has no waiting period. You have a meeting in an hour. You specifically asked me to be here for the meeting in case you needed some help convincing him to leave."

Kace scowled. "I can leave after the meeting, then."

"Which defeats the purpose of this whole plan to make Michelle squirm."

"You could attend the meeting on my behalf and torment Michelle for me. You can tell her I've kidnapped her sister and won't be giving her back. I'll give you the keys to the Audi, and you can give them to Michelle so she can get home. I'll bring Ginger back to work tomorrow. Would that appease you?"

Juliette considered Kace, her eyes narrowing. Then, with a sly smile, she nodded. "As a matter of fact, yes."

The elevator dinged and swung open, and my sister stormed into the reception. "Kace Dannicks, you are a menace!"

"Your plan just exploded in your face, I'm afraid." Juliette patted Kace's shoulder. "It'll work out."

"What's going to work out? Nothing is going to work out for you ever again, Kace. I'm going to murder you. You got everyone a Carter jacket! In red. To be spiteful and evil."

"Actually, I did that," I announced, raising my hand. "Juliette seduced me with clothes, and the next thing I knew, I was seducing your business partner. I couldn't help it. He kept saying nice things to me."

The moment my sister comprehended what I said, her expression went blank. I waited for her brain to finish rebooting. After a few minutes, I began to worry, and I waved my hand in front of her face.

"You did what with my business partner?"

"I seduced him."

"You, who can't stand Kace, are claiming to have seduced him? Okay, I get that you're mad at me, but come on. That's just ridiculous. You wouldn't seduce Kace. Hell, I can't even get you to try a blind date. I can't even get you two to share the same room without one of you wanting to commit murder."

Next time, I wouldn't bother with preplanned revenge. Spontaneous oversharing seemed to do the trick. "Not only did I seduce him, I did so in your shower. There's a reason he was mostly naked in your chair. I'd tired him out *that* much."

Kace's brows shot up. "That was ruthless even for you."

My sister's eyes widened, and she jerked her head in Kace's direction. "Kace?"

He shrugged and held his hands up in surrender. "I can't help it I think your sister is smart and beautiful. I've been lusting after her for years. All I did was unbutton my shirt a little because it was a little warm in your house. As for the towels, I stole them because they participated in my seduction of your sister in your shower. I wanted to keep them as a cherished memento."

Susan made a choking sound, sat down at her desk, and tried her best to keep from laughing. She failed. Juliette covered her mouth with a hand. "Now you've done it, Kace."

"I'm strongly considering ditching work today, kidnapping your sister, and carting her to the nearest state without a waiting period for marriages so I can make her fully mine. I'm a jealous man, and I don't give up my captured women readily. And make no mistake, Michelle. I've thoroughly charmed and captured her. She's mine. But it gets better."

"Better?" My sister pointed at me. "You did *what* with my sister and my towels? And you think this gets *better*?"

"She's my new executive secretary, and she's taking over the office that connects to mine. My work life is going to be as amazing as my home life, and there's nobody better qualified to be my executive secretary than her."

While my sister could handle a lot life had to offer, the news of me being Kace's new executive secretary overwhelmed her. After witnessing my brother-in-law faint over the Fist, I was prepared, catching her under her arms before she cracked her head open on the shiny floor.

The elevator dinged. My brother-in-law stepped out, raising a brow as he took in the sight of his wife sprawled on the floor. "Did Michelle finally figure out you're sleeping with her sister, Kace?"

What the hell? I left my sister slumped on the floor and gaped at my brother-in-law. "What?"

He grinned and shrugged. "Kace is happy, you are happy, you were completely flustered over the new-car situation, which told me that you already had some form of vehicle arrangement, and the kids have been bouncing balls of excitement. I'm of the opinion only sex, marriage, or the formation of a relationship can make everyone happy like that all at one time, and my children are many things, but they really like you both, so only you two shacking up would make them that happy. Well, getting married if you weren't caught shacking up. Close enough. Am I right?"

Susan giggled and peeked over the top of her tall desk. "It was the news Mr. Dannicks hired Miss Harriet to be his executive secretary that did her in, but they are debating skipping out on work and getting married, as it seems Mr. Dannicks really does not want to let her get away."

Juliette dug out a box from her purse and held it out to Kace. "I anticipated something like this happening, and I got her ring size while she was sick. I will bill you for the rings once you're back. You are well aware of when I got yours. While my son and daughter-in-law waited for their actual marriage, I had the feeling you'd rather be sure she'd marry you than wallow unhappily and anxiously until you got a ring or two on her finger. I know your type. You're a man of action. I'll stand in for your meeting as long as you don't mind me using your office for my work. I do have a job. I'm also going to have to steal printer paper, pencils, and anything that could possibly be used to design clothes. I want my minions to like me tomorrow."

"Make sure Juliette has everything she needs today, Susan. Leave Michelle on the floor or something. If she asks where I went, just tell her I'm eloping for the rest of the day."

"Why did you bother making any plans at all today?" Susan complained.

"I really thought I'd last more than a few hours," he admitted. "But then I realized Juliette designed all of her clothes, she owns a lot of red now, and I need a ring on her finger to deter other men."

"I design such wonderful clothes." Juliette rubbed her hands together. "I particularly like when my clothes marry people. It's one of my joys in life. Mission accomplished. I'd say my work here is done, but I agreed to pretend to be you today. That was really foolish of me."

"You're the best, Juliette."

"I do try, and you looked so sad and desperate I just had to help. Honestly, I expected her to put up more of a fight, but then again, I shouldn't have been surprised. She's a smart one, and she only needed a chance to see what was right in front of her all along."

As the woman was right, I shrugged, dug out the keys to my new Audi, and dropped them onto my sister. "Don't you let her scratch my new car, Mitchel. It seems I have some important business to attend to today."

"When you're finished with him, try to impress upon him we do have actual work to do around here, okay?"

Before I could throttle my brother-in-law for being a jerk, Kace wrapped his arm around my waist and dragged me to the elevator. "I'll try to return her tomorrow less likely to snap, Mitchel."

"You better, or I'll have to beat you for not making her happy."

I waited for the elevator door to close before laughing. "All you have to do to make me happy is take off your shirt."

"I think I can do a little better than that, and I look forward to spending the rest of our lives proving it."

Merry Christmas to me, along with a happy New Year.

About the Author

Bernadette Franklin is a figment of imagination owned and operated by two cats, some plants, and a human.
 The human also writes as RJ Blain and Susan Copperfield.

Want to hear from the author when a new book releases? Sign up here! Please note this newsletter is operated by the Furred & Frond Management. Expect to be sassed by a cat. (With guest features of other animals, including dogs.)

For a complete list of books written by RJ and her various pen names, please click here.

RJ BLAIN suffers from a Moleskine journal obsession, a pen fixation, and a terrible tendency to pun without warning.

When she isn't playing pretend, she likes to think she's a cartographer and a sumi-e painter.

In her spare time, she daydreams about being a spy. Should that fail, her contingency plan involves tying her best of enemies to spinning wheels and quoting James Bond villains until she is satisfied.

RJ also writes as Susan Copperfield and Bernadette Franklin.

Visit RJ and her pets (the Management) at thesneakykittycritic.com.

✼✼✼

FOLLOW RJ & HER ALTER EGOS ON BOOKBUB:
RJ BLAIN
SUSAN COPPERFIELD
BERNADETTE FRANKLIN